## Praise for Valerie Wilcox
## and Her Debut Sailing Mystery
### *Sins of Silence*

"Kellie Montgomery is a welcome addition to the roster of female sleuths. You will like her brain, and her heart, and her tongue, which is as salty as the sound on which she sails her sloop. An impressive debut . . . I look forward to seeing Kellie again. And again and again and again."

—Stephen Greenleaf, author of *Strawberry Sunday*

"Wilcox's debut sails smoothly through a sea of dark secrets and murky death."

—Mary Daheim, author of *Legs Benedict*

"With her meaningful plot and earthy, likable sailing instructor heroine, Wilcox treats us to an adventure that resonates long after we've finished reading."

—Earlene Fowler, author of *Mariner's Compass*

# SINS OF BETRAYAL

## VALERIE WILCOX

BERKLEY PRIME CRIME, NEW YORK

SINS OF BETRAYAL

A Berkley Prime Crime Book / published by arrangement with the author

PRINTING HISTORY
Berkley Prime Crime edition / July 1999

All rights reserved.
Copyright © 1999 by Valerie Wilcox.
This book may not be reproduced in whole or in part, by mimeograph or any other means, without permission. For information address: The Berkley Publishing Group, a division of Penguin Putnam Inc., 375 Hudson Street, New York, New York 10014.

The Penguin Putnam Inc. World Wide Web site address is http://www.penguinputnam.com

ISBN: 0-425-16963-4

Berkley Prime Crime Books are published by The Berkley Publishing Group, a division of Penguin Putnam Inc., 375 Hudson Street, New York, New York 10014. The name BERKLEY PRIME CRIME and the BERKLEY PRIME CRIME design are trademarks belonging to Penguin Putnam Inc.

PRINTED IN THE UNITED STATES OF AMERICA

10  9  8  7  6  5  4  3  2  1

*For my mother, Laura McConnell Worthington*
*and*
*In memory of my father, James W. Worthington*

# ACKNOWLEDGMENTS

A SPECIAL THANKS to the following people who helped make this book possible: Rita Gardner, Janet Beatty, and Julia Stroud, Ph.D., for reading and editing the early drafts; John Wilcox for his biblical insights; Maureen O'Hara for answering my many questions about Judaism with patience and good humor; Margie Newman, for contributing to my understanding of sign language and the challenges facing the hearing impaired; Steve Cook and Herb Florer of the Island Sailing Club and Nicki Ehrlich DeBoard and Ruth DiDomenico of the Tacoma Women's Sailing Association for sharing their sailing expertise; Lt. Steve Bourgette and the men and women of the Bellevue Citizen Police Academy for their outstanding community education program; my agents, Anna Cottle and Mary Alice Kier of Cine/Lit Representation, and my editor, Judith Palais, for their invaluable advice and support; my daughters, Maryanne, Julie, Linda, Dawn, and JoAnn for putting up with this crazy roller-coaster ride, and my husband, David, for always being there with big arms and a big heart.

# SINS OF BETRAYAL

# ONE

ON THE WATER everything is clear. It is a gift for the soul; a clarity born of sea and salt air that touches the small inner voice within us that has been too long silenced by the chaos of life. It is a gift that heals; that gives us power to rid ourselves of confusion, worry, guilt, and regret; that gives us faith in ourselves and our dreams. But if we refuse to heed the gift of clarity, if we deny the inner voice that tells us who we are, then we will wither and die before our time. For when we kill the dream within us, we kill ourselves.

We may be breathing, and the blood may be flowing through our veins, but it is not living. It is merely busyness disguised as living—from children who are shuttled from one organized activity to another without a single moment simply to be themselves, to play, or to let their imaginations run free, to adults who scurry from store to store, buying whatever their money or credit will allow in the false hope that material acquisitions will somehow deaden their pain. The pain may go away for a while, but it always returns. For nothing can satisfy a dream unfulfilled, a life unlived.

On the water everything is clear. It gives us power to climb the wind and soar.

*You want to be happy, Kellie, darlin'? Then find the wind, find where it's coming from and where it's going. For it is only when your boat has a bellyful of wind in her sails and her hull is ripping through the sea, and the salt spray is stinging your face, that you will know you're alive. You will know who you are and where you're going. You will know your dream.*

"HEATHEN BITCH!"

"Actually, the name's Kellie. Kellie Montgomery."

"Sinner slut!"

The guy calling me names was crazy. That he was also dangerous hadn't occurred to me until he'd wheedled his way into my office. By the time the name-calling started, it was too late to reconsider. He'd persuaded me to open the door by claiming he wanted to sign up for sailing lessons, which sounded reasonable enough, considering I run a sailing school. The part about God having personally sent him to my doorstep should've set off a few warning bells. But it was six o'clock on a rainy Sunday morning, and I wasn't thinking too clearly. Okay. I wasn't thinking at all.

I'd come into the office at that distasteful hour out of some perverse notion that if I were in the office making like a workaholic, I might actually have something to do. It was May and the opening of boating season, but Seattle's blustery, winterlike spring had turned off even the die-hard sailing enthusiasts. After two weeks of steady rain, the only thing still dry at Larstad's Marina was my bank account, so I wasn't about to ask too many questions of a potential customer—crazy or not.

He looked rather endearing when he first came to the door. Dressed in a gray woolen sweater with obligatory elbow patches, a wrinkled white shirt, and garish plaid trousers that stopped just short of his bare ankles, he reminded me of an aging, absentminded college professor I once had. The poor man seemed tired, as if his clothes were too heavy for his short, wiry frame to carry. And, despite the soggy weather, he wore no hat or coat which, combined with the unruly white frizz atop his head, gave him a distinctly wet and wild look. Albert Einstein on crack.

Once inside, he shook himself off like a dog, plopped a battered leather briefcase on my desk, and sat down in the chair opposite mine.

"God sent me," he said again. A gust of wind rattled the front windowpane as if to emphasize his point.

"Yes, sir." Who was I to argue? Considering all the rain we'd had lately, his name was probably Noah. I riffled through my file drawer and found a standard registration form which I slid across the desk.

"Let's get you registered," I said eagerly.

He pushed up his wire-rimmed glasses with the tip of his index finger and considered the form. Taking his time, he puffed thoughtfully on a meerschaum pipe he'd pulled from his shirt pocket. As I waited, a lazy spiral of smoke drifted from his pipe and filled the room with the sweet smell of cherries. When he finally looked up, his face was the color of gutter water and carried an expression as blank as the paper in front of him.

"Oh, I'm sorry," I said. Where *was* my brain? "You'll need a pen." I grabbed a couple from a lop-sided ceramic pot-cum-pencil-holder that my daughter had made eons ago, but he declined the offer.

"That won't be necessary," he said, digging into his briefcase.

He hadn't impressed me as the fussy type, but Larstad's Marina tends to attract a more upscale clientele. It wasn't uncommon for my students to eschew the cheap ballpoints I carry in favor of their own Mont Blancs. It was just a simple registration form, but if it made him feel better to use his own pen, so be it. Whatever floats your boat.

I crammed the pens back in the pot just as he found what he was looking for in his briefcase. Only it wasn't a Mont Blanc that he now held in his hand—it was a Colt .45. I knew the weapon well, having taken a bullet from one a few months back. Another instance of misjudging a dangerous situation.

"Hey," I said, raising my hands palm-side out. "No problem. You don't have to sign the form. Consider yourself registered."

He aimed the pistol at me. "You can cut the chatter now. I don't want sailing lessons."

"If it's money you're after, feel free to help yourself." I motioned to my handbag lying on top of the file cabinet. "There's not much cash, and the credit cards are tapped out, but hey, it's all yours."

He glared at me indignantly. "God doesn't want your money."

Tell that to the televangelists. "What *does* He want?"

A smug smile. "That's for me to know and you to find out."

Slowly I lowered my hands and rubbed my shoulder. Just looking down the barrel of the Colt had been enough to cause the pain of the old injury to flare up again. I winced, but Noah didn't seem to notice.

He leaned back in his chair, the pistol ever vigilant. "Well?" he said.

At forty I was too old to be playing games, especially at the point of a gun. "Well, what?" I replied irritably.

"What do you think God wants?"

Despite my parents' best efforts, I've never considered myself particularly religious. My father was a devout Catholic, and my mother was an equally devout Mormon, which meant I'd spent most of my formative years shuffling between one church or the other. But I abandoned churchgoing altogether after my parents were killed when I was thirteen. The confusion caused by their untimely deaths, plus the unresolved issues surrounding their battles over which church represented God's one true religion, had left me spiritually bereft. I had no idea what this guy *or* God could possibly want, but I struggled to think of something that might placate both of them. My mind drew a blank.

"Uh, I'm not sure."

He frowned, frizzy white eyebrows arched at a menacing angle. He yanked the pipe out of his mouth and slammed it onto the desk.

"Unacceptable!" he shouted, waving the gun wildly with his other hand. "Try again."

I flinched at his outburst, feeling like a disobedient child who'd disappointed her teacher.

"Obedience?" I ventured timidly.

"Excellent." He rewarded my scholarship with a crooked, toothy grin. A piece of gristle or something clung to one of his incisors. "And what else?" he asked, working at the irritant with the tip of his tongue.

Having exhausted the store of my knowledge of things godly, I hemmed and hawed for a few more uncomfortable seconds. Then the phone rang, startling us both. Without thinking, I said, "That must be God now." Bizarre as it sounded to my own ears, Noah seemed to accept the suggestion as perfectly plausible. He waited while I answered.

"Uh, hello?" I said.

"Kellie?" It was my sister Mary Kathleen. "You sound strange," she said. "Did I catch you at a bad time?" That she should be calling me at six o'clock on a Sunday morning seemed almost as bizarre as having God on the line. Kate is one of those people whose biorhythms are more in tune with night owls, bats, and teenagers. "If It's Before Noon, It's Too Soon" could've been her theme song.

"Yes, God. We were just talking about you."

Noah nodded agreeably.

"God?" asked Kate.

"That's right. Your messenger came as you requested. In fact, he's sitting in front of me as we speak."

"What are you talking about?"

"No problem, God. Always good to hear from you." I glanced at Noah with a reassuring smile.

"And I thought *I* was Looney Tunes in the morning!" she said, laughing. "What the hell's the matter with you?"

"He asked me to explain what you want, but the gun he's pointing at me is too distracting."

Noah blinked nervously, but kept the Colt steady.

"Gun? Uh . . . Kellie, are you in some kind of trouble?"

By Jove, I think she's got it. "Yes, definitely!"

"Oh, shit. Listen, sis, I'm going to hang up and get some help. Okay?"

"I understand." I kept on talking to the dial tone after she'd disconnected. "Yes, sir. I'll be sure and tell him."

Noah scooted to the edge of his chair. "Tell me what?"

I put one hand over the receiver and said, "He says you should leave now."

"What? That can't be."

I offered him the phone. "If you don't believe me, talk to Him yourself."

He hesitated briefly, muttering something under his breath. Then, with the Colt still leveled at me, he leaned across the desk with his free hand to take the phone. But I slammed the receiver onto the desk much like he'd done earlier with his pipe. The move so startled him that he jerked his hand away, knocking the pipe onto the floor. Instinctively he bent over to pick it up.

Momentarily out of his line of sight, I jumped up and grabbed the receiver. Then, with both hands wrapped around it like a baseball bat, I swung at the Colt with all the strength I could muster. Unfortunately the pistol did not conveniently fly out of his hand. It must have hurt, though, because he yelped like a wounded pup before bolting out of his chair and sprinting around the desk to confront me.

"Heathen bitch!"

That's when I introduced myself. When all else fails, try manners.

He wasn't impressed. "Sinner slut!" he yelled. Up to this point, his voice had been merely creepy—a high, raspy twang that sounded like a violin with a bad cold. But the yelling had deepened the tone somehow, dripping venom with every syllable.

If I'd been rattled by the sight of the .45, it was the hatred now spewing out of the guy's mouth that set my heart to racing. I retreated a step and tried to keep my cool, figuring help would come charging through the office door at any minute.

He was in my face, his breath as foul as a clogged-up sewer. The Colt was just inches from my stomach.

"Listen," I said evenly. "We've obviously gotten off to a bad start here. Perhaps if we both sat down again and—"

A noise at the door. *Finally!* I held my breath and waited for the rescue.

Tap-tap. Tap-tap. The knock was very soft, very polite. The police were *knocking?* Whatever happened to kicking down the door and storming the joint?

Noah gripped my arm and twisted me around so that I was in front of him, the pistol jammed into my lower back.

"We'll answer it together," he growled, shoving me forward. As we lurched across the room, the door swung open and I caught a glimpse of my rescue team—and the certain knowledge that I was doomed.

The storm troopers I'd been hoping for had come in the persona of one Todd L. Wilmington, a.k.a. the Weasel. A tall, gangly, Ichabod Crane type, Wilmington's main problem was that he suffered from delusions of adequacy. The *L* in his name stood for Larstad, which meant he had connections. As the nephew of the marina's owner, old man Larstad, Todd L. Wilmington didn't have a real job. Unless you consider hanging out at the marina and messing with everyone's head a proper job description. As usual, he strode into the room with a self-important air that only the truly incompetent can pull off.

We all froze where we were, staring at one another. This lasted for a couple of unnerving moments until Noah took charge of the situation. Squeezing my arm roughly with one hand, he brandished the pistol at the Weasel with the other. "Shut the friggin' door, you faggot!"

Wilmington responded predictably—he fainted.

The trouble with someone taking a dive is that they tend to fall where they shouldn't oughta. In this case— on me. I tumbled backward like a wobbly bowling pin and fell spread-eagled on a toppled Noah. This time the pistol flew out of his hand and landed just beyond reach of our tangled heap.

Wilmington was out for the count, but Noah and I squirmed around on the floor like a couple of lusty lovers. Trying to pry ourselves from the Weasel's dead weight wasn't easy, but I had the advantage. With just the one body on top of me, I was able to extricate an arm and a leg, which I knew would be enough to free myself. I'd had my share of wrestling matches growing up. As the youngest and puniest of six kids, I always wound up on the bottom of the pile, and quickly discovered what it took to survive.

With my newly liberated limbs, I got enough leverage to start rocking Wilmington. I rocked 'n' rolled, rolled 'n' rocked, until I'd tipped his bony carcass onto the floor. Noah was wriggling and flailing the whole time, but I didn't let him pull the same trick on me. Once I was clear of the Weasel, I flipped onto my feet like a pancake turning on a hot grill. The ease with which I'd carried off the stunt made me grin. I grinned even wider when I saw what was lying right next to my feet.

Noah spotted the pistol at the same time. He quickly rolled over and grabbed for it, but by then I'd already scooped it up and had it pointed at his head.

"Freeze!" I yelled, amazed at the gutsy way I sounded.

He froze.

Despite having gained the upper hand, I wasn't feeling all that confident. Guns—whether in my hand or someone else's—make me nervous. Shaky nervous. So shaky that Noah dropped to his knees and started praying. It was probably a good idea. Given my agitated state, I wasn't sure what I'd do. But I was still holding him at bay when the cavalry finally arrived.

First on the scene was Bert Foster, the marina's harbormaster, followed shortly by two of Seattle P.D.'s finest and a smattering of weekend marina personnel who'd stumbled onto the scene as they were headed to work. The arrest itself was straightforward and over quickly, but my role in the affair took a while.

I had to endure an extensive round of questioning by the police—the part about God's intervention by phone had them confused. Then amused. I have to admit I hammed it up a bit, especially when I described the Weasel's aborted rescue attempt. Relating the tale helped to calm my frazzled nerves, and the cops seemed to enjoy the story so much that I couldn't resist a few embellishments—even when I was asked to repeat the whole episode about a zillion times. Must have been a slow crime day.

The Weasel recovered from his fainting spell after the officers arrived. As soon as he realized that he was no longer in danger, he tried to take credit for the rescue.

The only person who seemed interested in what he had to say was a stringer for the local newspaper. She was a sweet young thing who'd hurried over to the marina as soon as she heard that a hostage situation was in progress. Since nobody would talk to her or to the Weasel, they naturally gravitated toward one another. Last I saw of them they were heading out the door arm in arm.

I'd just finished signing an official statement when the phone rang. It was my sister Kate again. The police had intercepted three other calls from her, but I answered this one myself.

"*Finally.* I can't believe I actually got through to you. How're you doing?"

"Just fine," I said, nodding to the officers as they let themselves out the door. "All the excitement's over." I wasn't exactly fine, but I didn't want to alarm her. Since the police hadn't given Kate much information, I gave her a quick rundown on the morning's events. As before, talking about what had happened seemed to help settle my nerves.

"So who was the guy? A deranged boater?"

To Kate, all boaters were a little nuts. How else would you explain someone who'd shell out thousands of dollars and then some on "a pointy thing that floats" when you could get a mighty nice sparkler on your finger at a fraction of the cost. What she didn't seem to understand was that buying a boat—any boat—is about as rational as falling in love. The bigger and fancier the toy, the better the affair.

"No, he wasn't a boater. Or a sailboater, either, although that's what he initially claimed he was interested in. Turns out he was some paranoid yahoo from the Blue Water Warriors."

"The blue water what?"

"It's an extremist branch of a local environmental group opposed to just about everything. But this fruit-cake had mixed environmental fervor with a somewhat warped religious viewpoint. He had a real problem with marinas.''

"Why was that?"

"The guy was delusional. He spouted all kinds of drivel before they hauled him out of here, but it basically boiled down to the belief that marinas are the devil's playground." I chuckled. "Get this: He thought I was the devil's whore because I worked here. He thought he'd been personally chosen by God to clean up the situation at Larstad's.''

"What situation?"

"Water pollution. He was convinced the marina was 'desecrating' the sacred waters of Puget Sound.''

"You're kidding . . . So what'd the weirdo intend to do? Kill you in the name of God and clean water?"

"Apparently. But thanks to your timely phone call and a little luck on my part, he never got the chance. By the way, why *did* you call so early?"

I could hear her tapping her long, French-wrapped acrylics on the receiver. "To invite you to lunch."

"Come on, Kate. Since when do you get up at six A.M. to make a luncheon date?"

"Since . . . Well, it's too complicated to get into on the phone. Meet me for lunch at the Pacific Broiler and I'll tell you all about it."

"The Broiler?" I groaned. The marina's fancy restaurant wasn't my favorite dining spot. Besides having a ridiculously overpriced menu, they expected you to dress up, factors that strained both my thin wardrobe and even thinner wallet.

"Don't be difficult. It'll be my treat. You deserve some pampering after what you went through this morning. And the Broiler is just the place to indulge yourself.''

I had my doubts, but we agreed to meet at noon. I was looking forward to seeing her again. She lived nearby, but aside from a short visit when I was recuperating from my last dance with a Colt .45, it'd been several months since we'd gotten together—not since a family Christmas gathering had ended on a sour note when I stomped out, furious with our older sister, Donna, for meddling in my affairs.

Kate and I were only a year apart and often mistaken for twins as kids, but the close relationship we had involved much more than physical similarities. For one thing, she never messed with my head like Donna always seemed to do. The worst I could expect from Kate was an ear-bending litany of woe about her love life. She'd been married three times and had recently dumped the guy who was supposed to be husband number four. I suspected that the real motive behind the invite was nothing more than the need for a sympathetic shoulder to cry on.

As it turned out, I was wrong.

Dead wrong.

# TWO

I LOCKED UP the office at 11:30 so that I could change my clothes before meeting Kate at the Broiler. I've called Larstad's Marina my home for the past three and a half years, ever since I moved aboard *Second Wind*—a forty-foot sloop that's moored at the end of K Dock. *Second Wind* was the life ring I grabbed in the aftermath of my husband's death. Wendell's losing battle with a brain tumor at age thirty-six caused me to take a good hard look at how I wanted to live the rest of my life, however long that might be. The upshot was that I wanted to be doing what I loved most—sailing.

Within months of burying Wendell, I'd quit my job teaching high-school science, sold my house, and cashed in all my savings to buy *Second Wind.* I couldn't have shocked my family more had I run off with the parish priest. ''Holy Mother of God, you've done *what?''* pretty much sums up the general reaction. Words such as ''irresponsible'' and ''selfish'' still ring in my ears, but despite the family uproar, I know with every fiber of my being that buying *Second Wind* was the right decision.

It was the affirmation of all that my grandfather had

ever taught me. *Sailing is a vision, Kellie, darlin'. And your boat is the physical realization of that vision—a spiritual blending of wind, tides, and salt air with self-reliance, with mastery over yourself, with survival.* To me, *Second Wind* is more than just a sailboat; more than rigging and winches, cleats and billowing sails. It is the ever-changing wind. It is the ebb and flood of the sea. It is silence and great peace at the bottom of my soul. It is who I am.

Sailing represents life as my grandfather always said it should be, as it has to be. It is real. It is authentic. It is the life we all crave, the life that stirs within us and will not die unless we let ourselves succumb to the desperation born of life's minutiae, killing us every hour of every day, a little at a time as surely as the insidious disease that killed my husband.

So here I was, three-plus years into my authentic lifestyle—hurrying down the dock toward my boat in a torrential downpour without an umbrella. Can't get much more real than that. The marina was practically deserted. Normally at this time of year the place would be hopping with activity. But even for Seattleites, the incessant rain had been a bit much. The unusually wet spring had dampened spirits as well as everything else. The smart folks had found a dry place and were staying put. The best I could do was pull my jacket collar up and cover my head with an old newspaper. Big deal. I was soaking wet by the time I got to K Dock.

"Hey, Montgomery! This your cat?" yelled Stubbs Dahlquist. He pointed with a metal boat hook at a scrawny gray cat sitting atop his sailboat's canvas-covered boom. The cat, studiously ignoring Stubbs, was busily licking its paw.

"Not really."

Stubbs wasn't convinced. "Hmmf. The little shit came tearing out of your cockpit like a bat outta hell a half-hour ago. It's been making itself comfortable up there ever since." He took a swipe at the cat with the boat hook. She hissed and growled at him, but never budged an inch. Stubbs swore under his breath. "Stupid fucker doesn't even know enough to get itself out of the rain."

I assumed he meant the cat. Stubbs was a former used car salesman in his late sixties who'd hit the big time when he parlayed his modest retirement money into a fortune. He invested in Microsoft some years back when the stock was under thirty dollars a share, and has been bragging about it ever since. But, according to his ex-wife, it'd all been a mistake—his broker thought he'd said, "Buy Microsoft, you idiot!!" when he actually said, "Buy Microsoft?? You idiot!!"

"Maybe I can help you, Stubbs."

He chomped down on the unlit cigar stub at the corner of his mouth and shrugged. "Be my guest."

I climbed aboard and waved off his attempt to hand me the boat hook. I knew the cat and figured I could handle her without resorting to force. She wasn't mine, but we had a history of sorts. The first time I saw her she was in the drink at the end of K Dock, frantically struggling to keep her head above water—and losing. I'd plucked her out, dried her off, and tried to send her on her way, but she dug her tiny claws into my sweat-shirt and wouldn't let go. She's been hanging out with me ever since, but so far neither of us has been ready to commit to a long-term relationship.

I approached the boom and called her name softly. "Pan-Pan. Come on, Pan-Pan. It's time to go home."

She studied me a moment, then pulled herself upright and leaped onto the deck next to my feet. I picked her up, and we exchanged a quick greeting—a couple of strokes on her neck from me and a tongue-licking on my cheek from her.

Stubbs snorted. "Not yours, huh?"

I took her back to *Second Wind*, where I found a couple of towels to dry us off. I've always had a pet of some sort around, but when I moved aboard my boat I made a conscious decision to forgo the responsibility that comes with pet ownership. I liked being able to set sail at a moment's notice without having some animal depending on me to feed it or change its litter box. It was a freedom I cherished. But there was something about Pan-Pan's big green eyes that had gotten to me. Whenever I'd think about kicking her out, she'd give me one of her how-could-you stares and I was hooked.

At first I just called her Kitty, but that seemed too ordinary, so we settled on Pan-Pan for the panicky way she had clung to me after her watery rescue. Also, I suppose, for the sobering moment bordering on panic when I realized that my youthful fears had finally come to pass: I was a forty-year-old (ancient by kid standards) woman living alone with nothing but a mangy cat to keep her company. Oh, well . . . at least I still had all my own teeth.

Pan-Pan curled up on my bed and fell asleep while I rummaged around in the closet for something present-able to wear to lunch. It wasn't easy. Due to space restrictions aboard the sloop, I don't own an extensive wardrobe. To be truthful, I've never owned an extensive wardrobe. Luckily jeans and sweatshirts serve me very well around the marina. In spite of the weather, I chose a silky Johnny Was sundress with cap sleeves, some-thing I'd been dying to wear ever since I'd bought it on sale at the Bon Marché. That was back when I thought summer was just around the corner. Ha! Buying a sun-dress in Seattle has the same effect on the weather as washing your car.

I'd just slipped into my nylons when Pan-Pan woke up from her nap, refreshed and frisky. She head-nudged my legs, but I swatted her away. "I don't have time to play with you. I'm already late as it is." I grabbed a hairbrush and tried to do something with my hair. It's short and naturally curly, which means it takes care of itself most of the time, but the rain had done a number on it—my head looked like a frizzy red beach ball with eyes.

Meanwhile, Pan-Pan had grown weary playing by herself and shifted from frisky to attack mode, claws fully operational. She started with the nylons and quickly moved onto the dress. In a matter of seconds I looked like I'd been run through a paper shredder.

"Stubbs was right!" I screamed. "You *are* a little shit." I locked her in the forward cabin, grabbed an umbrella, and stomped off the boat, not bothering to change into something else.

"DOES MADAM HAVE a reservation?" The Pacific Broiler's maitre d' had a phony French accent and a nose about a mile high. He looked me over, with his eyebrow cocked at a disapproving angle.

"No, but my sister probably does," I said, shaking the water from my umbrella. "I'm meeting her here."

He sighed heavily. So dreary dealing with the masses. "And her name would be?"

"Rossiter. Mary Kathleen Rossiter."

He made a big show out of consulting his appointment book, slowly running his finger down the page. "Sorry." He managed a tight smile and took in my hair and dress again. "There doesn't seem to be a Rossiter listed here. Are you sure you're not meeting her at the Topside?"

The Topside Bar and Grill was the marina's other restaurant. It'd been a warehouse at one time and, despite extensive renovations, still retained enough of its former roots to give it a casual, working-class atmosphere. It was my favorite hangout, but I didn't much care for anyone assuming that's where I belonged.

"Why don't you take another look in your book. It's Rossiter. R-o-s-s-i—"

"I know how to spell it."

"Great. Then you should be able to find it."

"Madam, that would be an impossibility. The name simply isn't in my book."

Piss on it. It'd been a rough morning. "Tell you what. Forget your book. I'll just take a gander at the dining room." He stepped forward as if to stop me, then thought better of it.

Larstad's Marina was one of Seattle's ritziest, with pricey moorage rates and amenities like the Pacific Broiler to prove it. In keeping with the marina's upscale image, the Broiler's decor was fashionably elegant, which meant a lot of money had been thrown around for crystal chandeliers, Oriental rugs, and mahogany and teak everything. The overall effect was a staid and stodgy look that seemed rather fitting, given the rich old duffers who usually hung out there. So I was more than a little surprised to see that the conservative dining room had gone "ethnic." Brightly colored piñatas hung from the chandeliers, and several posters of bullfighters and Mexican street scenes dominated the walls. The motif looked about as Mexican as Taco Bell.

I stopped one of the waiters who used to work at the Topside. "What's going on here, Ralph?"

He shrugged, obviously embarrassed. "We got a new manager—he's into theme menus." He tugged at his sombrero. "You should've been here in March. He had us all wearing silly little green hats like we were leprechauns or something." He glanced over his shoulder before adding, "But I'm hitting the road if he ever does a Scottish theme. I draw the line at kilts."

I headed for the dining room's smoking section—Kate's been a two-pack-a-day smoker for years—but didn't find her amongst the puffing hordes. The non-smokers' part of the room was even more crowded, but it wasn't hard to spot Kate. Even at forty-one she was easily the prettiest woman in the place. Always the beauty of the family, the years had been kind to her even if her love life hadn't. She was just five foot two, but she always seemed much taller. Trained as an actress, she carried herself like a runway model and dressed the part—meaning she was graceful and glamourous and everything I wasn't. But I wasn't jealous . . . well, not much.

For today's lunch she sported a casual look—an ivory silk blouse under a classic double-breasted red blazer with peaked lapels and gold buttons. Her auburn hair looked as if she'd just had it cut—a short new style that flattered her oval face. She sat at a window table with her shapely legs crossed, her gray gabardine skirt tastefully covering her knees.

I hesitated a moment before approaching the table, painfully aware of how shabby I looked compared to Kate. "What happened to you?" she asked when I joined her.

I fingered one of the snags in my dress. "Let's just say I'm giving serious thought to placing a Found Cat ad in the *Seattle Times*." As I sat down I said, "It's lucky I found you. The maitre d' insisted that your name wasn't on the reservation list."

Kate shrugged. "I told him I was Kate Larstad. Thought a little name dropping might get us a better table."

Her ruse must have worked for we had a terrific view of downtown Seattle and Mount Rainier, but we might as well have been in a closet. The only thing Kate seemed to notice was the margarita in front of her. She drained the last of it as soon as I sat down, and then signaled a waiter for another. Kate wasn't much of a drinker. In fact, she hardly drank at all. She was allergic to wine, hated beer, and considered herself overdoing it if she took a brandy after dinner.

"Jeez, Kate. What's up with the booze?"

She ran a finger over the salted rim of her empty glass, but said nothing. A waiter in a purple sombrero two sizes too big arrived with her drink order. She licked the salt from her finger and gulped the margarita as if it were water.

The waiter turned to me. "And what can I get for you?"

I ordered some iced tea and perused one of the menus he left for us.

Kate suddenly set her glass down. "Oh-my-god, I can't believe he's here."

I looked up from the menu. "Who?"

She motioned to a corner booth several tables away where a middle-aged man sat by himself, reading the same menu I had in front of me. I was surprised that Kate recognized him. Dennis Lancaster was the owner of Maritime Enviro Services and the moving force behind an effort to oust live-aboards like me from the marina. I'd managed to steer clear of the guy, but several of the other live-aboards had had plenty of run-ins with him.

"Oh, yeah," I said. "Dennis Lancaster. He has a yacht moored here. Thinks live-aboards are trailer trash or some such nonsense. If he gets his way, I could be looking for new living quarters soon."

Kate didn't seem to hear me. "Why is he following me?"

"Following you?"

She took another drink. "Listen, Kellie, I don't trust the guy."

"Well, you're not alone. But I wasn't aware that you even knew him."

"The jerk lives in my building."

That explained it. Dennis Lancaster fancied himself something of a ladies' man, and since Kate attracts men like cat hair to a sweater—a tight sweater—he'd probably hit on her at their condo. He was good-looking in that he was taller than the average Joe, with all the requisite manly features—strong, square-jawed face, tanned and well-built body, neatly trimmed hair and beard with just a hint of gray, and deep-set dark eyes. But there was something else about him, a dangerous and unpredictable look that belied his flirty smile and teasing banter.

The waiter returned with a bowl of chips and some salsa, then asked if we were ready to order lunch. Kate opted for a small taco salad while I went for the works: a combo plate with taco, burrito, chimichanga, rice, and beans. I was suddenly ravenous and dug into the chips and salsa. However tacky the Broiler's new decor, the salsa was great. It had just the right amount of cilantro, lime, and serrano chile to keep me eating right up until our lunch arrived.

Whatever Kate's problem with Lancaster was, she didn't elaborate further. Our conversation was mostly confined to the ordinary intermixed with a little family gossip—the unsurprising scoop being that our sister, Donna, was going in for another round of liposuction. We were midway through our meal when I saw Lancaster stand up. He'd been joined by none other than the Weasel and the young newspaper reporter. "My, my. That's interesting," I said.

"What?" asked Kate.

"Lancaster is on the selection committee for the marina's general manager position. Looks like Todd Wilmington is doing some hustling for his vote."

Kate looked over at the trio and frowned. "The Weasel is an idiot in search of a village. How does he possibly think he'll get selected?"

I laughed. "Who knows? Though I've always said he should go far—and the sooner the better."

That drew a smile from Kate, the first since we'd begun lunch. "Just be glad you're not on the selection committee," she said. "He'd be trying to suck up to you as well."

I nodded, but not for the reason she thought. Besides Wilmington, Rose Randall, the marina's accountant, and Bert Foster, the harbormaster, were also vying for the same job. Rose was my best friend, but Bert was the main reason I was able to live at a marina like Larstad's. He was Donna's ex-husband and the only one who'd supported my decision to buy *Second Wind*. He'd gotten me a mooring slip at Larstad's at a drastically reduced rate and even arranged for me to teach at the sailing school. I owed him big time, but I was also very fond of Rose, who was extremely qualified to be general manager. I was glad I wouldn't have to put my loyalties to the test.

"How about some dessert?" I asked Kate. She immediately summoned our waiter, but instead of ordering dessert she asked for another drink.

"I don't get it, Kate," I said. "Why are you drinking your lunch?"

She smiled sheepishly and pushed up her sleeve to expose a small tan patch on her arm. "Can you believe it? I'm finally doing something about kicking the habit."

"Congratulations," I said, sincerely pleased. "But I still don't get it. Are you saying that you've switched your drug of choice? From nicotine to alcohol?"

"Hardly."

"Then why all the booze?"

"Well, I guess you could say the moment of truth finally arrived."

Before she could explain further, our waiter brought my dessert—a scrumptious flan—and Kate changed the subject. "Enough about me," she said. "I want to talk about Pearl."

"What's she up to now? Climbing in the Himalayas?" Pearl Danielson was a former sailing student of mine and Kate's next-door neighbor—a feisty, fiercely independent seventy-five-year-old who took up sailing at age seventy because she was bored with fly fishing.

"She's missing."

"What do you mean, *missing?*"

"As in *poof!* She's gone. Disappeared. Vanished without a trace . . ."

I rolled my eyes. "Get real, Kate. With Pearl, anything's possible. What makes you think she's not just off on one of her little adventures? Remember the time she signed up for a cruise and we thought she was going on a luxury liner to someplace like the Caribbean? It wasn't until she got back that we learned her so-called cruise had been a canoe trip down the Amazon."

"Yeah, I remember. It took us all by surprise."

"Well, there you go."

"No, Kellie, this is different. She isn't off on some exotic trip—unless you consider Salem, Oregon, exotic."

"Isn't that where her daughter lives?"

"Right." Kate nodded. "Little Adrienne, the tight-ass Republican. The thing is, she's never gotten along with Pearl—or her liberal-leaning politics. But according to Pearl, Adrienne's been after her to move to Salem, ostensibly to be closer to the family."

"What'd Pearl think of the idea?"

"Not much. She was just going to Salem for a visit. Wasn't supposed to be gone more than a couple of days, but it's been over two weeks now and she's not back yet."

"So? Maybe she just decided to extend her visit— spend a little more time with Adrienne and her family."

"That's what I thought at first. But then the police showed up, asking all kinds of questions about her. Apparently she never made it to Salem, and Adrienne filed a missing persons report."

"Hmm."

"So, what do you think?"

"About what?"

"About finding Pearl?"

"I'm sure she'll turn up eventually, especially if the police are involved."

Kate sighed and looked down at the table. "I was afraid you'd say that."

I had to laugh. "You sound as if you don't want her found."

"Of course I do. It's just that I thought you might want to help find her."

"Me? Why would you think that?"

She shot me an exasperated look. "I swear to God, Kellie, I can't believe you sometimes. This is Pearl Danielson we're talking about—the woman is like a mother to us. Didn't you jump at the chance to solve the Moyer murders a few months back? You hardly even knew them, but you sure got yourself involved in the investigation."

I rubbed my shoulder. "Yeah, and what did my little investigation get me? A stay in the hospital and a bum shoulder that still hurts like crazy whenever it rains." I looked out the window at the dark clouds hovering over the city like a giant black umbrella. "Which is just about constantly these days."

"All I know is that you're good at figuring things out. And this isn't a murder case. It can't possibly be all that dangerous. Besides, you're Pearl's only hope. Adrienne and her family don't want her found."

"Why do you say that? They contacted the police, filed a missing persons report. What more do you want them to do?"

"Oh, I don't know. Something besides sit around on their butts waiting for the police to do all the work."

"That's what the police get paid for."

"If it's just money you're concerned about, I'd be more than willing to pay you for your efforts."

Her offer annoyed me. Kate was comfortably well off,

each of her three divorces having left her with substantial settlements, and—although I hated to admit it—my sister was no different from many of the rich people I'd met at the marina. She truly believed that money could solve any problem. Trying to keep the irritation out of my voice, I said, "It's not the money, Kate. I have a job here. Tracking down Pearl—as much as I love her—would take time."

"I thought you said things were a little slow right now," she said, pouting.

"That's true, but this weather can't last forever."

"Nothing's happening today, is it?"

"No, but—"

"Then come back to Palisades with me now," she pleaded. "Take a look at Pearl's condo. See if there's anything there that the police may have overlooked. That's all I'm asking. Just a quick look. What can it hurt?"

"And just how do you propose that we get into her condo? I'm not about to get arrested for breaking and entering even if you can afford the bail."

She ignored the dig and said, "I have access to a key."

I considered Kate's request. Maybe her concerns were valid—she was certainly upset about Pearl. But I couldn't shake the feeling that there was something else troubling her as well. "Okay," I said finally. "Just a quick look. Nothing more."

# THREE

AS I EXPECTED, Kate started feeling the effects of her three-margarita lunch as soon as we left the Broiler. Before I could suggest it, she threw me the keys to her car and ordered me to drive. Her car was a brand-new Mercedes S500 which, given our destination, seemed only slightly less fitting than a limo. My sister and Pearl Danielson lived at Palisades West, a hoity-toity condominium located near the newly constructed Bell Street Pier and within walking distance of the Pike Place Market. Recipient of countless architectural awards, the Palisades had one of the most sweeping views of Elliott Bay and the Olympic Mountains that the city had to offer. Because of the choice views from virtually every unit and the exclusive appointments, the Palisades was home to some of Seattle's wealthiest citizens.

Kate lived there by virtue of her marriage to husband number two, a Texas oilman who could've bought the entire building and never felt a dent in his portfolio. He and Kate had lived in the 5,000-square-foot penthouse suite during their brief marriage, and after the divorce, Kate wound up with the whole shebang. She opted to sell the penthouse at a substantial profit and bought a smaller unit—a mere 3,000 square feet—right next door to Pearl Danielson.

Pearl had lived in the building since it opened. Unlike me, she was a widow with money. And unlike Kate, she'd earned most of it herself. She was notoriously tight-lipped about her personal life, but it was no secret that Pearl Danielson was a self-made millionaire. Her success story began in 1945 when she turned a long-time hobby—portrait photography—into one of Seattle's most successful entrepreneurial efforts. Before hanging up her camera case a few years back, she'd taken Photos by Pearl public and authorized the development of a string of studio franchises across the U.S. and Canada.

Palisades West wasn't far from the marina, but it took us quite a while to get there. Every two blocks or so, I had to pull over to the curb so Kate could upchuck her lunch. By the time we finally arrived, she looked miserable and smelled even worse. Tony Carmine, the building's superintendent, met us at the lobby entrance.

An ex-Marine, Tony was forty-five, short, and as stocky as a bulldog. He had a little round face with little round eyes that were always on you—sort of like in those trick paintings, the ones where you swear the eyes follow your every move. Kate thought he was the greatest, but I couldn't get past those eyes—or the fifty pounds of Brylcreem he favored. Despite a no-nonsense crew cut, he'd smeared enough grease on his thick black hair to fry up a dozen eggs.

Dressed in white overalls and carrying a bucket of paint in each hand, he was giving orders to a couple of similarly attired teenagers when we came in. As soon as he saw Kate, though, he thrust the buckets at one of the kids and sprinted across the lobby like Michael Johnson going for the gold.

"Hey, whatsa matter with my girl?" he asked. His concerned expression confirmed my long-held belief about the man. Dennis Lancaster might have the hots for Kate, but Tony Carmine was absolutely in love with her. He'd served in Vietnam with one of Kate's husbands and had barely made it out alive. With nothing but a couple of medals to show for his troubles, he'd wrapped himself around a whiskey bottle and never let go, flitting from one low-paying job to another for years—until he met Kate. She got him into AA and convinced the management at Palisades to give him a chance. He'd been hovering around her like a love-struck teenager ever since.

"Nothing that a little bed rest won't cure," I said, steering Kate toward the elevator. Getting my sister moving in the right direction, though, was akin to propelling a boat across Elliott Bay without a rudder. To keep her upright, I grabbed hold of one arm while Tony grabbed the other. Kate clung to us as though we'd offered her a life ring.

When we reached the elevator, Tony punched the button for the ninth floor. "You want I should get you something?" he asked Kate as we waited.

She groaned a little which Tony took as a yes. "Whatcha want, sweetheart? Aspirin, Alka-Seltzer®, you name it, you got it."

"Key," she sputtered.

Tony's dark eyes registered momentary confusion. "Oh, I get it," he said, snapping his fingers. "You forgot your house key again, is that it?"

The elevator doors slid open as Kate shook her head. "Pearl's."

So that's what she'd meant by "having access." I thought Pearl had given her a key so that she could water the plants or something. Instead, she'd counted on Tony to get us into her condo. "Kate," I said, "I don't think this is such a good idea."

But Tony had already pulled a large metal ring crammed with keys out of his pocket. He quickly pried open the ring and handed one of the keys to Kate. "Here ya go. Pearl Danielson. Numero 925."

"Oh, God," moaned Kate. "What I really need is a cigarette."

I fully expected him to produce one of those as well. Instead he looked down at the elevator floor, suddenly interested in a small rip in the carpet. "Aw, Kate," he said, poking at the frayed fabric with his shoe, "you know what the doctor told you."

"What doctor?" I asked.

Tony and Kate exchanged glances. "She doesn't know, does she?" he said.

When Kate failed to respond, I said, "You're talking about the patch, right?"

If my sister had been nauseous in the Mercedes, her condition became even more acute following the elevator ride. Tony and I managed to get her into her condo just before she delivered up the rest of her lunch. I was beginning to feel a little queasy myself and, after cleaning up the mess on the entryway floor, went into the kitchen for a drink of water. Meanwhile, Tony had eased Kate onto the living room couch. When I returned, he was wiping her forehead with a handkerchief.

"How's she doing?" I asked.

"Not so good." He picked up a prescription bottle from the coffee table and shook out two pills. "Need some water," he said, hurrying out to the kitchen.

I sat down next to Kate and examined the prescription label. I didn't recognize the medication. "Kate? What's going on?"

She pressed Pearl's key into my hand. "You'll have to go by yourself, sis. I can't make it."

"I'm not going anywhere until you tell me what's the matter with you."

"Too much to drink."

I fingered the prescription bottle. "Yeah, right."

Tony hustled into the room with a glass of water.

"Here ya go, sweetheart," he said, handing her the glass and pills. "See if you can get these down."

I held her head while she sipped the water and swallowed both pills. "What's the prescription for, Kate?" I asked.

"I can't talk about it right now," she said, closing her eyes. "Go take a look at Pearl's condo. We'll talk when you get back."

"But—"

"It's all right," Tony said. "I'll stay here with her."

"Yeah," echoed Kate, pushing me away. "Tony knows what to do. So, go on. Get yourself out of here."

I started to argue, but it was apparent from the set of her jaw that it would be a pointless exercise. Her determined look told me that nothing had changed since we were kids—I could badger my sister all day long, but if I didn't do what she wanted, she'd never tell me anything. "Okay," I said. Then, unable to suppress the teacher in me, I added, "But when I return, I want an explanation." Since Kate had closed her eyes again, I wagged a finger at Tony. "A *full* explanation."

I was almost out the door when he said, "There is one little thing . . ."

"What's that?"

"Four-five-four-seven."

"Say again?"

"The security code. You'll need it once you're inside Mrs. Danielson's."

One "little thing" indeed. I wondered how he knew her code, but didn't press the issue. "Thanks for sharing."

"Four-five-four-seven," he repeated. "Don't forget, or there'll be hell to pay if that alarm goes off."

Hell I could handle. The police were another matter.

•   •   •   •

I COULDN'T HAVE felt more guilty about letting myself into Pearl's condo than if I'd jimmied the lock. Despite the difference in our ages and our markedly disparate economic circumstances, Pearl and I had become good friends—on and off the water—but in all the time that I'd known her, she'd never invited me to her home. And now here I was, inviting myself in like a common thief. Never mind that I had a key. I was nothing more than a trespasser. An interloper. A snoop. The fact that she was supposedly missing did nothing to quell my uneasiness over being in her home without permission. I figured I'd take a quick peek around and get out as fast as I could.

After I opened the front door and slipped inside, I located the security keypad and quickly entered the numerical code Tony had given me. With the alarm safely disarmed, I stood in the marbled entry a few moments to get my bearings. The air was stale; as dry and lifeless as the roses that adorned a nearby table. The room's musty odor was not surprising considering that the place had been closed up for over two weeks. But there was something else that hit me as soon as I walked in—a suffocating tightness in my chest that left me gasping for breath. It was eerie, as if all the oxygen had been sucked out of the room during Pearl's absence.

Still feeling like an intruder, I was reluctant to touch anything, including the light switch—a reluctance that was a little silly since I could hardly see a thing. But after a moment or two, my eyes adjusted to the low light spilling out from the edges of the heavily draped windows and I was able to see well enough for my purposes. Which, my guilty feelings notwithstanding, included a certain curiosity about how the rich folk lived.

What a disappointment. For someone with Pearl's net worth, her furnishings didn't seem all that opulent. Oh, she had fine taste, evidenced by the exquisite plush carpeting, oil paintings, and antiques—but they were hardly examples of conspicuous consumption. I'd seen more elaborate furnishings in some of the yachts moored at Larstad's. The more I thought about it, though, the more the simple decor made sense. Her home was just like Pearl herself—warm, comfortable, and easy to like.

Since Kate and Pearl were next-door neighbors, I'd expected the units to have similar floor plans. At first glance, the layout was indeed the same: formal dining room to my right, office/den to my left, and immediately ahead, an expansive great room with adjoining gourmet kitchen. Beyond the great room on the left was a hallway that led to a small guest bathroom; further on, three bedrooms. Just your basic little condo.

Pearl's unit was even larger than Kate's 3,000-square-foot nest. A white spiral staircase to the right of the great room led to a second floor. Since my initial look-see downstairs hadn't turned up anything remotely helpful, I decided to check out what lay above. At the top of the stairs, I found myself in a huge loft overlooking the great room. Grampy always said that the heart of a home was the kitchen, but if he'd been with me this day he'd have said we were looking into Pearl's soul.

Two of the three walls were occupied by floor-to-ceiling bookcases crammed with hundreds of books, *National Geographic*s, several vintage cameras, and a hodgepodge of souvenirs from Pearl's travels around the world—including a model of *Star Runner,* the ketch Pearl had sailed single-handedly from Seattle to Hawaii three years before.

The third wall was covered with black-and-white portraits, some framed and titled, but most not. The subjects were varied and offered a striking retrospective of Pearl's artistry through the decades—a young bride waiting in front of a church, an old man toting a fishing pole, a schoolgirl playing hopscotch, a couple of street people sharing a smoke. As I studied the portraits, it suddenly occurred to me why Pearl had enjoyed such financial success. Through the simple click of a shutter, she had created a lasting link between the thin thread of memory and a fleeting moment in time.

The only furniture in the loft consisted of a cream-colored leather recliner, a square end table, and a floor lamp grouped alongside the railing. A variety of magazines and books—mostly travel- and sailing-related—were piled atop the table. One of the books—*The Sparrow* by Mary Doria Russell—was open, its pages secured with a pair of reading glasses. I could picture Pearl sitting in the chair, a cup of tea on the table, the book in her hands, reading glasses perched halfway down her nose, a contented smile on her face. What I couldn't picture was anything amiss. Except for a little dust, the loft, like the rest of the condo, was immaculate. If there were any clues to Pearl Danielson's disappearance here, they sure weren't popping out at me.

As I debated whether or not to check out the rest of the upstairs or simply bag the whole thing, I heard a noise at the front door. I held my breath and hoped it was just someone passing by in the hall outside. No such luck. Voices—male voices—were in the entryway now. And I was knee-deep in guano. With absolutely no desire to make my presence known, I immediately hit the deck—quietly, of course—and laid stomach-side down facing the railing.

Two men entered the great room, and although I couldn't see their faces without exposing myself, I had no trouble hearing them. Their voices were loud and rough and, in the case of one of them, surprisingly familiar.

"How many times I gotta tell you, shit brain? Always lock the door."

"Fuck you. I locked it."

"Yeah, yeah. And I suppose you reset the alarm, too."

"Right."

"You hear any little beep-beep sound going off?"

A pause. "Must be something wrong with the system."

"With *your* system, you mean."

"Fuck you."

"Let's get this over with. Where'd you say you saw it?"

"The den."

They backtracked to the entryway and presumably the den. I could've stayed put, probably should've stayed put, but these guys were obviously after something, and I damn well wasn't going to cower in a corner until they found it—or me. I crept down the staircase and inched my way across the great room. I was within spitting distance of the front door and a clean getaway when all the lights went on in the den. Scarcely breathing, I flattened myself against the nearest wall.

I thought I'd recognized Dennis Lancaster's voice earlier. Now I was positive. I poked my head around the corner and saw him standing at Pearl's rolltop desk, pulling out one drawer after another. I didn't know the guy with him, but he was giving a small oak cabinet the same treatment. I figured I had two choices in this situation: get the hell out while I still could or stick around and see what Lancaster and his pal were up to. I chose door number two.

The entryway table didn't make for an ideal hiding spot, but I decided to chance it. Crouching low, I watched nervously as the two men ransacked Pearl's den. Their search was a hurried and haphazard rifling that culminated in a furious dumping of papers onto the floor.

"It's not here," said Lancaster's buddy disgustedly. "Are you sure you even saw it?"

"I said I did, didn't I?"

"Yeah, but what you say and what you do are two different—"

"Shit," said Lancaster, tugging on his beard.

"What?"

"Maybe she took it with her."

"Why would she do that?"

"Who knows? I tell you, man, she's getting loonier and loonier every day. Get this: One day I'm over here, can't remember why, but the point is, she offers me some tea. Last thing I want is to have tea with the old biddy, but I figure, what the hell? Won't hurt me to humor her a bit. You know, maybe get on her good side for a change."

"Are you going somewhere with this story?"

Lancaster made like a traffic cop and held both hands in the air. "Just hold on," he said. "The old gal serves up the tea all nice and proper like. I mean, we're talking fancy here—silver tray, cream and sugar, linen napkins, the works. But then she goes and pulls a weirdo on me."

"What the hell are you talking about?"

"The sugar bowl," said Lancaster. "She dips into the goddamn bowl and spoons out her house keys."

"Damn. If she's really getting that bad, then it could be anywhere. We're going to have to tear this place apart."

I took that as my cue to leave. But when I stood, I bumped into the table. It was just a slight tap, but it was enough: The vase of roses teetered, then crashed to the floor.

# FOUR

GLASS SHATTERED IN a million directions as the vase hit the marble floor. I couldn't have announced my presence better if I'd waved my arms and yelled, Hey, fellas, I'm over here!

Dennis Lancaster bolted out of the den to investigate and stopped abruptly when he saw me. "Well, well, well," he drawled in a deep, manly-man sort of voice that, despite the circumstances, exuded a raw sexiness. "What have we got here?"

He didn't seem particularly threatening, but my throat constricted and I couldn't say a thing. I stood rooted to the floor, unable to decide whether I should cover myself or spit in his face as he ogled me from head to toe. Laughter flickered in his eyes as he winked. Where did he think we were? A pickup bar? I brushed him off with a get-lost look, which did nothing to diffuse the situation.

"Hey, Phil," he called over his shoulder. "You should see this. We got ourselves a pussy burglar. Emphasis on pussy."

His partner was not amused. He exited the den and snapped, "What the hell's going on?" He was a tall man, nearly the same size as Lancaster, but the stoop-shouldered way he carried himself made him seem shorter, softer, and, despite his bold talk, sort of vulnerable.

Lancaster gave me another once-over. "I know her," he said. Having essentially stripped me naked, he seemed disgusted by what he'd found.

"Who is she?" asked Phil.

"Some chick from the marina. I think she's one of those live-aboard types."

They yakked back and forth a moment, talking about me as if I weren't even there—which is exactly what I wished. Thinking that a way out of the situation would somehow present itself sooner or later, I refrained from jumping into the conversation.

The Phil guy looked me over. His gaze, unlike Lancaster's, didn't make me uncomfortable. He wore a confused expression, like someone trying to figure out how dog poop had wound up on his brand-new shoes. He was about Lancaster's age—late forties to mid-fifties—but he lacked the same good looks, mainly because of the deeply pitted scars covering his face like an old orange peel. Must have been one heck of a case of teenage acne. He was dressed in a lightweight summer suit that projected a smart, businesslike image. "Does she know Pearl?" he asked.

I was tired of listening to them talk around me. "As a matter of fact, I do," I said. "She's a friend of mine."

Lancaster took a step forward. "Oh, yeah? You make a habit of breaking into your friends' homes?"

Phil winced, clearly bothered by the tough-guy attitude. He placed a hand on Lancaster's shoulder. "Cut the crap, Denny," he said. "She hardly looks like a threat."

"But—"

"I mean it," he said.

Lancaster brushed Phil's hand away and stepped

aside. "Fine," he said, giving me a sour look. "You talk to the bitch."

Phil regarded him briefly and then turned to me. "Now," he said, "suppose you tell us who you are and what you're doing here."

"You go first," I suggested.

Lancaster snorted. "Smart-ass."

Phil shot him a disapproving look. "That's not necessary, Denny." He smiled an apology to me. "Pearl Danielson is my mother-in-law." He motioned to Lancaster. "And Denny, here, is my brother."

I could sort of buy the son-in-law bit, but brothers? Give me a break. Other than size, the two men were polar opposites. Dennis Lancaster's dark hair and beard, swarthy complexion, and look-at-me-I'm-a-stud attitude contrasted sharply with his so-called brother's fair skin, blond hair, and businesslike demeanor.

He caught my dubious expression. "Same mother, different fathers," he explained. "I'm Phillip Coughlin. He's Dennis Lancaster. And you are?" he asked pleasantly, offering his hand.

"Embarrassed," I said, shaking his hand. "Kellie Montgomery."

"Well, isn't this just peachy keen?" chided Lancaster. "We're all properly introduced now. But you still haven't told us why you're here."

Neither had they, but I let the omission slide. "My sister asked me to check on things. She's worried about Pearl."

The two brothers exchanged glances. "And just who might your sister be?" asked Coughlin.

"Mary Kathleen Rossiter. I believe you know her? She lives right next door."

Lancaster's face registered disbelief bordering on shock. "No way," he said." He turned to his brother. "She's lying. There's no way this pipsqueak is related to that knockout."

I laughed in spite of the slam-dunk. "Strange as it may seem, we're sisters, all right." I looked at Coughlin. "Same mother, same father."

"You say your sister sent you over here," he said. "To do what, exactly?"

"She thought I might be able to find something that would help explain Pearl's absence. I understand she's been reported missing."

The two brothers exchanged glances again. "So?" said Lancaster.

The guy bugged me. That's the only explanation I can give for what I found myself blurting out next. "*So* . . . I plan to find her."

Lancaster laughed. "You can't be serious."

I looked him square in the face. "Oh yes, Denny, I am. Very serious."

Both men tensed visibly during the brief silence that followed. But it was Lancaster who let his feelings loose. "Bitch!" he snarled.

"Wait a minute," Phillip said, shooting a warning look at his brother. "Kellie, are you a detective?"

"No, I teach sailing at Larstad's Marina."

Phillip Coughlin's pitted face took on a sudden hardness that erased any hint of the vulnerability I'd sensed earlier. "Then I suggest you stick to what you do," he said curtly. He took me by the arm and quickly escorted me to the door. Giving my arm a sharp squeeze, he added, "And let the police do what they do."

His reaction egged me on. I twisted out of his grasp and said, "Oh, I will. But I don't intend to just stand by twiddling my thumbs." I opened the front door and stepped into the hall. "As I said, Pearl is my friend." I smiled broadly. "And there's nothing I wouldn't do for her."

Phillip returned my smile, a tight little lip action that had about as much warmth in it as an ice cube. "I understand," he said, leaning closer now, teeth clenched.

"But you need to understand this: The family doesn't want your help. We are cooperating with the police. End of discussion. If we find you trespassing again or interfering in the official investigation in any way, we'll have no recourse but to take legal action against you."

WHEN I GOT back to Kate's, she was asleep on the couch, and Tony was slouched in a nearby chair, idly thumbing through a magazine. He tossed it aside and stood up when I walked in. "How'd it go?" he asked quietly.

"Do you know a guy named Phillip Coughlin?"

Tony rolled his eyes. "Oh, yeah. He's Pearl's son-in-law and a real pain in the butt."

"How so?"

He glanced at Kate. "Come out to the kitchen where we can talk without disturbing her."

In the kitchen, he poured himself a cup of coffee while I put a teakettle on the stove. When we'd settled at a small table in the eating nook, I asked about Kate.

He avoided my eyes and drank his coffee. "She's okay now. Fell asleep right after you left." I waited, but he said nothing further until the kettle whistled, startling him. He jumped up and took it off the stove. "You want Earl Grey or something herbal?" he asked, rummaging through the basket Kate kept stocked with tea bags.

I opted for good old Earl. "So, Tony," I said after he'd returned to the table with my cup. "Before we get into why Coughlin is such a pain, why don't you tell me what's wrong with Kate?"

He shifted uncomfortably in his chair. "Uh, I think it'd be better if she told you that herself."

The aura of sadness that enveloped him frightened me. My heart beat faster and faster. I swallowed hard, then asked, "It's something serious, isn't it?"

He nodded slowly, confirming my worst suspicions. I

was numb. It couldn't be happening again. I'd lost my
husband to a brain tumor, Grampy to cancer. The possibility that Kate might be taken from me, too, was more
than I could bear. I had to think about something else.
I blew on my tea. "Okay. Let's get back to Phillip
Coughlin. What can you tell me about him?"

"A lot," Tony said, setting his cup down on the table.
"But I don't have that much time. I've got to get back
to work—those kids will sit around all day watching the
paint dry if I don't get on them."

"Just give me the *Reader's Digest* condensed version,
then."

Glancing at his watch, he said, "Phillip Coughlin is
co-owner of Maritime Enviro Services. The home office
is in Oregon, where he lives with his wife, Adrienne,
and their teenage daughter. The other owner, his brother,
Dennis, runs the Seattle office. An even worse pain in
the butt. Just ask Kate about him. Anyway, from what
I hear, business hasn't been all that great lately. Mrs.
Danielson never talks much about her family, but the
scuttlebutt is that Phillip and Dennis have been hounding
her to bail them out of their financial difficulties. Both
brothers are arrogant as hell and won't give me the time
of day." He stood up. "My advice is to steer clear of
them."

"Good advice," said Kate behind us. She came into
the kitchen and slowly eased herself into a chair at the
table. We watched her expectantly. Yawning, she said,
"Tony, before you leave, how about a cup of that coffee?"

"Sure thing, doll."

After Tony left, we sat drinking our tea and coffee
without speaking. I wanted to ask Kate one of the million questions zinging around in my head, but I just
couldn't get the words out. Although she looked better
than she had earlier, she still wasn't her normal self. She

broke the silence first. "How'd it go at Pearl's? Find anything useful?"

"Just the brothers grim—Dennis and Phillip. And they didn't much like the idea of my looking into Pearl's disappearance."

When I finished telling her about our encounter, she smiled at me over the rim of her cup. "You're going to do it, aren't you? You're going to find Pearl." She reached across the table and took my hand in hers. "I knew you wouldn't let Pearl down." She squeezed my hand. "Or me."

"Well," I said, "I admit I hadn't planned on it when I went over to her place. I didn't find anything out of the ordinary until the brothers showed up. Their behavior was very odd."

"I hear you," said Kate, nodding knowingly.

"Besides making a mess out of the den, they said some disturbing things about Pearl when they didn't know I was listening. And when I accidentally gave myself away, Lancaster tried to bully me."

"That doesn't surprise me. What'd Coughlin do?"

"He put the damper on his brother and was even sort of pleasant—until I said I was going to look for Pearl. Most people with missing relatives welcome any help they can get. Not so with Phillip Coughlin and company."

"I told you the family wasn't acting exactly kosher." She poured herself another cup of coffee. "So, what's your next move?"

"I haven't thought that far ahead yet, but I suppose I should talk to some of the residents here. Maybe someone saw Pearl before she left for Salem."

"Great idea! You can start with me."

"You saw her?"

"Better than that," Kate said with a grin. "I talked to her."

She knew she'd hooked me. "And?"

"And it was eight-thirty on a Friday morning about three weeks ago. Downstairs in the parking garage. My parking spot is right next to hers."

"Wait a minute," I said, setting my cup on the table. "You were up and at 'em at eight-thirty in the morning?"

She shrugged. "Doctor's appointment."

When she didn't elaborate, I said, "Okay, you were in the garage. What'd Pearl say to you?"

"At first, she just waved. She was lugging a small black suitcase—a Tumi, I think—and after she put it in the trunk of her Jaguar, I asked if she was going on a trip. That's when she told me her daughter had invited her to Salem for a visit."

"How did she seem to you?"

"What do you mean?"

"Was she excited about the trip? Happy? Sad?"

"I don't know. It wasn't a long conversation. I got the impression she was in a hurry, because she kept looking at her wristwatch."

"Did she happen to mention if she was planning to drive straight through to Salem or stop along the way somewhere?"

Kate smiled and said, "I knew you'd be good at this, Kellie. The police asked the very same question."

I looked at her expectantly. "So, what did you tell them?"

"Pearl didn't say anything about her itinerary."

"Great. That helps a lot."

"Maybe not, but I thought of something else after the police questioned me. It didn't mean anything to me at the time, but now I'm not so sure. During my short chitchat with Pearl, I made a comment about the weather. Something about picking a good day for taking a trip. That was right before we started getting all this rain. Anyway, Pearl said, 'Driving to Salem on a day like this is the last thing I want to be doing.' "

"Do you think she changed her mind and didn't go?"
Kate grimaced suddenly.

"Kate," I said softly. "Please tell me what's wrong. I'm so worried."

"Don't be."

"But Tony said—"

"Oh, don't listen to him. He exaggerates everything."

"Even what he told me about Dennis and Phillip?"

"Kellie," she sighed, "the situation is under control. It's true that I'm having a few problems right now, but it's nothing to get worked up about."

I didn't think that was the case and was tempted to tell her so. But I knew an argument was bound to result. I was already on the outs with my other sister. Jeopardizing my relationship with Kate, too, was something I wanted to avoid at all costs.

"Isn't there something I can do for you?" I asked.

"Absolutely," she said. "Find Pearl."

# FIVE

I TOYED WITH the idea of calling Allen Kingston to give me a ride back to the marina. Actually I'd been debating whether I should call him for the past two weeks. We've been "an item," as my daughter would call it, since last Christmas, but I've known him for some time. To our mutual surprise, we sort of fell into a relationship when I butted into a murder case he was investigating. Things got hot and heavy for a while, but lately he's been so busy with his job that we haven't seen much of each other.

As a homicide detective, Kingston is always busy, but ever since his partner, Brian Saunders, was promoted to sergeant a few months back, he's been even busier. My guess was that Kingston was having some major adjustments to make. Beyond the stress associated with breaking in a new partner, Brian Saunders had never been his favorite person, and now that he was Kingston's boss, things were . . . well, a little tense.

In any case, I was reluctant to call Kingston. The plain fact is, I've yet to fully embrace the nineties when it comes to male-female relationships. Things were so simple when Wendell and I were dating. You knew the rules, and although you might not like them, you knew what was what. Rule number one was that women didn't call men. I'd missed Kingston these past couple of weeks, but there was no way in hell I was going to call him first.

Since I was hopelessly trapped in a fifties time warp, the honor of escorting me home fell to my daughter, Cassie. She picked me up in my little Miata roadster—an all-too-quick ten minutes after I'd called her.

"What'd you do, set a new speed record?" I asked, hopping into the passenger seat. I knew the remark wouldn't be appreciated as soon as it popped out of my mouth. Our relationship has been rocky ever since her father died. Only sixteen at the time, she took his passing hard. I'd experienced the same thing when my parents were killed, but instead of blaming God as I did, Cassie focused her anger on me. It is only recently that we've begun to draw closer, but we're still not on firm ground yet. My flippancy didn't help matters.

"Oh, Mom, don't start."

"Sorry." I belted myself in without further comment, a remarkable feat given the fact that we nearly reached Mach 3 pulling away from the curb. Luckily we found ourselves mired in a traffic jam before Cassie could get us airborne. I took the opportunity to smooth things over. "So, how was your first day at work?"

She shrugged. "Okay, I guess." Cassie attends Rensselaer Polytechnic in Troy, New York, on a full scholarship, but she'd snagged a job at the Topside for the summer. Although I made no comment regarding her lack of enthusiasm, she must have sensed I needed reassuring. "I mean, it's fine. Just fine."

"Good," I said. "I think."

"It really is good," she said. "Got lots of tips to prove it, too," she added, pointing to the small clutch purse she'd stashed between our seats. Something was on her mind, but I didn't press the issue. Sure enough, it wasn't more than a couple of minutes later that she got around to talking about it. "Mom, I . . . I found her."

*Her? Oh God . . . Her.* Wendell and I had adopted Cassie as an infant, and I'd bonded with her so completely that it sometimes slipped my mind that I hadn't given birth to her myself. It was only a few short months since Cassie told me that she was going to search for her birth mother. It had been a struggle to understand her decision at first, but eventually I accepted the idea and even encouraged her search. Still, her announcement caught me off guard. My heart rate shot sky high, and I folded my arms across my chest to keep from trembling.

"She lives in Portland," Cassie said. "Can you believe it? That's practically in our backyard."

"How'd you find her so fast?"

"I had the file, remember?"

I remembered very well. Her birth mother's maiden name was in an old file folder that Allen Kingston had rescued from the office of our attorney, Donald Moyer, following his murder. Only after reading through the twenty-year-old file did I discover that Cassie's mother had delivered twins. Cassie and her sister had been adopted at birth by separate families who were told nothing about each other's existence. "Wait a minute," I said. "Are you talking about your twin sister or your birth mother?"

"My sister. I figured it would be better to locate her first. Maybe the two of us can team up to find our mother. Besides, I'm really curious about what she looks like. I mean, wouldn't it be a kick if we're identical?"

I nodded slowly, feeling as though a weight had been lifted from my shoulders.

"Anyway," said Cassie, "according to Moyer's records, they were living in Portland at the time of the adoption. Within minutes of logging onto the Internet, I

found them. They have a different address now, but
they're still living in Portland. I figure their daughter
probably does, too. Unless, like me, she's going to college out of the area or something.''

"What do you plan to do?"

"I'm not sure, Mom. I'm real anxious to contact her,
but kind of scared, too. Does that make sense?"

"Perfect sense," I said, touching her shoulder.
"Maybe you just need some more time. There's a lot to
think about, especially how you'll handle the initial contact. If you'll recall, Lydia said that using an intermediary sometimes works best in these situations. Maybe
you ought to talk to her.''

Lydia was the leader of a support group that dealt with
birth-family reunions. Cassie and I had attended a few
sessions with the group the last time she was home from
college. I couldn't tell whether she was considering my
advice or not, since she didn't say anything further until
we got to the marina. By then she'd switched to a new
subject.

"Hey," she said with a grin, "I saw your friend Col-
umbo today.''

Cassie loved to tease me about Allen Kingston, especially regarding his shaggy hair and rumpled clothes.
She found his willful disregard for the Seattle P.D.'s
dress code amusing. But his sloppy ways were no laughing matter with the brass. Because of his outstanding
record with the department, though, they'd looked the
other way for years. According to Kingston, Brian Saunders wasn't proving to be so understanding. They'd already had more than one go-round over the issue since
he took charge of the unit.

Cassie shook her head. "Boy, he sure has changed!"

"What do you mean?"

"Come on, Mom. Give yourself some credit. Since
you've started dating, he's a new man. Even I have to
admit that he really looks great now—new haircut, new

clothes. Rumor has it that he's traded that old clunker of his for a bright red Porsche.''

A Porsche? No way. And what new haircut? What new clothes? "Actually, Cassie, I haven't seen much of Allen lately. He looked just the same the last time I saw him. But from what you say, it sounds as though his new boss has finally gotten him to clean up his act. Saunders is a stickler for things like that.''

Cassie seemed unconvinced. "Whatever.'' She shrugged.

"I take it you think otherwise.''

"Well,'' she said after a moment's hesitation, "it may have something to do with his new partner.''

"Mel Connor?''

"Yeah. They were at the Topside together.''

Wary at first about taking on a new partner, Kingston seemed to like the guy a lot. For weeks after they'd first teamed up, all I'd heard was Mel this and Mel that—ad nauseam. I'd yet to meet the guy and, frankly, I was more than a little curious. "What's he like?''

"Oh, Mom,'' Cassie said with a sigh. "I thought you knew.''

"Knew what?''

She flashed me a wary look. "Uh . . .''

"Come on, Cass. Spill it.''

"Mel Connor isn't a he. Her full name is Melody. Melody Connor.''

Talk about a whack on the head. "Okay . . . what's *she* like, then?''

Cassie squirmed visibly. "I don't know. She's just a cop.'' Then, a little too quickly she added, "But I don't think you have anything to worry about.''

Damn. I should've called him.


THE NEXT MORNING checked in gray and dreary. What can I say? It was just another rainy day in paradise.

Despite several cups of the strongest tea I could find, I had a hard time getting myself going. I'm normally an upbeat person, but this morning I felt as gloomy as the weather. Yesterday's tumultuous events had unsettled me more than I thought. By the time my first sailing class started, though, the rain had tapered off, and I'd mellowed out somewhat. It didn't last long. My improved mood, that is.

At first, everything was just fine. My class consisted of four enthusiastic beginning sailors—all ladies who were seventy years of age and older. Officially they were enrolled in the Sailing for Seniors program, but somewhere along the line the participants had dubbed the course Sailing for Tough Old Birds.

It had been Pearl Danielson who convinced me that I should have a program especially designed for older folks. It was her belief that sailing slowed the aging process. I was skeptical at first, but my research on the subject tended to back up her claim. What I found was that as we age, the larger muscles are the first to go. As Pearl says, "If you don't use it, you lose it." Since sailing *requires* you to use your muscles, it provides an excellent exercise regime. In addition, many older adults have balance problems that can result in falls. Continually adjusting for balance while the boat is moving through the water stimulates your reflexes.

As was my practice, I led the ladies in some stretching exercises before boarding the Catalina 25 I'd selected for our lesson. They were a fun group, and I was soon laughing in spite of my earlier mood. Once we were actually on the water, we had an even better time. The wind was brisk and afforded us ample opportunity to apply the sail trim techniques we'd talked about in the classroom.

"As you'll recall from our earlier discussion, if the angle of the sails to the wind is wrong, the boat slows down or may even stop." I turned to Lois at the helm and asked, "So how can you tell when you have a problem with sail trim before you come to a stop?"

She looked up at the mainsail. I could tell from her expression that she thought the answer sounded too easy. "Uh, look at the sails?"

"You've got it. Looking up at the sails is your best and fastest indication of improper trim." I went on to remind her and the rest of the group that sails can either be perfectly trimmed, undertrimmed, or overtrimmed. "What happens when a sail is undertrimmed?" I asked.

"It begins to luff," she said, checking the mainsail again.

"Right. Luffing means that the sail is spilling air and thus losing power. An overtrimmed sail—one that is pulled in too much—also slows you down, but it's harder to see because it still appears full. If you could see the air molecules as they travel over the sail, however, you would see that the airflow is stalled on an overtrimmed sail."

My explanation produced a few blank stares until Faith, the wife of a retired United Airlines pilot, stepped in. "It's just like what happens when an airplane stalls," she suggested. "The plane can't fly because the wings can't generate lift."

"That's a very good analogy," I said. "Lift is what makes a sailboat move."

"What about those little pieces of yarn on the sails?" asked one of the other students. "Aren't you supposed to pay attention to those, too?"

"Absolutely. The strands, or telltales, show you what the air molecules are actually doing. You can think of telltales as a kind of early-warning system. They are more sensitive to changes in the flow than the sail is, so they luff sooner than the sailcloth does."

At this point, everyone was looking at the telltales, and I had to remind them that it was also important to keep an eye out for what was happening on the water.

With the break in the weather, there was quite a bit of boating traffic on Elliott Bay. A big Cigarette boat was headed our way at a very fast clip.

Lois regarded the power boat for a moment. "Doesn't he see us?" she asked. "As a sailboat, we have the right of way."

"Don't always count on power boaters to remember that rule," I said. "And if there's a collision, the skippers of both boats are equally responsible."

"Shouldn't Lois turn or something?" asked Faith.

The boat was still half a mile away, doing maybe thirty knots. "Let's hold our course a bit longer," I said. "The stand-on boat—that's us—is supposed to maintain course and speed so that the give-way boat doesn't have to guess what you're going to do. He may yet turn." I'd no sooner said that, however, than the Cigarette boat picked up speed. Its engines roared like a locomotive as it headed straight for us. Holding our course was no longer an option.

"Lois! Turn the wheel to port! Ladies, hurry up with the lines! We're coming about right now!"

Faith manned the jib sheet, but the emergency had her rattled, and she froze. I quickly took over her job and let the sheet go. It wasn't a precision tack, but we'd avoided a collision. Instead of passing well behind us, though, the boat's skipper suddenly turned and headed directly toward us again. I couldn't believe what I was seeing—he deliberately maneuvered his craft so that he came within half a boat length of our stern. "Hang on, ladies!" I cried. "We've got a nutcase on our tail."

As I feared, the ensuing wake caused the Catalina to buck and pitch violently. The women dropped to the deck and grabbed the lifelines and whatever else they could find to keep from being flung about or, worse yet, falling overboard. I took the wheel from Lois and craned my neck to get a better look at the Cigarette boat. As it roared off, the skipper raised his middle finger in the air and laughed. I thought I'd recognized him earlier, but now I was positive. Dennis Lancaster was just as unpleasant on the water as he was on land.

# SIX

MY STUDENTS WERE a hardy lot and recovered rapidly from our experience with Dennis Lancaster. I, on the other hand, could barely keep my anger in check. I was still seething over his childish recklessness when the class ended. After the ladies docked the Catalina and we said our goodbyes, I headed straight for Bert Foster's office. Although Bert was the harbormaster, I knew there wasn't anything he could do about Lancaster's behavior on the water. All I wanted at that moment was a sympathetic ear. Venting is good for the soul.

I'd just reached the administration building when a commotion in the parking lot caught my attention. Three men were shouting at one another and, judging by their body language, were about to come to blows. The prospect was intriguing since one of the warring parties was none other than the Weasel. Thinking this was too good to miss, I staked out a spot near the threesome to watch the show.

The long and lanky Weasel was seriously outmuscled by the other two men. But what he lacked in bulk, he more than made up for in volume. "I don't care what you say!" he screamed at the larger of his two opponents. "That car is in violation of marina policy! It has to be towed right now."

As I expected, the recipient of his outburst—a beefy marina security guard named Bruno—was not intimidated by the Weasel's high-pitched voice and skinny clenched fists. "Back off, Jack!" he shouted. "This is my job. I decide what gets towed around here. Not you."

The Weasel tried puffing up his chest, but came off looking like an anorexic blowfish. "Don't you know who I am?" he asked. This was a vintage Weasel tactic. Whenever he couldn't get someone to listen to him, he brought up his relationship to the marina's owner.

Bruno snorted derisively, then quickly turned his attention to the tow-truck driver. "Hey, man. Sorry you made a trip for nothing. The car stays put."

The driver shrugged. "No problem." But to the Weasel he said, "Next time, try checking with your boss before calling."

"*I* don't have a boss," the Weasel said haughtily.

The tow-truck driver had already begun to disengage the car in question from his rig, but he stopped and gave the Weasel a dead man's stare. "Then I guess *you* can pay the bill for my time today."

The Weasel stamped his foot like a little kid who'd just been kicked out of the sandbox, then beat a hasty retreat.

"What was that all about?" I asked Bruno.

"Just the usual. Todd Wilmington trying to make like he's somebody important."

I gestured toward the dirty green Jaguar that had caused all the fuss. "It has a marina parking permit in the windshield. What was Wilmington's problem?"

"New policy just went into effect. If you're going to park your vehicle at the marina for over two weeks, you have to get a long-term sticker from the office. The Jag's been here for almost three weeks now, so the owner couldn't have known about the change in policy. But that little fact didn't stop Wilmington. He insisted on flexing his baby muscles to get it towed, anyway."

I took another look at the Jag. "If I didn't know better, I'd say that car belongs to Pearl Danielson."

"It's not as clean as she usually keeps it," Bruno said, "but considering how long it's been here, that's understandable."

"Wait a minute. Are you saying that the car *does* belong to Pearl?"

"Yeah, those are her wheels. Sweet, huh?"

THERE ARE OVER a thousand mooring slips at Larstad's Marina, and, unless you're a dock attendant charged with the responsibility of tracking such things, it is nearly impossible to know which boats are in port at any one time. If pressed, I could probably give a fairly accurate port status for the boats on K Dock since that's where my own sloop is moored. But Pearl's sailboat, *Picture Perfect*, was moored clear across the marina at B Dock. Until Bruno confirmed that it was her car in the parking lot, it had never even occurred to me to check on whether her sailboat was in port.

What was that remark Pearl had made to Kate in the garage? Something about not wanting to drive to Salem. Perhaps she'd decided to go sailing instead. It wouldn't be the first time Pearl had changed her mind at the last moment. If I had to choose an adjective that would best describe Pearl Danielson, it would be "impulsive." Couple that with her love of sailing, and the scenario didn't seem so far-fetched. In fact, it made perfect sense. Within minutes of hustling down to B Dock, I had the confirmation I sought: Except for a few ducks splashing about in the water, *Picture Perfect*'s slip was empty.

I was still gawking at the ducks when Fred Slocum stopped to say hello. A fellow live-aboard, Fred was a friendly sort in his late seventies. "Whatcha doin' on B Dock, Kellie? Slumming?"

"Looking for *Picture Perfect*," I said, gesturing to the empty slip. "But it looks like Pearl's taken her out somewhere."

"Sure did. As a matter of fact, I lent her a hand casting off." He scratched his snow-white beard. "Mercy, that was almost three weeks ago. Time sure does have a way of getting away from a body."

"Fred, this is very important. Did Pearl happen to mention where she was headed?"

"Nope. But she weren't going on no little day sail."

"How do you figure?"

"Cuz she loaded a suitcase and several bags of groceries on board."

"What time of day was this?"

"Don't recall exactly, but it had to be close to noon. I realized I was hungry soon's I saw them grocery bags she was totin'. And I didn't have a blasted thing on board *Sallie Anne* to eat."

"Was anyone with Pearl?"

"Nah," he said, shaking his head. "I offered to keep her company, but she weren't interested. How 'bout you, Kellie?" he asked with a playful wink. "Care to join me on *Sallie Anne?* We could break open a bottle of Gallo. I think I even have some clean glasses on board."

I laughed and said, "The offer's real appealing, Fred, but not today."

"Okay," he said, feigning disappointment. "Had your chance and muffed it."

WHEN AN AIRPLANE goes missing, the first question searchers ask is whether the pilot filed a flight plan. Unfortunately there is no equivalent document for boaters. Searchers have to rely on family and friends for information regarding the skipper's intentions. But as far as

I could tell, Pearl's decision to go sailing that day was a spur-of-the-moment thing. I doubted her family had any idea that she was aboard her boat. Not only aboard, but—based on what Fred had said about the groceries she'd bought—most likely sailing all the way to Oregon.

Although Oregon is south of Washington, she would have had to begin her trip by sailing north through the Strait of Juan de Fuca, then west to the Pacific Ocean, and finally south along the coast. Her destination would undoubtedly have been Portland, since Salem, where her daughter lived, is an inland city some forty miles farther south. Sailing from Seattle to Portland isn't an easy trip, but, barring any unforeseen problems, she should've made it in about forty-eight hours.

Convinced now that Portland was Pearl's intended destination, I decided to trace her probable course. I began by heading back to *Second Wind* to consult the nautical charts I always keep aboard. The indisputable chart authority is the federal government, with the National Ocean Service publishing about 1,000 charts for U.S. waters and the Defense Mapping Agency issuing additional charts of the high seas and other countries' waters. That's a lot of charts. Fortunately I didn't need that many. The charts for the Pacific Northwest, Region 15 (Puget Sound to Vancouver) would tell me all I needed to know.

As I examined the charts, I realized that I'd have to make some assumptions, any one of which could seriously affect whether I'd be able to locate Pearl. The first assumption was that she hadn't had any mishaps along the way. This seemed reasonable since a call to Bert's office confirmed that the Coast Guard hadn't reported any serious boating incidents in the area for the last two or three weeks. If *Picture Perfect* had run into trouble of any sort, Pearl would've radioed for help. She had a full complement of electronic gear aboard with which to summon assistance in the event of an emergency. Although the sloop could've broken down and forced Pearl to pull in to some port along the way, I didn't think that was the case either, since she hadn't alerted her daughter to a possible delay in her arrival.

The second assumption was based on my knowledge of Pearl and her vessel. I'd sailed with her aboard *Picture Perfect* many times and had a pretty good feel for her sailing habits. Although impulsive and in love with what she termed "the element of imminent danger" associated with sailing, she was not irresponsible. She would have charted her course with care and made allowances for the tides, currents, and weather. But most important, she would've avoided motoring, preferring instead to wait out a windless sky rather than crank up the sloop's engine. Even with favorable winds and tides, though, *Picture Perfect*, a forty-foot Hunter, had a top speed of eight knots. Since that speed would be impossible to maintain for the entire trip, I decided to base my calculations on an average speed of four or five knots. The assumption was important because it determined just how much distance Pearl would have covered in a day.

According to Fred, she had left the marina around noon. Knowing Pearl, she would've sailed as far as possible before pulling into a port for the night. I hoped that the port she chose was a marina and not some little cove or I'd never track her down. At an average speed of four or five knots she could've made it to Port Townsend at the north end of the Quimper Peninsula in about six hours, maybe sooner, depending on whether she hit the tides just right. I'd sailed to Port Townsend many times myself. The best example of a Victorian seacoast town north of San Francisco, it's a popular tourist spot and a haven for writers, craftspeople, and artists of all kinds. From past visits, I knew that two marinas bracket the waterfront—Point Hudson Harbor at the north end and Boat Haven to the south.

I used my Waggoner Cruising Guide to find the phone numbers for the marinas and called the facility operated by the Port of Port Townsend first. After introducing myself and explaining to the harbormaster why I needed the information, he said, "Sorry, but I have no record of any vessel called *Picture Perfect* having been moored here in the past three weeks. You might try Point Hudson." But I got the same story at the privately operated marina.

It was hard for me to believe that Pearl would've gotten much farther than Port Townsend in one afternoon. I looked at the chart again and backtracked twelve nautical miles south from Port Townsend to Port Ludlow— the next most logical place Pearl would've stopped for the night. In the 1800s, Port Ludlow was the site of a productive lumber mill and shipyard, but over time a dwindling lumber supply and a depressed market changed everything. It is now the site of a posh resort for vacationing and corporate conferences, including a year-round, 100-slip marina. I got the phone number from the Waggoner Guide again and called the harbormaster. This time I hit pay dirt.

"Sure, *Picture Perfect* was here. A couple of nights, in fact. Skippered by a real nice lady, too."

"Pearl Danielson."

"Right. That's the name."

I was surprised that she'd stayed more than one night and wondered if I'd been wrong about her sailing all the way to Portland. "Did she say where she was headed next?"

"No," he said. "She just paid for her moorage and left. But if she was any kind of sailor, she headed south."

"South? What makes you say that?"

"It was a flood tide when she left here. If she was heading north through Admiralty Inlet she'd have been fighting the current something fierce. I figured her for an experienced sailor. If so, she'd work with the tides, not against them.''

"That makes sense, but how do you remember what kind of tide it was back then?"

"She remarked on it to the old gent.''

"Old gent?''

"The fella who was with her. He wasn't a sailor and didn't know the significance of an ebb and flood tide until she explained it to him.''

"Do you know his name?"

"No, but he was attending the Pacific Rim Import/ Export conference here at the resort. The old guy didn't seem to be in all that good a shape healthwise, but your friend was real good with him. Hired a local kid to drive over to Port Townsend to get his oxygen bottle refilled before they took off.''

"Are you saying Pearl and this man left on *Picture Perfect* together?''

"Yep. Nice couple, those two.''

# SEVEN

SAILING THE WASHINGTON coast is a gutsy thing for anyone to tackle. There are lots of rocks offshore, and the water can get awfully rough and wild, especially if the weather turns foul as it had been lately. A couple of years ago three Coast Guard men drowned trying to rescue a sailboat in distress along the same waters Pearl would've traveled. And yet she had apparently taken on a passenger who not only didn't know how to sail but had health problems to boot. If the harbormaster's assumption was correct, though, and she had headed south from Port Ludlow, then she probably had some other destination in mind besides Portland. But where? Where would she have gone? I wrestled with that question while I made a pot of tea.

When I sat back down at the dinette table with the tea, I realized that the question was impossible to answer. The simple fact was, I had no idea where Pearl had gone. There were just too many unanswered questions: Who was the man she'd picked up in Port Ludlow? Had they just met or were they long-time friends? Was their meeting coincidental or previously arranged? Was he the reason she'd headed south instead of north toward the Strait of Juan de Fuca and the coast? Or had she never intended to go farther than Port Ludlow in the first place?

As I sipped my tea, I perused the nautical chart again as if the answers to the questions rattling around in my head would somehow leap off the page at me. Finally I decided that the only choice I had was to make some more phone calls. Just to verify that she hadn't continued sailing north, I called the marinas where she would've most likely stopped on her way to Oregon—Port Angeles, Neah Bay, and LaPush. Fifteen minutes later, I was convinced that the Port Ludlow harbormaster was correct—Pearl had probably headed south.

Unfortunately I was still stumped. Without knowing her probable destination, I had no idea which of the many marinas in the area she might have visited. I'd just finished a second cup of tea when a new possibility occurred to me. What if Pearl and her gentleman friend had sailed south as far as they could in Washington and then taken some other transportation to Oregon? It was a long shot, but if true, then I only had to call a few marinas in Tacoma and Olympia—the southernmost ports in the area. The first three calls got me nowhere fast. But I had a winner with call number four.

The Davis-Moore Marina was a newly constructed private facility located on the west side of Budd Inlet, a short distance from downtown Olympia, our state's capital. I'd never been to the marina, but according to Bert, who had toured the facility when it opened, it was a grand affair. Like Larstad's, the marina was a family-owned business. The harbormaster was Clyde Davis, the owner's grandfather-in-law. Grouchy grandfather. He answered the phone in a gravelly, unfriendly voice. Despite a tendency to mumble, he made it perfectly clear that he wasn't interested in handing out information about the marina's guests. That is, until I mentioned the name of Pearl's boat.

"Yeah, *Picture Perfect* was here," he admitted. "Is still here, in fact."

I punched the air with my fist. Yes! I couldn't get the next question out fast enough. "And her skipper, Pearl Danielson? Is she there, too?" I asked excitedly.

"Nah, she split as soon as she registered her rig. Seemed like such a classy lady, too. I never would've taken her for a deadbeat."

"What do you mean?"

"She paid for a week's moorage in advance. Said she'd be gone for just a few days, but I haven't heard from her since. Now that her moorage is two weeks overdue, we had to attach a chain and lock her boat to the dock. Your friend's not sneaking outta here without settling up."

"Don't worry about it," I said confidently. "Pearl Danielson will pay whatever she owes you."

"Damn tootin' she will," he grumbled.

If she's still alive and kicking, I thought. I wanted to believe that there was a reasonable explanation for Pearl's absence, but the harbormaster's words had a chilling effect on me. Pearl was independent and impulsive, but you could always count on what she said. If she told the harbormaster she would be back in a few days, then that is exactly what would happen. If her plans had changed, she would have called and made other arrangements for settling her moorage account. For the first time since Kate had pulled me into this search, I had a real fear for Pearl's safety.

I quickly asked, "You said Pearl paid her moorage and then left. Did she say where she was headed?"

"Nope."

I wondered if Pearl and the old man had parted ways at the marina or were still together. "Did you see anyone leave with her?"

An exasperated sigh came over the line. I could picture him rolling his eyes. "Lady, I don't have time for this right now. You may have nothing better to do, but I've got a marina to run.''

The scuttlebutt I'd heard was that the fledgling marina was hurting for business. If true, then he probably wasn't all that busy, but I kept that opinion to myself and acquiesced graciously. ''I understand,'' I said. After a beat I added, ''But do you think it would be all right if I came down to the marina and took a quick look around? The sooner I can get a line on Pearl's whereabouts, the sooner you'll have your money.''

''Okay,'' he said after a moment's hesitation. ''Take a look-see if you think it will help. Just don't bother our guests.''

''Thanks,'' I said. ''I'll be there in about an hour or so.''

I didn't know whether a visit to the marina would help or not, but it was the only lead I had at the moment. Besides, I had some time to spare. My next sailing class wasn't scheduled until four o'clock—if it didn't have to be postponed. I try very hard to avoid rescheduling classes, but the dark clouds rolling across the sky like gigantic bowling balls made the possibility of an afternoon sail a touch-and-go proposition at best.

If I hadn't been so worried about Pearl, and the weather had been better, I'd have sailed *Second Wind* down to Budd Inlet. It would have taken much longer than an hour, but under other circumstances, it would've been a pleasant trip. I shook my head as I thought about how little opportunity I'd had to sail for fun lately. You'd think a sailing instructor would have plenty of time to herself on the water, but it's like that old saying—The cobbler's children have no shoes to wear.

Almost exactly an hour to the minute later, I arrived at the Davis-Moore Marina. As far as marinas go, the 120-boat facility was impressive. The owners had obviously put out some dough to make the place attractive to boaters. Although too small to support amenities such as an on-site yacht brokerage, apparel shop, or sailing school, the facility did have a fuel dock, pump-out station, Laundromat, and a small bar and grill near the one-story brick building that housed the harbormaster's office. The clean, well-maintained marina reminded me a lot of Larstad's. But the similarity ended at the docks. Almost half of the mooring slips at the Davis-Moore Marina were empty. Moorage space can be hard to come by in Puget Sound, but there is a limit to what folks are willing or able to pay for spiffy concrete docks and hanging baskets on all the pilings.

I parked the Miata and followed a paved pathway to the gated but unlocked entrance to Dock 2. The harbormaster had said that *Picture Perfect* was moored halfway down the dock in slip number fifteen. The entire marina wasn't what you'd call a hotbed of activity, but Dock 2 was practically deserted. And eerily quiet. Only a wayward halyard slapping against a mast in the distance broke the silence. I found myself hurrying toward Pearl's boat with an uneasy urgency. As soon as I spotted *Picture Perfect* I realized I hadn't been uneasy for nothing—someone was aboard the sloop. And he didn't look like any frail old gentleman.

Nor did he look particularly sinister. In fact, from a distance he looked pretty good. His tall, tanned, and athletic build was what Kate would categorize as "a keeper." But my heart was still beating a mile a minute as I approached the slip. *Get a grip, Kellie*, I muttered to myself. The guy was probably just a marina employee. His white polo shirt, khaki shorts, and sandals didn't look like work clothes, but they could pass for a uniform of sorts. I'd just about talked myself out of being concerned when I suddenly realized what he was doing on Pearl's boat.

"Hey!" I shouted. "Cut that out!"

He stopped fiddling with the latch on the cabin door and whirled around to face me. "Whoa!" he said with a loopy grin. "You scared me." He gave me a quick once-over, then picked up a black carrying case before clambering onto the dock. "It's not a bad-looking boat," he said with a nod. "For a Hunter, that is."

Good grief, I thought, a snob as well as a trespasser. Although she could've easily afforded any sailing yacht on the market, Pearl chose a Hunter 40.5. Regarded derisively in some circles (mostly by those who'd never been aboard the craft) as a utilitarian, production-line model, the boat's smooth lines, easy maneuverability, and speed appealed to Pearl very much.

"Who are you?" I demanded. He could've passed for a younger, dark-haired Robert Redford.

He set his case on the dock and extended a big hand in my direction. "Cord Roberts. And you are?"

"Pissed," I said, ignoring his hand and engaging grin. "That's my friend's boat you were trying to break into."

An incredulous look spread across his face. "Hold on a minute," he said, raising both hands as if I'd pulled a gun on him. "You think that's what I was doing on board? Trying to break in?"

I nodded.

He tossed his head back and laughed heartily.

I hate it when I'm not taken seriously. Especially when I'm mad. I summoned a don't-mess-with-me look and said loudly, "This is hardly a laughing matter. I could have you arrested." So there.

He didn't look the least bit intimidated. Bored, maybe, but definitely not intimidated. "Listen," he said, "I've done a lot of dumb things in my time, but breaking and entering isn't one of them."

"Oh? Then what exactly *were* you doing on board *Picture Perfect?*"

"I've been thinking about buying a sailboat, and someone recommended a Hunter. I know I shouldn't have gone aboard without permission, but no one was around. I just wanted a quick look." He shrugged.

"That's all there was to it. Sorry if it looked like something different to you." He picked up his carrying case, slung the strap over his shoulder, and grinned.

Despite my scowl and tough-girl body language, he gave me a friendly, two-fingered salute and said, "You take care now." Then he stepped around me and ambled on down the dock.

"I hope you're not buying any of that bullshit."

The voice came from behind me. I turned around to find a woman scraping varnish off a little blue sailboat in the slip across from Pearl's. Although massive scarring had disfigured the right side of her face, she was an ebony beauty. She wore faded jeans and a T-shirt with "Trust in God but always wear a condom" printed on the front. I guessed her age at somewhere in the late twenties or early thirties.

"Excuse me?" I said.

She examined the spot where she'd been scraping and then ran her hand over it, testing for smoothness. "He's full of it, sister-girl," she said, jabbing her scraper in the air for emphasis. "Just like my good-for-nothing ex."

"You heard us talking, huh?"

She smiled and resumed scraping. "I heard you making a pitiful fuss and him feeding you a phony innocent line."

Her dead-on assessment of my exchange with Cord Roberts embarrassed me. "Well," I said, "at least he's gone now." She grunted. "What?" I asked. "You think he'll be back?"

"Maybe, maybe not," she said. "But you have to wonder why he was taking so many pictures of your friend's boat."

"Pictures?"

She gave me a look. "You know, like with a camera. Click, click."

I felt as dense as the wood she was working on. Of

course. The black case Roberts carried off the boat was a camera case. "Did you notice anything else about him?" I asked.

She shook her head. "Just that he was good lookin'. But ain't that the way it always goes?" She ran a slender hand over her scarred face. "My ex was a fine dude, too. And look what he did to me."

I didn't know what to say to that, so I told her I liked her boat. "My grandfather had a little sloop similar to yours," I said. "She's a Baba, right? About 1978?"

"You know your boats," she said with an approving nod.

"I learned to sail on a Baba. My grandfather called his *Bristol Bonnie*. After my grandmother, who was born in Bristol, England. Said he should've named the boat *Lotsa*. For lotsa teak, lotsa work."

She laughed. "I hear ya. This was a real tub when I bought her, but I've had a ball fixing her up." She gestured to the freshly painted lettering on the stern. "I call her *IFGAL*."

"*IFGAL?*"

"My ex was always telling me to get a life," she said. "So I did. Divorced the bum and bought this sailboat. *IFGAL* stands for *I Finally Got A Life*."

"That's terrific," I said. "By the way, my name's Kellie Montgomery."

"I'm Sasha Tichner," she said.

After we'd talked for a few more minutes, mostly about sailing and what it meant to us, Sasha invited me aboard. "You've got to see what I've done to the cabin. I completely gutted it and started over."

I looked at my watch. "I'd really like to, Sasha, but I'm sort of pressed for time. And it's *Picture Perfect* that I really need to go aboard. The owner, Pearl Danielson, is missing, and I'm hoping that her boat may give me some clue as to what happened to her."

"I met Pearl. She's a real friendly lady. Smart, too.

She gave me a few pointers on how to repair the cracked varnish around the toe rail. You say she's missing?''

"Her family hasn't heard from her in almost three weeks. According to the harbormaster here, she paid her moorage fee and said she'd be back in a few days. But she never showed and now she's in arrears.''

"So that explains why old Clyde chained her boat to the dock.''

"Did Pearl say anything to you about where she might be going?''

"No, but she used my cell phone to call a taxi. Then she and her gentleman friend headed up to the parking lot. That's the last I saw of them.''

"Did she seem upset or anything?''

"Not that I could tell.''

"What about her friend? Did you catch his name?''

"Sorry. I never even spoke to him.''

I asked Sasha a few more questions, but she didn't have much more to add to what she'd already told me, so I thanked her for her help and then climbed aboard *Picture Perfect*. The lock that Roberts had tried to open was a combination lock. I hadn't been aboard the sloop for a while, but I remembered the combination real well—54, 40, 5. I may forget names, but I never forget a number. Pearl is just the opposite. She said the only way she remembered the combination was to recite the slogan, "Fifty-four forty, or fight.'' I reached for the lock and discovered that I didn't need to remember any numbers at all—it wasn't latched. I examined the lock closely, but as far as I could tell, it hadn't been tampered with. It was just hanging there open. Strange, I thought.

Once inside the cabin, I saw that I hadn't been the only visitor—and he or she hadn't been concerned with disguising the fact. Charts and papers had been pulled from the captain's table and tossed onto the floor, stowage lockers emptied, and cushions and pillows upended. In short, Pearl's usually neat and tidy cabin was a mess.

I flashed on yesterday's encounter with Dennis Lancaster and Phillip Coughlin. They'd been searching Pearl's den. Had they somehow found her boat and searched it, too? Were they trying to locate something to lead them to Pearl, or were they looking for something else? I thought Cord Roberts had been trying to break into the cabin. Maybe he'd already been inside. Could he have robbed the place and stashed the goods inside that camera case of his?

I took a few moments to look around, but I couldn't tell if anything was missing. Nor did I have any answers for the questions running through my mind. I sat down at the dinette table and tried to think of what to do next. I decided against reporting the "break-in" to the harbormaster. The lock hadn't been jimmied, and there were no other signs of forcible entry. Neither were there any clues as to where Pearl and her friend had gone.

*Face it Kellie, you're clueless.* I berated myself for a moment—something along the lines of "You fool, you couldn't find a clue if it jumped out and bit you." Then, for want of anything better to do, I picked up a couple of the charts and put them back on the captain's table. As I did, it occurred to me that my initial assumption could still be valid—namely, that Pearl had gone to Oregon. That's where she was headed before she decided to go sailing, and, unless she'd had another change of heart, there was a good possibility that her daughter's place in Salem, Oregon, was still Pearl's intended destination. Why she hadn't made it to Salem was another matter.

Sasha said Pearl and the old man had left by taxi. Were they going to the airport? With her resources, Pearl could have hired a private plane. Or made the taxi driver's day and paid for a long-distance fare. I checked my watch. It was almost two-thirty. There was no way I could track down all the possibilities and still make it back to Larstad's in time for my four o'clock class. The least I could do was tidy up the place before I left. As I reached for another chart, I spotted a wadded-up piece of paper sticking out from underneath a cushion.

When I smoothed it out, I discovered a Greyhound bus schedule with the departure times for Oregon highlighted with a yellow marking pen.

Hot damn. I'd found a clue after all.

# EIGHT

IT WAS DRIZZLING lightly when I left the Davis-Moore Marina. I set the windshield wipers on intermittent and wound my way through the downtown traffic mess to the bus station. After parking the Miata, I dashed inside the building just as the rain got serious. My afternoon sailing lesson was beginning to look like a no-go.

Once inside, I took a moment to get my bearings. I hadn't spent any time at a bus station since the early days of my marriage to Wendell, but things hadn't changed all that much. The arcade games and pay-per-view TV sets mounted on some of the chairs were new, but the general feel of the place was the same. Anyone who knows me would say I'm an outdoors person, but I liked it here. I inhaled deeply, feeling oddly energized by the cacophony of sights and sounds and the smell of sweat, diesel, cigarettes, and fast food.

Today's crowd was a mixed bag. Except for the bum who'd made a bed on a couple of hard plastic chairs lining the wall, the paying customers waiting in line at the ticket counter included college kids, military types, couples with toddlers in tow, and more than a few folks eligible for the senior discount program.

Pearl Danielson certainly qualified for the senior rates, but I couldn't figure out why someone with her wealth would travel by bus. Nor could I figure out what could have possibly happened to her—despite her penchant for adventure, she had always let someone know where she'd be and when she'd be back. The circumstances surrounding her disappearance were becoming more unusual and disturbing by the moment.

That I'd gotten myself involved in this situation wasn't a bit unusual. Whether or not it was disturbing depended upon your point of view. I'd meant it when I told Phillip Coughlin that I'd do anything for Pearl. But after my last foray into police matters, I'd promised myself (and Homicide Detective Allen Kingston) that I wouldn't do anything that remotely infringed on his territory. But this was a missing persons case. Surely that didn't count, did it?

I approached the customer service window, where a harried young woman in an ink-stained white blouse sat at the counter, shuffling a stack of papers like a Vegas card shark. Without looking up, she asked, "How can I help you?"

"I need to talk to one of your drivers."

She shuffled the papers around some more and then stacked them on top of a towering out-basket to her left. The look she gave me probably wasn't what they recommended in the customer service manual. "Which driver?" she asked. "We only have about a hundred or so."

"I don't know the driver's name. Just the route: Seattle to Salem, Oregon, about three weeks ago." I'd checked the schedule board in the lobby and saw that the route stopped in Olympia. "If they haven't changed the schedule, it departed at eight A.M."

"That'd be Ben Givens," she said. Grabbing a clipboard, she flipped through several pages. "But, according to this, he's on vacation. Sorry." She tossed the clipboard aside and grabbed another stack of papers to shuffle.

"When's he due back?"

She heaved an exasperated sigh and consulted the clipboard again. Running her finger down the top page, she said, "He gets back today. Should be reporting in any time now." She smiled, a surprisingly nice, friendly smile that belied the words that came next. "But he won't talk to you."

"How come?"

She paused a moment. "Let's just say Ben is the strong, silent type. Stone-silent."

I tried to pry some more info out of her—like a description of the guy and where I might find him, but she cut me off with a shrug. Having apparently stretched customer service to its limits, I was left to my own devices. Meaning I was stumped. I also had to go to the bathroom. Since that's where I do my best thinking, I located the women's facility and did my thing. By the time I was done, I not only knew where to find Ben Givens but exactly what he looked like. Sometimes I amaze myself. In this case, though, it was Stella Brodowski who was amazing. She was mopping the rest room floor when I met her and, unlike my customer service pal, she was a talkative sort. Stella willingly told me what I wanted to know—and a little more. Stone-silent or not, Ben Givens was mine.

I found the door labeled Employees Only and opened it. According to Stella, friends and relatives were always popping in and out to visit with the drivers during their break, and no one would question my presence. But the moment I walked into the small smoke-filled room I got the "evil eye" from half a dozen different directions. And the evilest of looks was courtesy of one Benjamin P. Givens.

He was just as Stella had described him—lanky and cranky. Although dressed in the same uniform as his fellow employees—dark blue pants and matching short-sleeve shirt—he looked as if he should be driving cattle instead of a bus. His face was a narrow, craggy leather strap that had seen fifty years and then some. While the others in the room chatted, smoked, or played cards, he sat by himself at a small table near the back of the room hunched over some kind of paperwork.

The scowl he'd given me earlier was still planted on his face when I joined him at the table. He tugged at the cervical collar around his neck but didn't make eye contact.

"Those things can be a pain," I said, gesturing to the collar. "Makes you wonder which is worse, the injury or the cure."

Stone-silent he was not. He grunted loudly in response, a guttural mishmash that nevertheless got his point across: *I* was the pain. And, judging by the looks of him, Givens was well-acquainted with pain. Besides the cervical collar, he sported a head bandage and a mouthful of metal wires that clamped his upper and lower jaws together.

While I still had his attention, I said, "Sorry about your accident." Stella had told me that his vacation had come to an abrupt end when the horse he'd been riding spooked and bolted, tossing him headfirst onto the ground. Hence the collar, bandage, and wires. "You're lucky to be alive."

Givens nodded grimly.

"Can you work?" I asked.

Wrong question. His scowl deepened, and his face flushed. Grunting again, he grabbed the papers from the table and waved them at me.

Time to regroup. Thanks to what Stella had told me about Givens's wife, I was convinced I could get him to talk to me. I just had to make it a little easier on him.

"Listen," I said, motioning to the papers still clenched in his fist. "I don't want to intrude, but perhaps I can help with those."

He grunted again, obviously unconvinced.

"I know sign language," I said, signing as I talked. I'd learned to communicate in sign language when I had a deaf student in one of my sailing classes a couple of years ago. The extra effort gained me a new friend and a reputation as an instructor who wasn't afraid to take on new challenges. Since then I've had several deaf students in my classes.

Givens stared at me for so long that I wondered if Stella had been wrong about him. Maybe his wife wasn't deaf. Maybe he didn't know sign language. Then, seeming to relax somewhat, he tossed the papers aside and signed, "Do I know you?"

I shook my head. Since he could hear me, I didn't sign my response. "I'm Kellie Montgomery," I said, offering him my hand.

He shook it warily and signed, "Why are you here?"

"I need to ask you some questions," I said.

"You with Greyhound?" He didn't wait for my response, his hands gesturing rapidly. As is the case with American Sign Language, Givens used short phrasing and somewhat stilted syntax, but I had no trouble filling in the blanks as he signed. "I don't care what that SOB supervisor says, I can still drive."

"I'm from Larstad's Marina."

That brought him up short. He shrugged the equivalent of "Huh?"

"I'm trying to find a friend. She was last seen on your bus about two weeks ago. She got on at Olympia with an elderly man—possibly with an oxygen tank."

"You talking about an old lady?"

"She's seventy-five. Short, with white curly hair."

"Wears her glasses on a chain around her neck?"

"That's Pearl. You remember her, then?"

He nodded. "She wasn't dressed in a fancy outfit or sporting expensive jewelry, but there was something very classy about her." He tugged at his collar. "I wondered when someone would get around to asking about her and the old gent."

"Why do you say that?"

He glanced at the papers spread across the table. "Were you just making nice talk or did you mean it when you offered to help me?"

"I meant it."

He paused, his fingers intertwined and quiet. Finally he signed, "Never thought they'd cut me loose like this."

"What do you mean?"

"They say I have to go out on sick leave until the wires come off. That's six weeks from now. I have to get back to work before then, but I can't make my boss understand that." Givens glanced at the papers again. "He doesn't have a lot of patience with my henscratched notes."

"So you want me to interpret for you, explain your position? That it?"

He nodded.

"And if I do that for you—talk to your boss—you'll tell me about Pearl?"

Ben Givens leaned back in his chair and looked around the room. Most of the other employees had cleared out shortly after I arrived. Those who remained were so engrossed in a hot game of poker that Givens and I were essentially by ourselves.

Sitting upright again, he rapidly signed, "First let me tell you about this couple I knew a long time ago. Young, good-looking couple." The story he told me was this: The bride was the most beautiful woman the young man had ever seen. Being deaf, she'd never heard his proposal or any of the sweet words he'd uttered to win her. But they'd fallen in love and married.

Driving down the road in a busy convention-filled city on their wedding night, they looked for a motel room in which to celebrate their first night together. After finding the last available room in the entire town, the young guy swooped up his bride and carried her across the threshold.

He paused to see if I was following him.

I said, "Go on."

He continued signing.

The groom was eager to begin their first night as husband and wife. But his bride insisted on a bottle of champagne to make their wedding night complete. So the groom grudgingly left their motel room and drove to an all-night store to buy a chilled bottle. When he got back to the motel, he couldn't remember the room in which his bride was waiting and he couldn't ask anyone since the motel office was closed for the night. After a moment of pondering, he came up with a plan.

With a shiny metal grin, Givens signed, "What do you think he did?"

I figured this was some kind of test and I'd better get it right. I thought of my sailing student and tried to picture how he'd handle the situation. After a moment, I said, "He honked his car horn."

Givens laughed through his wires. "Until every light in every room in that motel came on."

"Except one," I said. "His bride couldn't hear the horn and didn't turn on the light."

"True story," he signed. "And here's another one. Your friend Pearl, and the old man with her, fell in love on my bus."

"What?"

"Being married to a deaf person, I've gotten so I can read faces and body language pretty good. And what I read on that couple was love."

"But Pearl wasn't on the bus when it arrived in Salem."

"Neither was her gentleman friend. They got off together when we stopped in Portland."

I was dumbfounded. Pearl in love? They hadn't been together *that* long. Pearl is impulsive, but this was too much. She had to have known the guy before she met up with him in Port Ludlow. "Do you have any idea who the man was? Or where they went?"

"Nope. But if I was trying to find someone, I'd honk a few horns."

I eyed him carefully. "And just where might I honk these horns?"

"Try the Church of the Passionate Life." He caught my confused look. "The old couple didn't leave the bus by themselves. They were accompanied by a young, clean-cut fellow. Didn't catch his name, but the back of his leather jacket was a billboard of sorts. Had a big gold cross with the words Church of the Passionate Life inscribed around it like a heart." He looked up as the door to the lounge opened. "Now, it's your turn," he signed as he stood up. "Here comes my boss."

I spent another half-hour with Givens and his supervisor before heading back to the marina. I'd valiantly translated Givens's signing, but in the end his plea fell on—excuse the pun—deaf ears. He was ordered to take sick leave for the full six weeks.

# NINE

DESPITE INTERMITTENT RAIN showers, enough students showed up for lessons the next day to keep me busy most of the morning. At noon, I stopped by the Topside, found a table in Cassie's section and ordered the first thing I saw on the menu—a Dungeness crab sandwich with cole slaw—and wolfed it down.

My appetite tends to be directly proportional to the amount of worry I'm carrying. And I was shouldering a boatload. Besides stewing about Pearl's disappearance, I couldn't get Kate's mysterious illness and Allen Kingston's new partner off my mind.

When Cassie stopped by my table to pour me another glass of iced tea she said, "What's wrong, Mom? You look down." I brushed the question aside, but she persisted. "You worried about Pearl Danielson?"

"Sure, I'm worried." I worked an ice cube out of the glass and sucked on it.

Cassie glanced at another customer two tables over who was waving his arms frantically. "Look, I can't talk right now, but there may be a way I can help. Could you stick around for another ten minutes or so—until I take my break?"

I could and did. When she returned to my table, she got right to the point. "I have the next couple of days off. How'd you like it if I spent them helping out at the sailing school?"

Her proposal—while welcome—took me off guard. I'd been hoping that Cassie would work for me this summer. But I knew that boat wasn't going to float and I was right. As soon as she got home from college, she made tracks for the Topside and never looked back. She's never been too keen on sailing, but I suspected the real reason had more to do with our still-developing relationship. Although she hadn't said so, it seemed reasonable that living and working together every day might be pushing the envelope a tad too far for Cassie. So I found her change of heart perplexing.

"You just started work here," I said, "and they're already giving you two days off?"

"It's crazy, I know," she said with a dimpled grin, "but perfect for what I have in mind."

"Which is?"

"To hold down the fort at Sound Sailing while you go to Portland. That way you could check out the church you told me about."

"The Church of the Passionate Life?"

"Right. Maybe they'll have a lead on Pearl."

I'd have been touched by her thoughtfulness if I hadn't known my daughter so well: There was more to this plan she'd hatched than concern over my concern for Pearl.

"And?" I asked.

"And what?"

"What else did you have in mind?"

"Well," she said, eyeing me cautiously, "I've been thinking about what you said the other day—about using an intermediary to contact my sister." She flashed a winning smile. "As long as you're going to be in Portland, anyway . . ."

"I might as well look her up."

She clapped her hands. "Exactly. I knew you'd see it my way."

"Wait a minute, Cass. I didn't say I'd do it." I wasn't necessarily opposed to the idea but I thought we should at least hash it over a little more.

"It's perfect, don't you see? Since I only have her parents' address, I'd have to go through them in order to find her. But that might be a little awkward—for them as well as for me."

"And you think it wouldn't be awkward for me?"

"Well, no," she admitted, "But as an adoptive parent yourself, you'd be able to connect with them better than I would—or anyone else for that matter." She looked at me pleadingly, her big brown eyes teary. "Please, Mom. Please do this for me."

So much for hashing things over.

After Cassie went back to work, I downed the last of the tea and paid my tab. I was collecting my change at the cashier's counter when Todd L. Wilmington and his young reporter friend came strolling through the door hand in hand. That he was favoring the Topside with his presence was surprising. The Weasel generally preferred rubbing elbows with the snob set, which meant that he spent most of his time hanging out at the Pacific Broiler. But, judging from the dazed way he looked at his pretty companion, he probably had no idea how far afield he'd wandered.

I did my best to avoid eye contact with him, which wasn't difficult given the Weasel's moony, schoolboy-in-love demeanor. But the object of his affection spotted me right away.

"Kellie? Kellie Montgomery?" she asked, jerking her hand out of Wilmington's grasp.

I acknowledged her with a quick nod and slung my handbag over my shoulder.

"Remember me?" she asked, extending a hand.

She was a perky little blonde with a grip like a stevedore. "The *Times* reporter," I said, wincing.

"Danielle Korb, but you can call me Dani. Everyone does. And, actually, I'm a freelancer."

At this point the Weasel came out of his trance. He blinked his beady eyes and put a protective arm around Ms. Korb. "You'll have to excuse us now, we have a luncheon appointment," he said airily.

Danielle Korb shook herself free of the Weasel with practiced ease. "Kellie, I'd like to talk to you a moment. For an article I'm doing."

I had no intention of talking to a reporter about anything, but I couldn't resist playing off the Weasel's dismissive attitude.

"What kind of article?" I asked.

"An environmental piece," she said enthusiastically. "It's not really an exposé or anything, but the focus will have tremendous local and possibly even national interest."

"How so?"

She hedged with a non-answer. "I'm not really at liberty to say. But I can assure you that your side will be fairly represented."

"My side?"

The Weasel had had enough. He stepped between us and said, "Dani, we really must go now. They won't hold our reservation."

Lame excuse (especially since the Topside doesn't take reservations), but it seemed to work.

"Okay, okay," said Dani, slipping me a business card. "Please give me a call at your earliest convenience. I'm available any time, night or day."

Not if the Weasel had anything to do with it. He forced his gaunt face into a tight smile and quickly steered her toward the bar. "Day or night," she called over her shoulder.

The entire exchange struck me as bizarre. But then,

all encounters with the Weasel struck me that way. He obviously thought he had a girlfriend. I wondered what she thought she had.

CASSIE MET ME at Sound Sailing after she got off work, and I briefed her on what to do while I was gone. Not that it was all that complicated. Because of the iffy weather, I didn't have a lot of classes on tap. Cassie's main job would be to call the few students I did have and postpone things until I got back.

By six o'clock, I'd packed for my trip and was feeling antsy. Once I decide to go somewhere, I just want to get going. I suppose I could've left for Portland right then and there, but I preferred to get a fresh start in the morning. Since I had some time on my hands, I made a stab at cleaning up the boat. With Pan-Pan hot on my heels, though, I didn't get much accomplished. She's a fussy eater, and I'd made the mistake of giving in to her whims early on. Now it's chopped liver or nothing. Since nothing was exactly what I had available, I hopped in the Miata and headed for Safeway.

The rain-slicked streets, ever-present construction projects, and commuter traffic made for a nasty drive. I patiently put up with the mess until I got stopped by a roadblock near the Kingdome. Thanks to a Mariners game, all traffic was being rerouted a hundred miles out of my way. I made a U-turn on Alaska Way and found my own alternate route—which took me right by Kate's condo. I'd planned to call her later, but as long as I was in the neighborhood, so to speak, I decided to pop in.

For once I lucked out and slipped into a parking spot right in front of the building. Just ahead was a long black limousine that gave new meaning to the term "stretch." At first glance, the presence of the fancy car and driver hardly seemed unusual, given that the combined annual income of the residents at Palisades West was probably more than the operating budgets of most countries.

But there was something about the uniformed driver that didn't seem quite right. He stood curbside smoking a cigarette, but quickly tossed it aside and trotted right over as soon as I'd climbed out of the car. Up close and personal, the man was as big as an ox. But uglier.

"Hope you don't plan on bein' long," he said.

"Excuse me?"

"The dipstick there," he said, waving a huge fist in the general direction of my car. "Unless it's a hemorrhoid, get it the hell off my ass."

I'm fiercely protective of my little roadster. She has over a hundred thousand miles on her, but she'd been Wendell's pride and joy. It probably sounds weird, but I sometimes feel as though he's sitting right next to me when I drive her. I planted my feet firmly in front of the car. "It's called a Miata. And it's legally parked."

"That ain't the point," he said, moving in closer. He patted the unmistakable bulge of a shoulder holster for emphasis. If he was trying to be intimidating, he was succeeding.

Nevertheless, I gave him some of the sass I usually reserve for the Weasel. "Only point that counts is one that's sharp," I said, smiling sweetly.

His scrunched his beefy face into a puzzled frown. *Did she just insult me or not?* "Listen lady," he said after a moment's consideration, "I ain't gonna argue with ya. The Man's inside. When he's finished takin' care of business, we're outta here—Mee-ah-ta or no Mee-ah-ta." He laughed heartily at his little joke. "Get it? No Mee-ah-ta?"

I didn't get it, but I laughed along with him. "Now, will you please step aside?"

"Sure thing," he said, grinning.

Sheesh. What a girl has to go through to get a decent parking spot in this city. Inside, Beethoven's Fifth serenaded a deserted lobby. As I waited for the elevator to arrive, the door to Tony's corner office swung open. A man in a dark pinstripe suit paused in the entry and looked left and right. He was only about five feet nothing, but there was something about his demeanor that was more menacing than the hulk outside. He caught me staring and frowned. I quickly looked away, punching the elevator button again in a futile attempt to hurry the thing along.

"Excuse me, miss." The little guy was at my side now, acting very polite. "I'm sorry to bother you, but do you happen to know a Mr. Antonio Carmine? Tony Carmine?"

I hesitated, unsure as to whether I should 'fess up. According to Kate, Tony's past was littered with questionable characters. From where I stood, this guy fit the profile.

"It's a simple question," he said. "Do you know the man or not?"

"Sort of."

The elevator arrived, but he stopped me from entering by extending his arm in front of the door. "Sort of? What kind of an answer is that?"

"An honest one. I don't live in the building, but I understand that Mr. Carmine is the superintendent here." I nodded at the elevator. "Now, if you'll excuse me."

"Sure, sure," he said, still blocking my way. After the elevator door finally closed, he lowered his arm and adjusted his tie. "You can catch the next one."

I punched the elevator button.

"But if you should see Tony . . . Tony Carmine—the guy you sort of know—give him this message: It's not nice to fuck with Mother Nature. But it's fucking suicide to fuck with T-Bone. Ya got that?"

I punched the button a second time.

"Hey! Ya got that?"

The elevator arrived, and once again he stopped me from entering. "Say it," he demanded.

"Don't mess with T-Bone," I said.

"Or?"

"Tony's dead meat."

He laughed—a short bark without mirth—and let me enter. "Close enough."

I found Kate in the kitchen playing solitaire. She'd edged out a space for the cards on a table littered with several empty beer bottles and a nearly empty platter of chips slathered in some kind of cheese and hot pepper goop. A cigarette smoldered in a crystal ashtray at her fingertips. So much for the patch program. As I sat down at the table, she reached for the cigarette and took a long, hungry drag.

"What brings you here?" she asked, not bothering to blow the smoke away from my allergy-sensitive eyes. "Checking up on me?" Her tone was uncharacteristically sarcastic.

I fanned the smoke out of my face and curbed the urge to sling a few choice words back at her. "No, Kate. I was on a food run for Pan-Pan and got stuck in Mariners traffic. Since I wound up detouring right by your place I thought I'd drop in and tell you the latest about Pearl."

"I see," she said, taking another long drag. An awkward moment passed while she stubbed out the cigarette. "And your phone's not working, I suppose?"

She sounded just like our sister Donna. Same self-righteous attitude that we both hated. "Come on, Kate. What's your problem?"

"Oh, no problem," she said, lighting another cigarette.

"Yeah, right."

This time she blew the smoke directly at me. A purposeful, antagonistic gesture that brought me to my feet. "Listen, Kate, I'm sorry you're sick, but you don't have to act like a baby." I motioned to the stub-filled ashtray and beer bottles. "If all this is because of Pearl, you're not doing yourself or her any good."

"At least I care about her."

"That's not fair, and you know it. I'm just as worried about Pearl as you are. And, despite some serious misgivings, I've done everything you've asked me to do—including getting threatened with a lawsuit by her son-in-law and dodging Lancaster's juvenile antics on Elliott Bay."

I ignored her sour look and continued dishing. "I haven't had a moment to call since I started looking into this thing. But I'm here now. So, do you want to hear what I've found out or not?"

Kate left the dare-posing-as-a-question hanging unanswered while we stared at one another like two stubborn kids. The impasse was broken by the sound of a toilet flushing. "You have company?" I asked.

"Just Tony," she said.

"Someone mention my name?" he asked, strolling into the room. All gussied up in tan chinos and a hot-pink shirt, the guy fairly glowed with good cheer until he caught sight of Kate's frown. He glanced nervously at me as he joined her at the table. "What's up?" he asked.

"Kellie has some news about Pearl," offered Kate. Her face softened into an apologetic smile. "But I've been too bratty to listen." She patted the seat I'd vacated earlier and invited me to sit down. "Please tell us what you found out, Kellie."

"Before I get into all that, there's something I need to tell Tony."

He was twisting the cap off a beer and appeared not to hear me. I waited until he'd taken a hearty swig before adding, "A message, actually, from some goon downstairs."

"Huh?"

"You know someone named T-Bone?"

I didn't think it physically possible, but Tony's little round eyes got rounder. He set the beer on the table with a jolt. "What about T-Bone?"

"I don't know if the pint-sized guy strutting around the lobby like an ornery rooster is T-Bone, but he's looking for you. I saw him coming out of your office. He said to tell you not to mess with T-Bone if you know what's good for your health—or words to that effect."

Kate looked at Tony. "Who's T-Bone?"

Tony gulped the last of his beer. "Just some guy," he stuttered. "You got anymore of this stuff?" He waved the now-empty bottle.

Kate pointed to the fridge.

As he helped himself to two more bottles, he asked, "Mind if I hang out here awhile longer, Kate?"

She shrugged her approval and lit another cigarette. "You having problems again, Tony?"

"It's nothing. Just a little misunderstanding. I can clear it up real fast with one short phone call." He looked down the hall toward her den. "Okay if I use your phone?"

"Sure, Tony. Do what you have to do."

After he left to make his call, she sighed and stubbed out the half-smoked cigarette. "I think he's been gambling again."

From the looks of the ashtray, Tony wasn't the only one who'd suffered a relapse. But I kept those thoughts to myself and said, "Looks like he's drinking again, too."

"No," she said, catching my glance at the ashtray. "I've had a smoke or two today, but Tony's still on the wagon." She caught my skeptical look as I surveyed the collection of empty beer bottles. "It's just near-beer, Kellie. But this T-Bone thing . . . I'm afraid it's bad news." She shook her head sadly and said, "So, tell me some good news. You *do* have good news about Pearl, I hope?''

"I don't know," I admitted. "But I have a lead on her whereabouts."

Kate listened attentively while I summarized what I'd learned so far. When I was through, she said, "Who do you think the old guy with her is?"

"That's what I was hoping you'd tell me. The bus driver seemed convinced they were in love. Do you know if Pearl has been seeing anyone?"

Chuckling, Kate asked, "You mean, like dating?"

"Why are you so amused? Pearl isn't that far over the hill."

"I know but . . . I just never thought someone her age would be interested in sex."

I eyed her ring finger which was encircled by a band of white skin, a still-visible reminder of her impetuous and stormy marriage to husband number three. "I never said anything about sex. But so what?"

"Okay, okay. Sex is for everyone. Me. You. Pearl. Some old geezer. I don't really care. The point is, where is she doing it? In Portland?"

"That's where Givens said they got off the bus. And the first place I plan to look."

"You're going to Portland?" she asked.

"Tomorrow morning. Cassie's going to sub for me at the sailing school."

"How'd you get her to agree to that?"

"It was her idea. She just found out that her twin sister's adoptive parents live in Portland and she wants me to talk to them while I'm there. Sort of pave the way for Cassie to meet her twin."

"Really? And you're okay with that?"

"Sure." I shrugged. "It means a lot to Cassie."

Kate let the matter drop and asked, "What about this passionate church or whatever you called it?"

"The Church of the Passionate Life. According to

Givens, Pearl and her friend left the bus with some young guy whose jacket had the church's logo on it. It's a long shot, but there's a chance someone at the church might know who he is. Givens gave me a pretty good description of the guy. In any event, the church will be my first stop when I hit town."

"But how do you plan to—"

"Kate!" Tony called, striding into the kitchen. Clearly agitated, he rocked back and forth on his heels like a kid who desperately needed to pee. "We gotta talk." He glanced at me. "Alone."

Kate nodded sympathetically at him, but said, "We're sort of in the middle of something here, Tony."

"It's important," he pleaded.

I took pity on the guy and left. It was either that or watch a grown man wet his pants.

# TEN

IT WAS ALMOST eight o'clock by the time I got back to the marina, but there was still enough daylight left to take a bead on the clouds scudding across the sky to the west. Grampy claimed that a good mariner should be able to forecast the weather—*Look to the sky, Kellie darlin'. The clouds and the wind will tell you everything you need to know.*

Grampy had drilled me until I was able to identify the four basic formations—cirrus, cumulus, stratus, and nimbus—in my sleep. He contended that weather changes are almost always heralded well in advance and usually come with the wind. If there is rain in the morning with winds from northeast to south, as we had today, and the wind begins to shift to western points, as it was doing right now, then the rain would soon be ending. I looked heavenward. Right, Grampy?

I climbed aboard *Second Wind* and found a note from Cassie taped to the cabin door. Despite protection from the elements by a canvas dodger, the wind had torn part of the paper loose. As near as I could tell, the message read: "Gone to dinner and a movie with Tyler. Will be back late. See you in the morning. Luv, Cass." I was disappointed, but before I could dwell on it, Pan-Pan meowed loudly from below. Once I was inside the cabin, she instantly wrapped herself around my legs, her meowing growing more desperate by the moment.

I put the cat on hold while I checked the answering machine for messages. Someone had called to offer me what every sailboat owner needs—a free chimney inspection. The rest of the tape was blank. I tried to convince myself that not hearing from Allen Kingston didn't mean anything. That his beautiful new partner was just that—a new partner. And how did I know she was beautiful? Cassie hadn't said that. No, Kingston was just busy. It was nothing more than work that was keeping us apart . . . Who was I kidding? We were history. And he was so wrapped up with this Melody person—this Seattle P.D. goddess—that he didn't even have the decency to tell me it was over between us.

Pan-Pan had had enough. While I was wallowing in self-pity about my miserable love life, she'd jumped onto the counter and was clawing the grocery bag. "Okay, okay," I said, rescuing the chopped liver and dishing it up for her. The meal looked about as appetizing as a dish of red mud, but it made me hungry. I surveyed the contents of the fridge for something I could eat and, finding nothing remotely enticing, headed straight for the Topside.

"Hey, Kellie!" Rose Randall and Bert Foster called in unison. They'd spotted me as soon as I walked in and waved me over to their table. I usually don't mind eating alone, but since my spirits were hovering right around sea level, I needed company. Especially theirs.

Bert and Rose are a likable but unlikely couple. Most of us who live and/or work at the marina have gotten used to seeing them together, but they still draw stares from outsiders. Rose is twenty-five, blond, and drop-dead gorgeous, while Bert is fifty-something, balding, and burdened by a layer of fat cells, mostly around the belly. The college kids who make up the majority of the marina's staff have affectionately dubbed them B&B or Beauty and the Beast.

They were in a festive mood, drinking champagne, telling outrageous jokes, and generally acting as goofy as teenagers in love. "What's with you two tonight, anyway?" I asked. "Celebrating something?"

They looked at each other and broke into giggles.

"Did I say something funny?"

"No," said Rose. "We're just winding down." She nudged Bert. "Been sort of a stressful day, hasn't it?"

Bert sighed. "Yeah, you could say that."

"Anyone care to fill me in?"

"Round one of the general manager interviews was held today," explained Rose.

I'd forgotten all about the interviews. The new position was a big deal at the marina. The small family operation that old man Larstad started several years ago had become one of Seattle's most successful marinas. So successful, in fact, that Larstad had seriously considered selling out to a Japanese conglomerate. He backed out at the last moment, but the negotiation process had pointed out the need for a more sophisticated approach to day-to-day management. Hence, creation of the general manager position.

I knew how much the job meant to Bert and Rose and I was embarrassed that I hadn't been more supportive. I asked somewhat belatedly, "How'd it go?"

"We both made the cut."

"Congratulations! That's really great." I lifted my glass and offered a salute to both of them. Frankly I was amazed at the lack of tension between them. I'd have thought competing for the same job would put some pressure on the relationship. If it had, they were sure good at hiding it.

"You won't believe who else is moving on to round two," said Rose with a wry grin.

"No way," I said. "Not the Weasel."

"The very one," Bert said, laughing.

"And we think he'll be tapped for the job," added Rose.

I thought she was kidding until I caught the looks on their faces. "Come on, guys. If brains were taxed, Todd Wilmington would get a rebate. The dope hasn't a chance against you two."

"Don't be so quick to judge him, Kellie," said Bert. "He's got the ear of Dennis Lancaster, head of the selection committee."

I flashed on yesterday's luncheon with Kate. "You're right about that. I saw Wilmington and Lancaster together at the Broiler yesterday. They looked real cozy."

Bert and Rose exchanged glances.

"But," I said, backpedaling, "Lancaster isn't the only one on the committee. Surely the others will see through the Weasel's act."

Rose shrugged. "Maybe, but don't count on it. Wilmington may not be the sharpest knife in the drawer, but he can still slice and dice. Especially when it comes to publicity. Have you seen that reporter he's been squiring around the marina?"

"Oh, yeah. Ms. Danielle Korb. Ran into Wilmington and her yesterday. The Weasel looked like he'd found his one true love. But she seemed more interested in me. Something about getting 'my side of things.' Whatever that meant."

"Kellie, be careful what you say around either one of them," warned Bert. "We think Wilmington's using the live-aboard issue to gain support from Lancaster."

"That's no big surprise. The Weasel would love to see me out of here. What better way than to cast his lot with the opposition? And Dennis Lancaster is definitely my opposition, especially after yesterday."

"Why? What happened?" asked Rose.

I explained about Pearl Danielson and my run-in with

Lancaster and his brother at her condo. Bert knew that Pearl was missing, but Rose was visibly shaken by the news.

"You know, that old gal is something else," said Bert. "She may just turn up on her own. I remember the first time I met her. She was making her way down A Dock, toting a canvas bag about ten times bigger than she was. She seemed to be struggling, so I caught up with her and tried to take the bag from her." Bert laughed. "She practically bit my head off. Said, 'I may be old, but I'm tough. A tough old bird. So, thank you very much, but no, thanks.' " Bert shook his head. "Yeah, she may be missing, but I have to believe that she can take care of herself."

"That's probably true, but I'm going to Portland tomorrow, anyway." I explained about Ben Givens and the old gent he saw Pearl with on the bus. "There's something else," I said. "They were last seen in the company of a young fellow from the Church of the Passionate Life."

"Uh-oh," said Rose.

Bert and I both turned toward her with raised eyebrows.

"It's not really a church. It's a cult."

"A cult?" said Bert. "You mean like that Hale-Bopp Comet group, the ones who committed suicide so they could meet up with a spaceship?"

"I wouldn't say the Passionates—that's what they call themselves—are that far gone, but they're definitely borderline. My brother got mixed up with them in Denver."

As best friends, Rose and I shared everything, but this was the first time I'd ever heard about a brother. So far as I knew, Rose's only sibling was a younger sister. Rose caught my surprised look. "I've never talked about him, Kellie. Too painful."

"Tell me what you can," I said gently.

"I could write a book about what Jimmy's involvement with the Passionates did to our family. My mother's still grieving, and it's been over five years now since Jimmy took off. That's what they do—get you hooked on their brand of religion, then separate you from your family. If you have any money, you can kiss it goodbye. But Jimmy was a baby, just sixteen. What did he know? Anyway, he thought the Reverend Paul St. Paul was the answer to all his problems.

"And I have to admit, Jimmy did seem to come out of his shell after he joined the group. He'd always been kind of shy. An introvert, really, who spent hours and hours in his room with his computer. Until he joined up with the so-called Reverend. Suddenly it was like he was on some kind of permanent high. In any case, he wasn't shy anymore. In fact, he never shut up. But all he wanted to talk about was that church."

Fighting back tears, Rose sipped her champagne. After a moment, she said, "I didn't pay enough attention. I should've listened to what he was saying. Maybe I could've done something to stop Jimmy."

"Stop him from what?"

"From leaving home. He'd been with the group about six months when the Reverend St. Paul up and moved the whole congregation out of Denver like a thief in the night. We didn't even know Jimmy was gone until it was too late. By the time we tracked down the group, they were in Houston, and Jimmy had turned eighteen. The police said there was nothing we could do. He was of legal age and if he wanted to stay with the group, that was his choice."

"You say this Reverend St. Paul is in Houston?"

"Yes, but from what I've been able to gather, the group moves around a lot. It's part of their philosophy— seeking the passionate life, wherever that takes them."

"It sounds like they might be in Portland now," I said.

Rose rummaged through her handbag and pulled out a faded photo. "This is an old school photo of Jimmy. He's twenty-one now." She thrust the photo into my hand. "If you find the church, could you ask around? Maybe Jimmy is there."

I assured her that I would be glad to find out what I could.

"Tell him his sister says hi." She paused a moment. "And that I love him."

We tried to recapture the convivial mood we'd enjoyed earlier—Bert told a few lame jokes and we laughed when we were supposed to—but it wasn't the same. After dinner, we skipped dessert (a first for Bert) and hurriedly said our goodbyes.

I was halfway down the dock when Rose caught up with me. "Kellie, wait up. I didn't want to say anything in front of Bert. He's such a worrywart. But you need to know something else about that cult."

"What's that?"

"Their leader, the Reverend Paul St. Paul? He has a criminal record."

"What kind of record?"

"He was convicted of murder."

"Murder? Then why isn't he in jail?"

"He got off on some kind of technicality. I don't know all the details, but the point is, he's no minister. He's a monster."

Rose isn't one to exaggerate. In fact, she's about as straight a shooter as anyone I know. But, in this case, I felt her judgment might be somewhat skewed. So when I got back to *Second Wind*, I logged onto the Internet. I figured if Cassie could track down her twin sister via cyberspace, I could at least get some background information on the Reverend Paul St. Paul.

Considering how many organizations and businesses tout their wares and/or philosophies on the World Wide Web these days, I was not surprised to find that the

Church of the Passionate Life had its own home page. And a rather impressive home page at that. All the bells and whistles took a while to download, but it was worth it: the Reverend Paul St. Paul in living color, talking to me in his own voice.

The photo showed a short, round man with a full head of snow-white hair and a neatly trimmed mustache and beard. An urbane Santa in a natty suit. I clicked on the audio button to hear what he had to say. "My ministry is about challenging people to find their passion in life. If you're looking for a more meaningful existence, a life that will ultimately help you to develop a fuller, more personal relationship with God and His son, Jesus Christ, then I welcome you to our church fellowship."

Information on how to contact him or a church missionary followed the spiel. I spent a few minutes checking out some of the links that highlighted the various programs that the church sponsored. From what I read, the reverend put heavy emphasis on ministering to drug addicts, alcoholics, unwed mothers, and the homeless— anyone who was experiencing life's difficulties.

I didn't expect the church's home page to have any derogatory material on it, so I used a keyword search that I thought might yield a hit. What I found was a litany of accusations from a variety of critics, the gist of which asserted that the reverend was, to say the least, guilty of poor leadership in fund-raising and financial stewardship. Some reports, citing unnamed sources, supported Rose's claim that the reverend had once been convicted of murder. But I found no factual data to back it up.

Nevertheless, Rose's fears were still on my mind at six o'clock the next morning. Hoping to get an early start on my trip, I skipped breakfast, kissed a still-sleeping Cassie good-bye, and headed off to the parking lot. I'd just loaded my duffel bag in the Miata's trunk when I spotted Kingston hauling his long legs out of a snazzy red Porsche. At least I thought it was Kingston. Cassie had said he'd changed, but this was more like a complete transformation.

His dark hair had been cut brutally short, a regulation-style number that was actually flattering. It got rid of the gray and made his forty-five-year-old face seem thinner and younger by about ten years. He'd traded his rumpled and crumpled all-purpose detective suit for something you'd expect to see on an up-and-coming corporate executive. He looked good. Real good.

But it was the blonde with him that had me holding my breath. Although she wore a conservative gray suit, she exuded sexuality. She was at least six feet tall and had the slender build of a runway model. I assumed she was the one and only Mel Connor. If so, she was everything I'd imagined and more. She said something to Kingston, and he looked at her as if he'd hit the partner jackpot. I slammed the lid down on the trunk and hopped into the Miata before they saw me.

# ELEVEN

WITH A LITTLE help from Rod Stewart blasting on the radio, I put Kingston and Melody Connor out of my mind. Pedal to the metal, I screamed down I-5 without stopping until I approached the Oregon border—a little over two hours later. A record of sorts for the aging Miata, and something of a miracle given the number of troopers that usually patrol the stretch between Seattle and Portland.

My radar-busting feat came to an end when I reached the bridge spanning the Columbia River between Washington and Oregon. A natural separation between the two states, the river is part of the 465-mile-long Columbia-Snake River inland waterway and some of the most spectacular scenery in the entire Pacific Northwest. I know, for I'd sailed the waters with Grampy many times.

Sunlight spilled out of the cloud-free sky, reflecting off the river with a blinding glare. As I'd predicted yesterday, the wind had brought a shift in the weather. Sometime during the night, the rain—like a war-weary soldier—finally ended its siege against the region. At last.

Keeping one hand on the steering wheel, I rummaged through my handbag and fished out my sunglasses. One lens was cracked, and I was about as tanned as Casper the Ghost, but I still felt like a California babe when I looked at myself in the rearview mirror. Okay, babe is probably a stretch, but I felt good.

After crossing the bridge, I pulled into the first restaurant I saw. Buddy's Diner was a popular truck stop if the number of big rigs in the parking lot was any indication. From the outside, the building looked like a large abandoned storefront with smoky windows. I entered to warmth, cigarette smoke, and a noise level equal to that of a bunch of seagulls on a feeding frenzy. Although the diner had its share of burly men in John Deere caps, the clientele was far more eclectic than I'd expected—yuppies in power suits, families with youngsters, an elderly couple or two, and a number of travelers like myself.

Bare of anything remotely decorative, the diner was twice the size of the Topside, but it seemed much smaller because of the crowd. I paused at the entrance and tried to gauge how long I'd have to wait. A big mahogany counter with red-upholstered stools stretched from one end of the room to the other, but every single stool was occupied. The picture was much the same at the tables. Arranged institution-style in several long, narrow rows, there must have been at least fifty or so—and all were filled.

When my name finally hit the top of the waiting list, a bosomy hostess with teased yellow hair and dark blue eye shadow led me to a booth upholstered in the same shade of red as the counter stools. I pushed a plastic ashtray out of my way—lining it up with a set of salt and pepper shakers and a bottle of Tabasco sauce—and studied the menu.

"Try the pancakes," said a voice to my left.

I looked up from the menu to find Cord Roberts, the

man I'd run off Pearl's boat, grinning at me. That he was in Buddy's Diner of all places, gesturing to his plate—and a half-eaten stack of pancakes—as if nothing had transpired between us, struck me as more than a little weird. Didn't he recognize me? I wondered.

"The buttermilk pancakes here are terrific," he said. "Famous, in fact."

I stared at him in stony silence, feeling too confused and more than a little angered to respond. But the guy's chutzpah was amazing. Undeterred by my lack of response, he continued to make polite chitchat. If I didn't know better, I'd have thought he was trying to pick me up.

"What are you doing here?" I finally asked.

He grinned again and said, "Same reason you're here, I would imagine. I was hungry." He made a sweeping gesture with his fork. "Why else would anyone hang out at Buddy's? For the atmosphere?"

I glanced around and stifled a laugh. The sparse decor gave new meaning to the term minimalist. The place didn't have much appeal, but I grudgingly had to admit that Cord Roberts did. Especially his big blue eyes. Despite our previous history, I found myself dangerously close to succumbing to his loopy grin and good-humored charm. Fortunately I caught myself in time. "Thanks for the tip about the pancakes," I said icily, "but I think I'll have an omelet."

He shrugged and took another mouthful of the fabulous pancakes. "Suit yourself," he said between bites.

After I'd ordered a cheddar cheese and bacon omelet, I took out the tattered city map I'd picked up at the cashier's counter, brushed off a layer of dust, and unfolded it atop the table. I'd gotten the address for the Church of the Passionate Life from their web site, but I was having difficulty locating the street on the map. I was studying it so intently that I almost jumped when

Roberts spoke again. He'd finished his meal and now stood alongside my table.

Eyeing the map, he asked, "Need some help?"

"No," I said irritably. I knew that I'd come across badly, but I didn't care. Despite his good looks and friendly manner, I didn't trust the guy. Besides, his question struck me the wrong way—like he'd pegged me for a helpless female, someone who couldn't find her way around an unfamiliar town without assistance from a man.

"Sorry," he said. "Don't mean to butt into your business." He turned as if to move on, then stopped and turned around. "But I have to ask. Did you get that map here at the diner?"

"Don't worry about it," I said with a dismissive wave. "I'm used to reading all kinds of maps and charts." I straightened my shoulders. "As a matter of fact, I teach celestial navigation."

He laughed.

"You find that amusing?"

"Not at all," he said, pointing to the map. "But your navigational skills might come in handy if you got that map here—knowing Buddy, it's at least twenty years out of date."

I felt my face flush as I turned the map over and found the pub date: 1963. Oops.

Roberts didn't wait for an apology. "I know we got off to a bad start yesterday," he said, "but I'm really not such a bad guy." He grinned and patted the back of the booth. "Mind if I sit down?"

*Oh, why not,* I thought. Maybe I could find out what he was really doing on Pearl's boat. I gave him a go-ahead nod, and he plunked the same black camera case he'd had with him yesterday onto the floor. After he'd settled himself, he offered me his hand across the table. "Name's Cord. Cord Roberts. I never caught yours."

"I remember your name," I said. "I'm Kellie Montgomery."

We made small talk for a few moments, sharing introductory stuff that seemed a lot like first date material. Cord Roberts was forty-four, divorced five years ago, no children, a native Oregonian, and a fellow sailor—an expert racer, as a matter of fact. I was thankful he didn't bring up my earlier crack about teaching celestial navigation.

"So, Kellie," he said. "What brings you to the City of Roses?"

"I'm looking for my friend." I locked onto his baby blues and added, "She owns the boat you were trying to break into."

He ran his hand through his thick black hair. "Jeez, not that again. I told you why I was on that boat. I'm thinking of buying a Hunter."

*Sure thing, fella. And I bet you didn't go inside the cabin, either.* "So you came all the way to Washington to look for a boat. Don't they have any Hunters in Oregon?"

"Hey, I was in Olympia on business. I happened to drive by the marina and decided to take a look around."

"And snap a few pictures?"

His face registered mild surprise. "Yeah, that's right," he said after a beat. "For comparison purposes."

Lame, lame, lame. But I said nothing, letting him squirm.

Roberts shifted gears back to Pearl. "Does your friend live in Portland?"

"No, but I think she may be in the Portland area." I was reluctant to say anything further, but decided to chance it to see his reaction. He listened intently as I told him what I knew about Pearl's disappearance and possible connection with the Church of the Passionate Life. "It's probably a long shot," I said, "but it's the best lead I have."

He was quiet a moment, then asked, "You say your friend's name is Pearl Danielson?"

I nodded.

"Pearl Danielson, the photographer?"

"That's right." Pearl's not exactly famous, but she is well-known in the Pacific Northwest as founder of the Photos by Pearl franchise. Still, I was surprised that he recognized her name. "Don't tell me you know Pearl?"

"Only by reputation. I'm a great admirer of her work." He paused to run a hand through his dark hair again. "Tell me something, Kellie—are you a detective?"

"Hardly."

"Working with the police?"

"Nope."

"Know the Portland area?"

"Not really." I gestured to the map still spread across the table. "But I just need a better map and I'll be fine."

"May I offer a suggestion?"

I gave him a wary look. "I guess."

"Let me tag along with you."

Wow. That was a request I hadn't expected. "You find me that irresistible, huh?"

He laughed—a little too heartily—and pulled out a photo ID tag from his camera case. "I'm a photographer with *The Oregonian*. Your search for Pearl Danielson sounds like a good human-interest story."

His credentials looked legitimate, but I didn't buy the human-interest angle—or his explanation for why he'd been snooping around Pearl's boat. I figured he knew more about Pearl Danielson than he was letting on. Still, I found the idea of spending a few hours with him tempting. Maybe I could get a better line on what was really going on.

The problem was, he *was* the press. I could just imagine how Lancaster and his brother might react if Roberts' reason for tagging along with me was on the up and up.

The more we hashed it over, though, the more I came around to Cord's way of thinking: that if there'd been more publicity about Pearl's disappearance in the first place, she might be back home right now.

"You're right about the publicity," I said. "But if you're going to get involved, there have to be some ground rules."

"Like what?" he asked.

"Like we travel in separate vehicles." He was a stranger, after all, and not a particularly trustworthy stranger at that. "And we keep the story angle low-key." I pointed to his camera case. "I don't want to scare off anyone who might have some information about Pearl."

"That sounds reasonable. Anything else?"

"I get to approve any photographs you submit to your editor for publication." A bold request, but I wanted to make sure that nothing got printed that put Pearl or me in a bad light. I was fairly confident that he wasn't some sleazy paparazzo, but there was no sense taking chances.

"No can do," he said. "Nothing personal, Kellie, but it's a matter of professional pride." He scooped up his ID tag. "If it makes you feel any better, I can assure you that I'll take no photographs that will embarrass you—or Pearl Danielson. My only goal is to help you find her as quickly as possible."

He seemed sincere, but I was still hesitant. "Well, I . . ."

"It's my job, Kellie." He leaned across the table. "And I'm damn good at it."

What can I say? I fell into his blue eyes. "Okay, let's go."

We paid our tab and left the restaurant. I wanted to stop at a 7-Eleven and buy an up-to-date map, but Cord told me not to bother—he knew exactly where the Church of the Passionate Life was located. As agreed, we drove our own cars. The route he took was somewhat complicated, but I had no difficulty following him—the heap he called a car left a smoke trail for miles.

After twenty minutes, he pulled to the curb in front of a high school and parked. There was no spot for the Miata, so I turned onto a side street and walked back to the school behind a group of teens smoking furtive, last-minute cigarettes.

"Ulysses S. Grant," said Cord when I joined him. "My alma mater."

The school was big, a sprawling redbrick building with white Doric columns marking the entrance. Despite the school's size, several portable units had been added to accommodate additional students. The homes surrounding the school were old but well maintained with lush green lawns and shrubbery, color-accented with a profusion of roses, hydrangeas, azaleas, and rhododendrons.

"Nice neighborhood. But where's the church?"

"Follow me," he said, slinging his camera case over his shoulder. We walked across the street and stopped in front of a two-story redbrick home. Like the school, the house had been enlarged, connected to similar houses on both sides by an enclosed glass walkway. A large, ornate brass sign in the yard said Church of the Passionate Life.

"Three houses?" I asked.

"Just temporary quarters, from what I've heard. If you can believe the literature they put out, they're one of the fastest growing churches in the city."

"What's the appeal?"

"Beats me. But they've got more missionaries combing the city than the Mormons."

"What about their leader, the Reverend Paul St. Paul? I've heard he's had some trouble with the law."

"You've done your homework," he said. "That's good." He adjusted his camera case and looked up at the house. I followed his gaze to a second-floor window where a shadowy figure stood behind a lacy white curtain. The curtain parted slightly and then closed.

Cord Roberts looked at me and winked. ''Ready to rock 'n' roll?''

# TWELVE

I MUMBLED A vague affirmative and stole another glimpse at the upstairs window. I'm not a woman who's easily spooked. I don't get queasy at the sight of blood and I don't worry much about meeting up with a mugger or the boogeyman. Guns and knives aren't my favorite things, but I've survived a couple of close calls that weren't nearly as terrifying as battling a raging storm at sea. Even as a kid, I wasn't one to scream at horror flicks, check underneath my bed for monsters, or run from the creepy-crawly things in life.

So it was hard to figure why, on a beautiful sunlit morning, in a charming, peaceful neighborhood, accompanied by a handsome (albeit untrustworthy) hunk, I suddenly felt uneasy. It wasn't a gut-cramping, heart-racing kind of moment. Just a fuzzy feeling. A quirky, ridiculous feeling, under the circumstances, that nevertheless had me rooted to the pavement, unable to get my feet going.

Cord picked up on my discomfort. "You're not nervous, are you?"

"No, of course not," I said, forcing a smile. Then,

with a confidence born of Irish pluck, I marched up the walkway to the main house.

Once at the door, I paused to consider the protocol for gaining entry to a church disguised as a house. Should I knock on the door, ring the doorbell, or simply walk in? I turned around to ask Cord, but he was still on the sidewalk, fiddling with his camera—a complicated affair with a telescopic lens that looked capable of filming craters on the moon, probably with more detail than a NASA space probe.

As soon as he saw me looking at him, he raised the camera and started snapping photos at a rapid, almost feverish pace. The clicking and whirring was mind-numbing. Jesus, Mary, and Joseph. "Cut that out!" I yelled.

I'm sure he heard me, but he kept on shooting as he advanced toward the porch. Every step was preceded by another round of clicking and whirring until I held my hands in front of my face. "Dammit, Cord! I said to stop."

He lowered the camera with an apologetic shrug. "Okay, okay. No need to get upset."

Upset? If he hadn't been holding the camera, I'd have stomped on it. "You promised me you'd be discreet with that thing. And here we are, not even inside the church yet, and you've already got your Kodak revved up and smoking."

He didn't say anything, just stared at me with the same loopy grin that he'd charmed me with at Buddy's Diner. *Nice try, guy.* The look struck me as condescending. "Well?" I asked.

"Well, what?"

"I know you couldn't have mistaken me for a fashion model. So just what did you think you were doing?"

Still grinning, he said, "My job."

"Hmmf."

Things could've gotten ugly, I suppose, but Cord was

just too amiable to rise to my bait. Besides, I'd no more started eyeing him like a petulant kid when the front door swung open.

At the entry stood a short, silver-haired woman with a soft round face and a similarly contoured body. She was dressed in a crisp black-and-white maid's uniform and smelled faintly of almonds.

"May I help you folks?" she asked, smiling pleasantly. Her dentures clicked when she talked, but her voice was silky and inviting.

The effect on my mood was immediate. Anger, and the edginess I'd felt earlier, drained out of me like water in a leaky bucket. Still, I glanced at Cord with a look that made my intentions clear: I was in charge here. "Yes," I said, "we'd like to speak with the Reverend Paul St. Paul."

She cupped a hand to her ear. "You'll have to speak up, sweetie. I'm afraid I'm a little hard of hearing. I suppose I oughta break down and get a hearing aid, but they're just so darn expensive."

I knew all about the high cost of living. Chapter and verse. I raised my voice before she could elaborate. "The Reverend Paul St. Paul? We'd like to see him if he's in."

"Is he expecting you?"

"No."

Her hands fluttered in the air. "Oh, my dear, I'm so sorry. The reverend doesn't see anyone without an appointment. Perhaps his assistant, Brother Matthews, could help you."

I could tell Cord was itching to say or do something. I didn't think he'd start shooting again, since he'd packed up his camera and slung the case over his shoulder. But the way he rocked back and forth on his heels made me nervous. I'd had students like him in my classes. They have such a hard time keeping their mouths shut that they have to get some part of their body moving or they'll bust.

As far as I was concerned, this Matthews fellow was better than nothing. "Sure," I said. "Brother Matthews will be—"

"Tell the reverend that the press is here," interrupted Cord, flashing his photo ID.

I nudged him with my elbow and whispered out of the side of my mouth, "What are you doing?"

"Did you say the press?" asked the maid.

*"The Oregonian,"* answered Cord with enthusiasm.

I groaned, thinking we'd never get in to see anyone now, but the maid's cordial demeanor never wavered. If anything, she was even more receptive. "Oh, really?" she said.

Cord nodded, warming to the subject. "We're here to do a photo shoot. For an upcoming story about the church's missionary program."

Oh, boy. *"Cord, stop this,"* I whispered through clenched teeth.

But the maid was already ushering him through the door. I followed, shaking my head at how easily he'd manipulated her. And me.

"You can wait in the library," she said, pointing to a room off the entry hall, "while I tell the reverend you're here."

The library was Old World atmosphere all the way. Twenty by thirty feet of floor-to-ceiling bookshelves (complete with movable ladder), wainscoting and floors all hewn of quarter-sawn oak, highly grained and varnished. I felt as though we'd wandered into one of those exclusive men's clubs where they sit around reading the *Wall Street Journal* and sipping Scotch. In fact, there was a wet bar plus several museum-quality sculptures, a leather couch, and a matching wing chair with ottoman and burnished-gold floor lamp. The library also doubled as an office with a desk, computer, fax machine, and copier.

Cord declared the room merely passable and perused the well-stocked bar. "Hey," he said, "if we play our cards right, maybe we can get the reverend to break open the Scotch. He's got some Glen Farclais here."

"I'd rather hear why you felt it necessary to tell that phony story to the maid."

He yawned and flopped onto the dark burgundy leather couch. "Now, this is luxury," he said, stretching out his long legs. "I think I'm in the wrong business. Saving souls is definitely the way to go."

The cheeky attitude was wearing thin. "Cord, let's get something straight," I said. "We're here to get a line on Pearl. Not to lounge around. Not to drink Scotch. Not to spout smart remarks. And certainly not to lie."

"Lie?" The question came from behind us.

I whirled around. A man in his mid-twenties stood in the doorway, his six-foot frame casually shouldered against the doorjamb, arms folded and ankles crossed. He was good-looking with short-cropped blond hair and a freshly scrubbed ruddy complexion. He flashed me a broad, toothy smile—a dazzling display of white that struck me as phony as Cord's story. The look he was obviously going for in his Wrangler jeans and Tommy Hilfiger shirt was the friendly, all-American boy. But his cold, stealthy eyes hinted at something else.

I gave him a polite nod and introduced myself.

"Brother Duncan Matthews," he said, entering the room. "But everyone calls me Dunc." We shook hands while Cord, still stretched out on the couch, propped himself up on one elbow to get a better look. Matthews eyed him expectantly but got no response.

I performed the honors. "And this is Cord," I said, waving a hand toward the couch. "Cord Roberts."

"Ah, yes. The one who lies."

"Only on couches," said Cord, pulling himself upright. When he stood, he was a couple of inches taller than Matthews. The two men were quiet a moment, taking each other's measure.

Cord broke the silence first. "The Reverend Paul St. Paul's assistant, I presume?"

"Assistant *and* supervisor for the Northwest Regional Missionary Program. Over one hundred baptisms this quarter." He was proud, this Duncan Matthews.

Cord chuckled and grabbed his camera case. "Dunk 'em Matthews, huh?"

A slight frown creased Matthews' otherwise wrinkle-free brow as he put a hand on Cord's arm. "No need to get your camera out just yet. The Reverend St. Paul has to approve all church photographs. He'll be here shortly."

"No problemo," said Cord, shrugging out of Matthews' grasp. "But I'm sure the good reverend won't mind if I just get things set up." He unfolded a tripod and began to fiddle with a light meter.

Left to ourselves, Matthews and I made small talk. He did most of the talking, slipping easily into his missionary role. I asked about Rose's brother, Jimmy, but he claimed that the membership rolls were confidential. Yet when I mentioned that I'd heard the church had a remarkable growth rate, he launched into an enthusiastic and lengthy description of the missionary program.

I cut him off before he had me scheduled for the next baptism, and asked the same question I'd asked Cord. "What's the appeal?"

"The Reverend Paul St. Paul."

"How so?"

The smile was back, a beatific wonder. "He's a prophet of God."

"A prophet? You mean like in the Old Testament?"

"I mean one who speaks for God. His word is divinely inspired."

"I see."

"Probably not. But you'll have a better understanding after you've met him."

"How did you meet the reverend?"

"He saved me. Literally." The life story he shared was a sordid tale of childhood abuse. At twelve he ran away from home and hitchhiked from L.A. to New York, staying alive any way he could. "It was just by chance that I met up with the Reverend Paul. He was standing on a street corner, preaching. I pretended to be interested in his message, but all I really wanted was to get close enough to pick his pocket." Matthews shook his head and laughed. "He made me right away. A cop on a horse came by and was all set to run me in, but the reverend intervened and took me home with him. I've been with him ever since. If it hadn't been for the reverend, I probably would've been dead by now. He got me out of that whole street scene."

"Sounds like quite a man."

"Not just a man—a prophet. Through him, God gave me back my life. But most important, He gave me a purpose for living: The Church of the Passionate Life."

I decided to force the issue. "You weren't bothered by the fact that the reverend, your rescuer and leader of your church, was convicted of murder?"

Duncan Matthews shrugged. "That rumor has been floating around for years."

"No truth to the tale?"

He shook his head vigorously. "Absolutely none." Casting a quick glance at Cord, he added, "No thanks to the press. They keep dredging up the same old dirt every chance they get. They're out of control."

Laughter rippled from the doorway. "But that's what makes it so much fun." The Reverend Paul St. Paul's Internet photo had accurately captured the bulk of the man, but none of the joy that radiated from his jowly face. He was outfitted in a summer suit nearly as white as his hair.

Matthews folded his hands as if to pray and bowed his head slightly as the man strode purposefully into the room. "The Reverend St. Paul," Matthews said. "My prophet, my leader, my savior."

# THIRTEEN

THE REVEREND EMBRACED Duncan Matthews, but the gesture came off contrived. A pro forma response to adulation. Matthews didn't seem to notice and returned the hug with genuine feeling. Quickly disengaging himself from his sidekick, the reverend said, "You'll have to forgive Brother Duncan's venerable introduction. He tends to get carried away at times. I'm just a simple man of God." He bowed slightly and extended a stubby, liver-spotted hand to me. "And you are?" he asked, pleasantly.

"Kellie Montgomery," I said. His grip was gentle and lingered a bit too long, a surprisingly sensual caress that I didn't find off-putting. I stared into his sky-blue eyes and returned his warm smile. I wondered if his appealing demeanor was calculated—an image designed to disarm his skeptics. Calculated or not, it was working.

I introduced Cord Roberts. He was still fussing with his camera and ignored the reverend's outstretched hand. It was a rude response, but I suspected he'd picked up on how easily I'd succumbed to the man's charms, and chose not to follow suit.

The Reverend St. Paul didn't look offended by the

snub, but Matthews was clearly angered. Despite a fixed smile, he looked like a cornered alley cat, ready to pounce at the slightest provocation. His dark eyes narrowed until they were just two unblinking black slits, while the cords in his neck throbbed furiously. When he spoke, his voice quivered. "He's pissed," Matthews said as if describing himself. His smiling lips curved into a sneer. "I told him he needed to get your permission first. Before taking any pictures, I mean."

"Nonsense," replied St. Paul. "What we need first is a drink. Must be five o'clock somewhere in the world." At the wet bar he waved a bottle at us and asked, "Scotch be all right?"

I declined the offer, but Roberts, suddenly finding his manners, said, "Perfect." After a quick wink delivered specifically for my benefit, he joined St. Paul at the bar. The reverend poured a healthy shot for both of them, and before they'd downed the first sip they were friends, joking and making nice.

I caught Cord's eye, mentally prodding him to take advantage of their instant camaraderie and get to the purpose of our visit, but he didn't acknowledge my signal.

Matthews continued to hover near the reverend's side like a leech until it became obvious that he'd been outmaneuvered by Cord. He quietly helped himself to a bottle of Perrier and slumped onto the couch.

The reverend caught me staring and asked, "Are you sure you don't want something to drink?"

Answers to a few questions about Pearl would be good. "No, thank you," I said. Time to get this show on the road. "But I would like to talk to you, Reverend." I glared at Cord. "About a friend of mine named Pearl Danielson."

Matthews suddenly straightened himself on the couch. The reverend shot him a quick glance and then stirred the ice in his glass. "Oh? I thought you were here to talk about our missionary program."

"Indeed," said Cord. "We're planning a feature story with a color photo layout. Front-page stuff." He downed the last of his drink and reached for his camera.

"Front page?" asked St. Paul, his interest evident.

"Absolutely. Let's start with some shots of you and Matthews over by the desk."

Matthews hesitated, his eyes focusing on the reverend. Approval was readily granted with a brief nod and the two men arranged themselves as Roberts directed.

"Reverend, could you lean over the desk a bit? Yes, that's better." St. Paul assumed his pose easily, but Matthews was as stiff as a statue. The anger that had surfaced earlier was still evident, and he wore his distrust of Cord like body armor.

My trust in Cord wasn't exactly on terra firma, either. I'd had enough of his manipulations. The show was getting away from me—again. When he aimed the camera to begin shooting, I blocked the shot with my body. "Wait," I said. "I don't work for *The Oregonian.*"

The reverend looked puzzled, but kept his pose intact.

"Right. She works for me," said Cord. "She's an assistant, like Duncan." He grabbed his camera case with his free hand and thrust it into my arms.

Now, I'm a reasonable woman. I'll give almost anyone the benefit of the doubt. What I won't do, though, is lie down and let them wipe their scruffy shoes on my backside. I let the case slip out of my arms, and it dropped on the floor with a real nice-sounding thud. "I'm not his assistant. I'm—"

"In need of a conference," said Cord, placing a firm hand on my arm. "Please excuse us a moment." He dragged me across the room until we were safely out of earshot and then asked, "What the hell do you think you're doing?"

I shrugged out of his grasp. "What am *I* doing? The question is what are *you* doing."

"Trying to help you find Pearl."

"No way. You're on your own mission here—sucking up to the reverend and snapping photos as if there's no tomorrow."

"Exactly. And I'll keep at it until we have the answers we need."

"I guess I'm missing something. How is a photo shoot for a bogus story going to lead me to Pearl?"

"It will. Just trust me on this. Okay?"

"No. It's not okay. You've blown the last of your trust account. Explain yourself right now, or I'll—"

"Fine. I'll explain," he said irritably. He glanced back at the two men. "But if we don't make this quick, we'll lose our edge."

"So talk."

"The good reverend is a publicity hound. Taking these photos will open doors for you."

"The door has already been opened. I just need to ask him a few questions and be on my way."

"Don't let his simple-man-of-God routine fool you. 'Ask and ye shall receive, knock and it shall be opened unto you' isn't in the reverend's prayer book. Front-page publicity is the main draw here. The sooner you realize that, the sooner you'll have your answers."

He glanced back at the desk again. Matthews shot us an impatient look while the reverend cleared his throat and looked pointedly at his watch. "The reverend and his cohort are getting restless," Cord said. He gave them a reassuring nod and leaned in closer. "Now, are you with me on this or not?"

I was inclined to refuse, to immediately disavow all connection with him, but my gut told me that he was right about St. Paul. The man took to the camera lens like a movie star. While he waited for us, he fetched a pocket mirror from the desk and fussed with his hair and beard. If shooting useless pictures of the reverend was what it took to find Pearl, then I'd play along. "With you, I guess."

"Good," he said. I turned to go, but he held onto my arm and pulled me so close that his lips brushed against my ear. "One other thing," he whispered, "about those answers you're looking for?"

"What about them?"

"My photos will help, but you'll have to do your part, too."

"Meaning?"

"Meaning, you should have an answer ready for the reverend. As it says in Proverbs, 'How delightful is a timely word.' "

"I don't get it."

"You will," he said, glancing at the reverend again. " 'And the truth shall make you free.' "

While Cord resumed his photo shoot, I sat on the couch and tried to make some sense out of what he'd said. Fifteen minutes later, the only conclusion I'd reached was that Cord Roberts was an enigma. On the one hand, he claimed he was trying to help me find Pearl. On the other, he was damn well acting like a man pursuing his own interests. Maybe the front-page story he'd claimed to be covering wasn't bogus. Maybe he was after some kind of scoop. A scoop that was somehow predicated on the outcome of my quest. No matter how hard I tried, I couldn't get a good handle on what Cord Roberts was up to except that his actions were giving me a headache.

My temples were still pounding like a jackhammer when Cord finally called the photo shoot a wrap. Matthews looked relieved, but the Reverend St. Paul was clearly disappointed. "If you want some outdoor shots, we could go into the garden," he suggested. "The roses are quite spectacular this year."

Matthews nodded his head vigorously. I didn't trust

the guy any more than I did Cord Roberts, but I sort of felt sorry for him. Like me, he'd gotten sidetracked by Cord's skilled manipulations and was desperately trying to make up for lost time. "Yes, yes," he said. "The rose garden. Great idea, Reverend." Spoken like a true suck-up.

The idea quickly died as Roberts packed up his camera case without responding. St. Paul watched him a moment, then wiped his brow with a monogrammed handkerchief. "Good Lord, Brother Duncan, it's hotter than Hades in here." He gestured toward the window with his handkerchief. "See if you can get that window pried open. Let a little fresh air into the room."

While Matthews played handyman with the window, the reverend made chitchat with Roberts, slapping him on the back as if they were old Army buddies and insisting that he join him in another round of drinks. And surprise, surprise, Cord readily accepted his offer. Since St. Paul hadn't seen fit to include Matthews and me, I helped myself to two bottles of Perrier from the bar's compact fridge.

I screwed the cap off one of the bottles and took it to Matthews, who, after a great deal of struggling, had succeeded in getting the window open. "Damn thing's been stuck ever since they painted the place," he said, slightly out of breath. I held out the bottled water. "Not fuckin' likely," he said, which I took as a "no, thank you." He hustled off to the bar, where he elbowed Cord out of the way and poured himself a generous shot of Southern Comfort.

I waited until we'd settled in with our drinks—the reverend sitting at the desk, Matthews in the wing chair beside him, and Cord and I on the couch—before launching into the purpose of *my* visit. "Reverend," I said, "do you know my friend Pearl Danielson?"

He sipped on his Scotch as if he hadn't heard the question. I knew he had, so I waited. It's hard to do.

The tendency is to get impatient or flustered and jump in with another question. I used to make that blunder all the time until I witnessed Allen Kingston, the master interrogator, in action. His suspect was Percy Phillips, a little unassuming guy who supposedly worked as a bee-keeper. Kingston believed Phillips was the mastermind behind a murder-for-hire ring, but there was no real evidence to support his theory.

Phillips kept a boat at Larstad's, and when Kingston first arrived at the marina to talk to him, he refused to even give his name. It took a while, but by the time Kingston got through with him, he'd not only given up his name, address, and all the aliases he'd ever used, but he'd also ratted on his gang, which included his sixty-two-year-old mother. No force. No intimidation. No threats. As Kingston says, power belongs to those who wait.

Matthews shifted in his chair, clearly bothered by the silence. But St. Paul seemed oblivious. He downed his drink, set the glass on the desk, and steepled his hands together under his chin.

Cord seemed as uncomfortable as Matthews. He shot me a raised eyebrow, which I brushed aside with a slight shake of my head. I kept my eyes focused on the reverend, who returned my concentrated stare.

"And if I do know your friend?" he answered at last.

"Then I have some questions for you," I said. "She's been missing for over two weeks now, and the last time anyone saw her she was with a young man who may be a member of your church." I looked squarely at Matthews. "In fact, he was said to have been a tall, blond-haired fellow wearing a leather jacket with the Church of Passionate Life insignia on the back."

Again the reverend was quiet. Again I waited.

Matthews couldn't tolerate our muted exchange. "So?" he demanded. "That doesn't mean we know—"

The reverend silenced him with an upraised hand. "Miss Montgomery, you may very well have come to the right place. I am acquainted with your friend Pearl Danielson."

*Yes!* "And do you know where she is right now?"

"Ah," said the Reverend St. Paul. "That may take some understanding on your part."

"What do you mean?"

"Let me ask you something first. What turns you on?"

"Excuse me?"

"What excites you? What motivates you? What brings you the greatest joy? What would you be doing right now if you were told that you had just days or, at most, a couple of weeks to live? In other words, Miss Montgomery, what is the passion in your life?"

My head still hurt, and I was feeling antsy, unable to think. St. Paul was looking at me expectantly. Waiting for something profound, I'm sure. What was that biblical quote Cord had spouted? Something about a timely word. I felt the muscles in my neck tense and made an effort to relax.

At the open window, gauzy white curtains billowed like sails in the gentle summer breeze. I closed my eyes and took several deep breaths to clear my mind. The air in the room was sweet with lilacs from a huge purple bush beneath the window, but it was the reverend's question that had miraculously transformed the scent of flowers to that of salt air.

"Miss Montgomery, are you with us?"

I shook my head. "Sorry. For a moment there I was aboard my sloop, *Second Wind.*"

"Tell me about your boat."

"She's a forty-foot Hinckley."

I could tell he knew something about sailboats, for he said, "A Hinckley? My, my. That must have set you back a pretty penny."

The Hinckley name is synonymous with quality workmanship—solidly built and beautifully finished—with a price tag that can easily reach half a million dollars. I quickly let the reverend know that I wasn't some rich blue blood. "I bought her used," I explained. "She was built in 1967 and needed a lot of work. She's in excellent condition now."

"And earlier, when you saw yourself sailing her, what was that like?"

"Her mainsail was set out to starboard, her jib to port—what we call sailing wing and wing. Above the sails, puffy clouds were blowing across a summer sky, and under the boom a lighthouse was visible on a point of land against a pale blue sea."

"Ah, yes, sailing. So peaceful, so tranquil."

"And so deceiving." I locked onto the reverend's eyes as I drove home my point. "Veer too far one way and the jib will lose its wind; veer too far the other way and the mainsail will crash across the deck."

"Exactly!" he exclaimed, clapping his hands. "You've hit on what most people miss when they describe their passion. Following your dream, your heart's desire, your passion, if you will, is not without an element of risk. Your friend Pearl Danielson knows this quite well."

A chill went through me. I moved to the edge of the couch and said, "Reverend, if you know where Pearl is, please tell me. Her family and friends are very worried about her."

He sipped his drink but didn't say anything further.

I tried to outwait him but failed miserably. "Please," I begged.

The reverend smiled. The tolerant father dealing with a foolish child. "Are you familiar with the term 'devil to pay'?" he asked.

I stared at him.

"It's an old seafaring term," he prompted. "As a sailor, I'm sure you've heard of it."

"It means very difficult or awkward."

"Go on."

"The devil was the caulker's name for the seam in the upper-deck planking next to a ship's waterways. It was given that name as there was very little space to get at this seam with a caulking iron, making it a particularly difficult and awkward job."

"Quite so. Devil to pay—a situation so difficult that no means of solving it is immediately apparent."

"Reverend, what exactly are you trying to tell me?"

"Just this: As a man of God, I've a sacred duty, a trust, if you will, to guide all who are seeking the truth to discover their true destiny, their raison d'être. And once this mission is accomplished, it is my calling to do whatever I can to help them keep their passion alive and growing for as long as they are bound by this earthly existence. My responsibility is inviolate. As are any confidences they share with me." He stroked his beard thoughtfully.

The man spoke in riddles. Was he going to tell me where Pearl was or not? I scrambled to think of something to say, but drew a blank.

"So let me get this straight," said Cord, sensing my confusion. "You know where Pearl is. But for some reason, a reason that has something to do with her life's passion, as you call it, you can't tell us. Because of your duty as a man of God, the keeper of confidences."

The reverend nodded. "You are a wise man, Cord Roberts."

He laughed and said, "There are some who'd question that assessment. But I do know that there's a simple solution to your dilemma."

"Which is?"

Cord pointed to the telephone sitting on the desk. "Call her up. Let Pearl decide if she wants to see Kellie."

# FOURTEEN

TWENTY MINUTES LATER, I was knocking on Pearl Danielson's door. She was staying in a suite at the Dover, one of Portland's swankiest hotels. According to Roberts, the hotel was originally the home of William P. Dover, a lumber baron from the early 1800s. Located on the banks of the Willamette River overlooking downtown Portland, the elegant redbrick building had once been prime demolition material. Saved from destruction by the efforts of the Oregon Historical Society, the building—now a registered historical landmark—was eventually acquired by a wealthy East Coast hotelier who spent a fortune transforming the former Dover family home into world-class accommodations.

The phone call that had brought me to Pearl's doorstep had been brief. The reverend Paul St. Paul ascertained that she was interested in meeting with me and received permission to divulge her whereabouts. And that was that. I still had no idea why she was hiding out from her family and friends nor, for that matter, how or why she'd hooked up with the Reverend.

"It's the money, honey," Cord had said as we left the church.

"What do you mean?"

"Think about it," he said. "Pearl Danielson is a very wealthy woman. The good reverend can preach all he wants to about being called by God to help others find their passion in life, but I'll guarantee you that it's their bank account *he's* interested in finding."

"That's kind of harsh," I said, remembering how I'd been drawn to the reverend myself.

"He's a con man, Kellie. I thought you'd see that right away. There's nothing spiritual about the guy."

I didn't exactly discount what Cord had to say, but I knew Pearl wasn't the type to fall for some fast-talker. She might be adventuresome, but she was prudent in business, especially when it came to parting with her money. No, there was more to her relationship with the Reverend Paul St. Paul than Cord suggested.

We argued about it (and whether Cord should accompany me to the Dover) all the way back to where we'd parked our cars. It wasn't much of an argument. The guy was something of a con man himself. I didn't trust his motives and I found his tactics annoying, but I still welcomed his company.

"Just let me do all the talking this time," I said after we arrived at the hotel. "And absolutely no photos."

"Camera's in the trunk," he assured me.

Once at Pearl's suite, he stood behind me like a shadow and let me do my thing. Pearl answered my knock almost immediately. She's a small woman, like me, but she's much slimmer, easily fitting into a size four—something I haven't been able to do since high school. She was dressed in a pastel blue skirt and a silky long-sleeved blouse with a floppy bow tie in place of a collar. Her glasses hung on a gold chain about her neck and, except for a large jade ring on her left hand, she wore no jewelry.

Although she knew I was coming, she seemed startled to find me at her door. I suddenly felt nervous and wondered if I'd made a mistake tracking her down. But after a moment's hesitation, she greeted me warmly. "Kellie, dear! Come in, come in."

"There's someone with me," I said, stepping aside so that she could get a good look at Cord. "A friend of mine." Not exactly true, but I didn't know what else to call him.

"Oh," she said, her hand flying to pursed lips. An awkward moment elapsed before she added, "Then he's a friend of mine, too."

After introductions were made, they shook hands and we entered the suite. The Dover was rated five stars, and it showed. Pearl's hideout was as spacious as her condo and just as well appointed. The decor was something along the lines of Classy Tudor meets Sensible Northwest—lots of warm earth and peach tones in the wallpaper, carpeting, and window treatments. Besides elegantly upholstered furniture, the sitting room included a baby grand piano, a stone fireplace, an antique Victrola, and enough framed art to furnish a small gallery.

All the appointments were breathtaking, but Cord was particularly taken with the artwork. He lingered in front of one gilt-framed piece until Pearl invited us to sit down.

We settled ourselves on a flowered love seat while she sat across from us on a similarly patterned couch. Her mood was hard to read. She seemed different somehow. Maybe it was just the room and its furnishings, but she had an air of formality about her that I'd never seen before. She made polite small talk about the welcome change in the weather and then offered us some refreshments that had been set out on a glass coffee table prior to our arrival. It was a light lunch consisting of fruit, cheese, crackers, and a selection of tea sandwiches.

Cord ate heartily, but I had no appetite. I nibbled on a sandwich just to be gracious and tried to figure out

what was going on. Pearl poured us iced tea from a
crystal pitcher, and we ate and drank in stilted silence
for a few minutes. Finally she smiled tightly and said,
"So tell me, Kellie dear. Why exactly are you here?"

I figured she'd get to the heart of the matter sooner
or later, but I delayed answering by taking the last bite
of my sandwich and then washing it down with a sip of
iced tea. The stall was a calculated effort on my part to
get the words just right. "Well, Pearl," I began, "everyone has been very worried about you. I came here to
make sure you're okay."

"Who's everyone?"

"Your family, Kate, me." I purposefully omitted
mentioning Dennis Lancaster and her son-in-law. I
didn't know how I was going to put a good spin on
meeting up with them at her condo. I figured I'd have
to explain the encounter eventually, but not now.

She shook her head. "Then you've all been worried
over nothing." She paused to wave a slender hand toward the room's elaborate furnishings. "As you can see,
I'm quite safe and comfortable."

I should be so lucky. "Right. And that's exactly what
I'll tell everyone."

She arched her back and snapped, "You'll do no such
thing."

"But the police are looking for you, Pearl. At least
let me inform them."

"The police?" She seemed genuinely surprised.

"Your daughter filed a missing persons report when
you failed to arrive in Salem as scheduled."

"Oh, dear," she said, fingering the gold chain that
held her glasses. "I never expected that."

She didn't? Seemed like a logical move for a daughter
to make as far as I was concerned. I'd sure expect Cassie
to call the police if I didn't get back from this little
expedition on time. "What *did* you think Adrienne
would do when you didn't show up?"

"I don't know. I wasn't thinking about her at all."

"Excuse me if I'm being presumptuous, Pearl, but what were you thinking about?"

"I . . . Oh, what difference does it make now?" She turned to Cord, who'd been remarkably successful in keeping his mouth shut during our entire exchange. "Would you like some more tea, Conrad?"

"Uh, it's Cord. And I'll pass on the tea."

This was going nowhere fast. Time to press the issue. "I understand that you weren't traveling alone. You were with a man you met in Port Ludlow."

She reached for the pitcher and carefully poured Cord the glass of iced tea that he'd just declined. "Yes, that's partly true," she said. "I was with a man on the bus. But we'd met long before Port Ludlow." She seemed about to say more, but didn't.

"And you got off the bus together. You and your gentleman friend and someone from the Church of the Passionate Life."

"Duncan Matthews," she said, her countenance brightening. "Such a nice young man. He's a missionary, you know."

"Yes, I know. Did Matthews introduce you to the Reverend Paul St. Paul? Or had you met him before, too?"

She sighed, "This is getting tiresome, all these questions. I don't mean to be contrary, Kellie, but I just don't understand your interest. What difference does it make to you or anyone else whom I met or when? Don't you think I'm entitled to my privacy?"

She was right, of course. I felt properly chastised. "I'm sorry, Pearl. I guess I got carried away. You're safe and well, and that's all that matters."

I rose from the couch and slung my bag over my shoulder. "Thanks for the lunch," I said. I motioned to Cord. "We'll see ourselves out."

"Wait a minute," Cord said. "There's something I'd like to say first."

Uh-oh. I should've known he couldn't leave without getting his two cents in.

He stood and faced Pearl. "Congratulations," he said. "Or is it best wishes? I always get confused when it comes to matters of etiquette." He grinned. "Except when it comes to kissing the bride, of course."

Pearl's face softened into a coy smile. "You want to kiss me, is that it?"

"Only if your husband doesn't mind."

Hello? What husband?

She looked over her shoulder toward the bedroom. "He's taking a nap right now. And what he doesn't know won't hurt him," she said with a giggle.

Cord leaned forward and bussed her on the cheek. "May your days together be long and happy."

"Thank you," said Pearl softly. Her small frame, held so stiffly earlier, relaxed noticeably. Tears welled in her eyes, but she was smiling.

"Excuse me," I said. "I seem to have missed something here." I looked at Cord and then at Pearl. "You're married?"

Pearl nodded. "Two weeks ago."

"The man on the bus?" I asked.

"Isaac Feldman. We've been friends for some time." She turned to Cord. "But how did you know we'd gotten married?"

Yeah. My question exactly.

"The *Ketubah*," he said.

"The what?" I asked.

Cord pointed to the gilt framed artwork he'd admired earlier. "The *Ketubah* is a marriage contract or agreement. The calligraphy is so ornate that it looks more like a beautiful design than actual writing. If you examine the work closely, though, you'll see it. This one is a little more modern—Hebrew on the right, English on the left. Rabbi Rosen is quite an artist.''

"Yes," agreed Pearl. "We think his work gives our suite a personal touch. You know Rabbi Rosen?" she asked Cord.

"He's my uncle."

I don't know why that news surprised me. Ever since I'd met up with him, Cord had been saying or doing unexpected things.

"Isaac will be so disappointed to learn that he missed your visit," said Pearl. "I know he would want to meet the nephew of Rabbi Rosen." She turned to me and took my hand in hers. "And I'd like you to meet my new husband, Kellie."

"I'd like that, too."

"Then let's make it happen," said Cord. "At dinner tonight."

"That would be lovely," agreed Pearl. "The two of you could join us at the White Cliffs. It's Isaac's favorite restaurant." She laughed softly. "He says it's because they serve a nice piece of fish, but I think he's taken with the name. Anyway, it's located right here at the hotel—the White Cliffs of Dover."

"We'd be delighted," said Cord.

"Absolutely," I said.

That settled, we took our leave. At the door, Pearl pulled me aside. "Kellie, I know you came here with the best intentions and I want you to know that I appreciate your concern. If I've seemed guarded or evasive, it was for a good reason. I suspect you're leaving with many questions still unanswered."

I nodded.

"That's why I must insist that you don't notify the police or anyone else about me just yet."

"But, Pearl—"

She cut me off with an upraised hand. "It's okay. I'll explain everything at dinner."

# FIFTEEN

CORD AND I parted ways at the hotel lobby. He claimed to have an urgent assignment across town, and I had an appointment with Flora Hampton—the adoptive mother of Cassie's twin sister. I'd called her before leaving Seattle and introduced myself as a relative of sorts who was tracing our family's roots. I was deliberately vague (blurting out the true nature of our relationship over the phone didn't strike me as a particularly smart move), but Flora Hampton wasn't put off at all. In fact, she seemed eager to meet me. I wondered, though, if she would've been quite so eager had I been totally upfront with her.

If she hadn't been expecting me, I'd have postponed our meeting until the following day. Besides having mixed feelings about my role as Cassie's intermediary, I was exhausted. If it's true that you're only as old as you feel, then I was proof that there were such things as the living dead. All I wanted to do was to check into a hotel and collapse. The Dover would've been nice, but a broom closet in that place would've required me to float a small loan. As they say, if you have to ask the price, you can't afford it. So I found a little mom-and-pop motel that looked decent and checked in without any embarrassing questions about my net worth.

Except for some fancy draperies, my room was a bare-bones affair. But it had enough of the basics to suit me. Namely, a bed. I looked at it longingly for a minute and then called Cassie. Collapsing would have to come later. Cassie wasn't at the sailing school or aboard *Second Wind*, so I left the motel phone number on both answering machines. I didn't want her to think I was checking up on her, but emergencies do happen. I took another look at the bed. Probably a hard mattress, I thought, heading out the door.

The Hampton family home was located in northeast Portland on a dead-end street that was within spitting distance of the airport. The street was so close to the cyclone fence that bordered the United terminal, it could've doubled as a runway. It was a respectable blue-collar neighborhood with trim, single-family homes on narrow but well-maintained lots. A market-savvy Realtor would play down the proximity to the airport and emphasize things like curb appeal and pride of ownership.

I slurped on a soda as I checked for house numbers. The temperature had shot up to a record-breaking 92 degrees, and I was wilting fast. I'd put the top down on the Miata when I left the motel, which turned out to be a big mistake. It was like driving inside a pizza oven. The only breeze was a blast of hot air sucked up from the heat radiating from the black-tar roadway.

Aside from a van that had been tailgating me for a couple of blocks, the Hamptons' street was relatively free of traffic. Just your basic kids on bikes and dogs running amok type neighborhood. When I stopped in front of the Hamptons' house, my tailgating friend and a jumbo jet took off at the same time. The roar of the plane's engines was so loud that my little roadster and I shook worse than if we'd been tapped for an IRS audit. I climbed out of the car just as another jet landed, and it occurred to me that survival in this neighborhood depended on an unlimited supply of earplugs.

The Hamptons' house looked pretty much like all the others on the block—a two-story, World-War-II-vintage clapboard with a cement front porch, aluminum awnings, and a brown shingled roof. The lawn was green and healthy-looking and smelled freshly mowed. A row of little yellow marigolds lined both sides of the walkway leading to the front porch. The door had been painted in the same shade as the flowers and had a ceramic plaque underneath the peephole that read WELCOME FRIENDS.

I looked at the doorbell and fidgeted with my bag a moment, shifting it from one shoulder to the other. Flora Hampton sounded nice over the phone, but I wasn't looking forward to meeting her. I had absolutely no idea what I was going to say to the woman, which ordinarily wouldn't have bothered me. Winging it and hoping for the best was my standard modus operandi. But this situation was different. There was a good chance that if I didn't handle things right I could blow Cassie's chances for a reunion with her twin.

I might've still been standing on the porch, finger poised over the doorbell like a gutless wonder, if the Hamptons' next-door neighbor hadn't come outside to water his lawn. He was about ninety-nine and moved at glacial speed, but he kept a watchful eye on me while he set his sprinkler. I smiled and gave him a friendly wave, which only served to tweak his interest. He was either the neighborhood watch captain or in desperate need of company. As soon as he'd gotten his sprinkler going, he started slowly heading my way. I rang the doorbell out of pure self-preservation.

When the door opened, I felt as though the earth had suddenly tilted on its axis and was spinning wildly out of control. There was no doubt that Cassie and the young woman who stood in front of me shared the same gene pool. I didn't think I'd faint, but I grabbed hold of the doorjamb to balance myself. My reaction wasn't lost on Cassie's twin.

A wrinkle creased her brow. "Are you okay?" she asked warily.

I stared at her like an openmouthed idiot, too preoccupied with inventorying her physical attributes to get a word out. The similarities were all there: five foot ten, thick hair, olive complexion, brown eyes, narrow nose, and dimples in both cheeks. But the differences were striking. Her hair was bleached blond (dark at the roots) and cropped extremely short. The style was hip, I suppose, but it was also spotty—so uneven that it looked as if she'd cut it herself. Either that, or the hairdresser couldn't find the scissors and made do with a razor. She was barefoot (purple toenails and a Tasmanian devil tattoo on her left ankle) and wore a hot-pink stretchy tank top and frayed, cutoff jeans. I wouldn't say her outfit was too tight, but the term "painted on" definitely came to mind.

I took several deep gulping breaths and tried to calm myself before she thought it necessary to call 9-1-1. "I'm fine," I said. "I just need to get out of the sun."

"Whatever," she said, shrugging.

I followed her into a small living room crammed with family photos, crocheted doilies, and too much furniture. I asked for some water. After a moment's hesitation— an interval marked by a look that said I was not only putting her out, but also keeping her from something of cosmic importance—she headed for the kitchen.

I settled myself on a lumpy, slipcovered couch. The place was tidy, but lived-in. Comfortable. The kind of place where you're not afraid to belch or fart for fear of breaking something. The kitchen was at the rear of the house, but cooking smells—stew or pot roast or something—poured into the living room on a savory tidal wave.

The air was stifling in spite of a big portable fan on the floor. I turned up the dial to full blast and positioned myself so that the air would hit me full in the face. I could hear angry-sounding voices through the thin walls but I couldn't decipher any of the words.

When Cassie's twin returned, she was accompanied by a plump, thick-waisted woman, who looked to be in her late sixties. She wore no-nonsense, black grandma-type shoes and thick support hose under a flowered dress that hung below her knees. Despite the weather, she had on a heavy white cable-knit cardigan.

"You must be Kellie," she said, handing me a tall Tupperware glass filled with water. "I'm Flora."

I quickly took a drink, more to hide my surprise than quench my thirst. I'd expected someone nearer my own age. Flora Hampton must have been in her forties when she adopted Cassie's sister. Disregarding the bleached hair and skimpy attire, though, the girl's features were surprisingly similar to those of her adoptive mother.

"And this is my daughter, Claudeen."

Claudeen rolled her eyes and scrunched up her face. The pouty-lipped, oh, Mother-please look that Cassie often favored me with. The two girls had perfected the look to an art form. "Deena," she said, irritably. "I go by Deena."

Flora gave me an embarrassed smile.

"Glad to meet you, Deena," I said.

"Same here," she said without enthusiasm. She glanced at her Mickey Mouse wristwatch. "Can I leave now?" she asked. Without waiting for an answer, she departed, taking the stairs two at a time to the upper floor.

"She has a date," explained Flora. "A good boy, from the neighborhood." She crossed herself. "Thank God." She studied me a moment. "How're you feeling?"

"Just fine now," I said, drinking the last of the water.

I set the empty glass on the large square coffee table in front of the couch. An intricately patterned doily served as coaster. "Thanks for the water. It helped a lot."

"Would you like another glass—or maybe some lemonade? It's no bother."

I shook my head. "I'm quite all right. Thank you very much."

She glanced at the fan noisily whirring at warp speed and then, pulling her sweater across her ample bosom, eased herself into an overstuffed rocker out of the direct line of fire.

"So," she said, eyeing me over the rim of her glasses. "You're a relative, huh? You don't look much like a Hampton. My husband's people were all tall and dark. Mine, too. Except for the Donatellis—my mother's kin. They're all short like you. Never knew of any redheads, though." She laughed.

I took a deep breath. "Flora," I said, "I'm not really related to you. Except through our daughters."

The puzzle quieted her a moment. Then a confused frown and, "Whatever are you talking about?"

"Adoption," I said softly.

"What?" she asked, cupping her hand to her ear.

I switched off the fan. "Adoption," I repeated. "I have reason to believe that your daughter and mine are twins. Separated at birth and adopted by your family and mine."

She drew a hand to her mouth and exclaimed, "No, that's not possible!"

"Claudeen is adopted, isn't she?"

Flora glanced at the stairs. "Please, keep your voice down," she pleaded.

"I'm sorry," I said. I dug into my bag and pulled out a photo of Cassie. "This is why I almost fainted when I first saw your daughter." I got up and handed her the picture. "Can you see the resemblance? They're identical. It's quite remarkable."

Her eyes widened as she studied the photo. In a shaky voice she said, "Oh, my God," and crossed herself.

"Are you okay?" I asked.

She nodded unconvincingly. "It's just that . . . Oh, my God. This is terrible." She stood up suddenly and bolted for the kitchen. For a large woman she moved awfully fast.

When I caught up with her, she was standing in front of a gas stove, vigorously stirring a simmering pot with a big wooden spoon. The kitchen was small and hot. Sweat dripped from Flora's brow as she stirred.

I ran some tap water and refilled the Tupperware glass that she'd given me earlier. "Won't you sit down?" I asked, motioning to a tiny alcove with a chrome dinette table and two chairs. "You look like you could use some of this water, too."

Flora turned the burner to low and joined me at the table. When we were both seated, she reached for the water glass and satisfied her thirst. Afterwards, she said, "Claudeen doesn't know she's adopted."

I stared at her in disbelief. That something so important had been kept from her daughter was unthinkable. I'd never actually sat down and told Cassie she was adopted, but I couldn't recall a time when she didn't know. It was just something that she understood about herself. Like knowing that you have brown eyes rather than blue.

I instantly flashed on an incident that occurred when she was only three. Cassie's preschool teacher drew me aside to tell me about a conversation she'd overhead that day between Cassie and three of her playmates: They were on the playground, boasting to one another about who had the best doll, the best this, the best that, when one of the girls said, "Well, that's nothing, I'm Irish." Another bragged, "I'm Italian" while the third informed the group with a superior air that she was Swedish. Cassie looked downcast as if she didn't quite know how to top all that. After a moment she looked up, and, with a triumphant grin, said, "But *I'm* 'dopted!"

Flora removed her glasses and wiped tears from her eyes with a paper napkin. "My husband, Claude, and I, we always meant to tell her, but we just never got around to it. Then he up and died. Heart attack." She crossed herself. "God rest his soul."

"I'm so very sorry to hear that. My husband died almost four years ago. Brain tumor."

She shook her head sadly. "Then you know what it's like. Claudeen was only thirteen at the time and very close to her daddy. They were really something, those two. Everyone thought we were too old to adopt a baby, but I can't begin to tell you how much joy that little girl brought into our lives."

"I have a pretty good idea."

"After Claude died, I couldn't bring myself to tell her about the adoption. It just seemed like another difficult burden for her to carry. She was already in trouble at school. Her grades dropped off, she started running with a bad crowd . . ." Flora took another drink. "I didn't know what to do. She wouldn't listen to a thing I said. It was as if she was deliberately trying to upset me. Her clothes. Her hair. She even got her tongue pierced, for heaven's sake. We went round and round about things." She sniffed into her tissue. "Still do."

Her story chilled me in spite of the heat. "My daughter had a hard time with her father's death, too," I said. "Blamed me somehow."

"Guess they're alike in more ways than just looks."

We were both quiet for a moment. Then Flora asked, "How did you find us?"

"The lawyer who handled Cassie's adoption was murdered, and a friend of mine was the detective assigned to investigate the case. He found the adoption records in the lawyer's files. Cassie's always known that she's adopted, but I had no idea that she was a twin until those files were opened.

"I told her as soon as I found out. That was back in December. She's been trying to locate her sister ever since. We had your name from the lawyer's old files, but your address had changed. She found your current address on the Internet."

"We moved into this house shortly after the adoption was final. Been here ever since." Flora twisted her tissue. "Why didn't your daughter—Cassie, is it?—come with you?"

"She wasn't sure if your daughter still lived at home. But I think she was just scared. She didn't know what kind of reception she'd receive, so rather than risk rejection, she asked me to contact you. She thought I might be able to explain things better. Adoptive mother to adoptive mother. Something like that."

"I see."

"What are you going to do?" I asked.

"Do?"

"Are you going to tell Deena that she's adopted? That she has a twin?"

Flora shrugged. "I don't know. I truly don't. You saw how she is. I'm afraid this kind of news would really set her off. Make her even harder to deal with than she is now."

"But then, it might not. It might be just what she needs."

"I don't understand."

"That same detective friend I told you about said that knowing who we are and where we come from is what grounds us, what gives our life meaning. As a Native American he believes that our heritage, our ancestry, is a spiritual thing. It's what defines us, what connects us with the rest of humanity. And if that knowledge is kept from us, legally or otherwise, we will always feel incomplete. He says it's a primal need. And denying that

need, no matter how well intentioned, is like denying
someone food and water.''

Flora thought that over a moment. ''I don't know,''
she said. ''What you say makes sense, but with Deena
so angry at me already . . .''

''You don't have to make any decisions today, Flora.
But let's do this.'' I took Cassie's photo out of my wallet
and pushed it across the table. ''I'll leave this with you.
If you decide to tell Deena about the adoption, show her
Cassie's picture. It might help her to know that she's
not alone in this. That she has a sister who has experi-
enced some of the very same things she's going through.
A sister who'd like to meet her.''

I gave her one of my cards from the sailing school
and wrote my home number on the back. ''Call me if
you'd like. I'd be happy to talk to you some more if you
feel the need.''

Flora ran her finger lightly across Cassie's photo.
''Okay,'' she said. ''But I can't make any promises.''

# SIXTEEN

I KNEW I was in trouble as soon as I left Flora's.

The white van with dirt-encrusted license plates that had tailgated me earlier was back. It was at the far end of the dead-end street, but as soon as I pulled away from the curb, its driver gunned the engine and came up behind me fast. It tailed me for two blocks, so close at times we actually touched bumpers. The first nudge was gentle, like a playful kiss. But when I turned onto Thirty-third Street and accelerated, things got rough.

I stopped for a red light at the intersection of Thirty-third and Killingsworth, and the van kept on coming, hitting the Miata's bumper so hard that the impact slammed me against the headrest.

Carjackers! It wasn't hard to guess why I'd been targeted. Woman alone. Driving a convertible. Out-of-state plates. Easy prey.

Dazed and seriously scared, I glanced in the rearview mirror. Within seconds, the van's door swung open, and a mountain of muscle in a black T-shirt and baggy jeans bounded out. He dashed toward my roadster with a fierce, athletic stride. He caught me eyeing him in the mirror and smiled. A twisted little smile that hinted of insanity.

I instantly pictured him as a little boy, pulling legs off grasshoppers and kicking puppies. He would've found it pleasurable, maybe even sensual. And he'd take perverse pleasure in doing the same to me. He'd grab me by the shoulders and jerk me out of the car, perhaps pausing long enough to stare at me with hooded, close-set eyes before shooting or stabbing me.

No way. No flippin' way. I shifted into first and sped into the busy intersection, narrowly missing two cars. Horns blared. Brakes squealed. Fingers gestured. I ignored them all and looked in the rearview mirror again.

The van was gone.

I was pumped. Energized. Adrenaline rushed through my veins like high octane gasoline. I'd survived a would-be carjacking! Based on how exhausted I was earlier in the day, you'd have thought the experience would render me comatose. But the human body is a wondrous thing. I was eighteen again and invincible.

The thought flashed through my mind that I ought to report the incident to the police, but I quickly discarded the idea as a waste of time. Instead, I drove back to the motel, stripped off my clothes and took a quick shower. Afterwards, I wrapped a towel around my head, slipped on a terry cloth robe, and cracked open a bottle of beer. I don't usually drink beer, but the Henry Weinhard's Private Reserve went down cool and smooth.

I'd bought a six-pack at the 7-Eleven where I'd stopped to assess the damage to the Miata's rear end. The crumpled bumper was still intact, but the middle part had been smashed flat against the trunk. It didn't look all that bad, but it would probably cost a fortune to fix. I tried to remember how much my deductible was.

Still keyed up, I paced back and forth in the room while I drank the beer. I put all thoughts about the damage to my car and bank account out of my mind. That wasn't as difficult as you'd imagine, mainly because I had a more pressing problem at the moment—what to wear to dinner. The White Cliffs of Dover was a cutesy name, but I was certain that a five-star hotel would have a snooty dress code. Something at least a notch or two above the *no shoes, no shirt, no service* standard that I was used to at the Topside.

Dress code aside, the plain truth was that I wanted to wear something that made me look good. Not just good—fantastic. Something that would get Cord to notice me. As irritating as he'd been today, I liked the guy. And even though good judgment told me to go slow, I wanted him to like me, too. Or at least find me attractive. Ever since I'd seen Kingston with Melody this morning, I'd felt like an old discarded shoe.

The problem was, I hadn't packed anything remotely suitable for what I had in mind, let alone a fine-dining experience. Since there wasn't enough time or money to go shopping for a sexy (or any other) dress, I settled on a scooped-neck gray tunic over a pair of black leotards. I didn't have a belt, so I made like Scarlett O'Hara and cinched the outfit together with a braided gold drapery cord snatched off the motel room window. For a final touch, I donned my good black leather sandals and a gold locket that Cassie had left behind when she last used my duffel bag.

I slung my bag over my shoulder and stood on the toilet seat to get a full-length view of myself in the bathroom mirror. What I saw was depressing. Cord Roberts probably wouldn't run from the restaurant when he saw me, but it was a safe bet he wouldn't stick around very long, either. Just like Allen Kingston.

As it turned out, I needn't have worried—at least about the dress code. The White Cliffs of Dover was not some stuffy place where incredibly snobby rich people wearing thousand-dollar suits and designer dresses sipped gin and tonics and talked about their latest trip to Europe. I wasn't the best-dressed woman in the place, but I blended with the crowd, which, for the most part, was casually attired.

The place was decorated like a quaint English pub. Lots of dark wood and leather, but nothing ostentatious. Not surprisingly, there was a big oil painting of the famous white cliffs at the restaurant entrance and several smaller paintings of the English countryside displayed on the other walls. The atmosphere was warm, friendly, and inviting.

Pearl Danielson and her new husband were already seated at a corner booth when I arrived at the restaurant. Pearl looked every bit as radiant as a new bride should be. She wore a black linen suit and light gray silk blouse with a strand of pearls—her trademark jewelry. The effect was casually elegant.

Isaac Feldman stood up when I approached the table, but it was a difficult maneuver. He was at least eighty and looked it: a frail, paper-thin little man with a weak handshake and whisper-soft voice. He was smartly dressed, though, in a black, custom-tailored suit. He didn't wear a tie, but his bald head was covered by a black silk skullcap.

"So nice to meet you," he said. A portable oxygen tank with plastic tubing was set on the floor next to the table. He pushed it aside with a curse as he sat down. "This contraption follows me everywhere."

"Doctor's orders," explained Pearl.

"The doctor," said Isaac with an exasperated shrug. "What does he know? He's just a kid. You should hear him talk, this kid, this doctor. He thinks anyone over the age of fifty is dying."

Isaac had worked himself into an agitated state, and Pearl gently stroked his hand to calm him. "Isaac, darling," she said softly, "the doctor is right. We begin dying the moment we're born."

The old man's eyes softened behind his glasses, and

he gazed at her with great affection. *"Kindila,* my *kin-dila,"* he said, drawing her hand to his lips. After a moment he turned from Pearl and looked at me. "Do you see why I could not let this woman get away? She is so smart, so wise, and so very, very beautiful. Do you see that?"

What I saw was love. Beauty. Poetry. *Grow old along with me, the best is yet to be.* My heart ached in sudden sorrow. For it was not Isaac and Pearl publicly sharing their love for one another. It was my husband and me—as we might have been. A gray-haired Wendell gazing into my tired eyes, stroking my frail hand, praising my wisdom and beauty. His untimely death had been a co-lossal storm, an irreversible wind that changed my destiny. *You didn't ask for it, Kellie, darlin', but it's your wind and you have to sail it.*

Grampy believed that the worst storm is not that which takes our lives, but that which casts us adrift on an empty sea deprived of our memories—be they of a lifetime or only a few short years. I shook off the mo-mentary melancholy that had enveloped me and wished Pearl and Isaac smooth sailing as they made their own memories together.

A ponytailed waiter with skinny arms and broad shoulders came to take our drink order. Isaac ordered a bottle of Erath Pinot Gris. "You think your friend will like it?" he asked me. "It's an Oregon label."

"I'm sure he will." I said. A smile masked my grow-ing irritation. I don't know which rankled me more: that Cord had set up this dinner party and then didn't have the courtesy to arrive on time or that I'd gone to so much trouble trying to pull myself together for him. "I'm sorry he's late. I can't imagine what's keeping him."

Pearl and Isaac made light of his tardiness, and I changed the subject by asking, "How did you two meet?"

They took turns telling the story. Isaac Feldman began

with how he'd become a widower so many years ago. His wife died in childbirth, and he raised his only child, Rachel, by himself. He described himself as a lonely man, but a busy one. A man who loved his work—an importer of china and glassware from the Far East and Europe.

"And he's still working," said Pearl. "Despite doctor's orders."

Isaac shrugged. "These doctors, what do they know of business? How can I not work? The Pacific Rim, it's a gold mine. But I knew this years ago. Anyone with good business sense could not help but know these things."

"Anyway," said Pearl, "you asked how we met. I can't remember what year it was, but we were both serving on the board of directors for HavenSafe."

I'd heard of the organization. It was dedicated to rescuing children who'd been orphaned due to the ravages of war. Monies were raised to provide food, clothing, medicine, or whatever was needed to keep the children safe and alive. Often the rescue involved removing the children from their homeland and bringing them to the U.S., where they could be adopted.

"It was love at first sight," said Isaac. He laughed and tapped his wire-framed glasses. "But my eyes, they don't work so well no more. Pearl's, too."

"He's trying to say it took a little time before we realized how much we cared for each other."

Our waiter returned with the bottle of wine. After toasting the newlyweds, I asked the question that had been on my mind since learning of Pearl's marriage. "When did you decide to get married? Sailing from Port Ludlow to Olympia or after you got on the Greyhound bus?"

They looked at each other and laughed. After a moment Pearl said, "I had no idea Isaac was going to be in Port Ludlow. It was just a coincidence that we ran into each other at the resort.''

''I was attending a conference there,'' explained Isaac.

''And I'd just planned to spend the night at the marina before heading on down the Washington coast. But I got a little sidetracked.''

''We *both* got a little sidetracked,'' Isaac said with a chuckle. He squeezed Pearl's hand. ''I even went sailing with this lovely captain.''

Pearl flashed her husband a loving smile. ''We didn't go to the coast, but it was a wonderful trip.''

I didn't want to spoil their mood, so I refrained from mentioning the overdue moorage or the mess I'd found in *Picture Perfect*'s cabin. ''Why'd you take the bus from Olympia?'' I asked.

Isaac shrugged. ''They were running a special double discount for seniors that week.''

Talk about frugality. The two of them had enough money to buy a fleet of buses. No wonder they were so rich.

''Isaac had business in Portland, and I was headed for Salem, where my daughter lives.''

''But she got off the bus and married me instead,'' said Isaac.

Cord still hadn't arrived when the waiter came to take our dinner order. It was now half past eight, and he was over an hour late. Since it looked as if he wasn't coming, we went ahead and gave the waiter our order.

After the waiter collected our menus and left, I steered the conversation back to the bus ride. ''And it was on this same bus that you met Duncan Matthews?''

''That's right,'' said Pearl. ''He was just the nicest young man. He saw that Isaac needed help—with his oxygen bottle, I mean—and stepped right in to lend a hand.''

Isaac laughed again. ''He thought we were already

married. Kept talking about how lucky our kids were to have parents as nice as us.''

"I think that's when the idea to get married first hit us," said Pearl.

They went on to explain that when Matthews learned they weren't married, he suggested that Pearl get off the bus with Issac in Portland. He wanted to introduce them to the Reverend Paul St. Paul. He said that the reverend would be honored to marry them.

"Which, as it turned out," said Pearl, "was exactly the case. The Reverend St. Paul was just as nice as Duncan Matthews. We married as soon as Oregon law allows."

The couple seemed inordinately taken with the Reverend St. Paul. They were especially impressed with the fact that his church had made donations to charitable organizations similar to HavenSafe. "The church has even contributed to several Jewish causes," said Isaac. He shook his head. "Who would have thought such a thing."

The more they talked about the reverend and his church, the more nervous I became. Maybe I was overreacting, but Cord's warning, coupled with what Rose had said about the man, caused me to ask, "What exactly is your relationship with the Reverend Paul St. Paul?"

The pair looked puzzled by the question. "We told you," said Pearl. "He married us."

"But," I said, remembering how Cord had learned of their marriage, "what about the *Ketubah*? It was signed by a rabbi."

Isaac shrugged. "We were married twice. By the Reverend St. Paul and Rabbi Rosen. The rabbi is a good friend of mine from many years."

"And the Reverend St. Paul? He's a good friend now, too?"

They both nodded slowly. "Of course."

"And yet he was quite reluctant to even admit that he knew you, Pearl."

"That was because we asked him to keep our marriage a secret."

"And our whereabouts," said Isaac.

"Why?"

Pearl eyed me carefully. "I promised I'd explain and I will. But first you have to promise me something."

"What's that?"

"That you won't, under any circumstances, tell anyone where I am—or with whom."

"Oh, Pearl, that's a difficult thing to promise. I told you earlier today that your family is very worried about you. Kate, too. In fact, she's the reason I'm here."

I looked at Isaac. "Does anyone in your family know *your* whereabouts?"

He shook his head. "Not exactly. Rachel thinks I'm on a business trip."

"How long do you think you can keep something like this a secret?"

"As long as we have to," answered Pearl. "We're very careful. We only use cash."

"No paper trail," added Isaac.

It occurred to me that with their resources and moxie they could keep this disappearing act running indefinitely. "Okay," I said, "but I have to ask this again: Why?"

"Because they'll try to break us apart."

"Who will?"

"Adrienne," said Pearl.

"Rachel," said Isaac.

"I'd think your daughters would be happy for you."

"Ah, my dear," said Pearl, "that's where you're wrong."

"I'm confused."

"But cute," said Cord Roberts, sliding into the booth next to me. The comment took me by surprise, but no more so than his arrival—on crutches. His left foot was in some kind of walking cast. Besides the cast and a dark blue sports coat, he wore a bandage around his forehead. "Sorry I'm late," he said, nodding to Isaac and Pearl.

"What happened to you?" I asked.

"Ran into a little trouble on the way over here."

A little trouble? The guy looked as though he'd been beaten to a pulp. His face was a bruised and swollen mess, and his nose looked slightly off center, probably broken.

Pearl and Isaac clucked sympathetically, but he brushed off their concern for his injuries. "Nothing serious," he said, extending a hand to Isaac. "Cord Roberts. Rabbi Rosen's nephew."

"Isaac Feldman."

The two men exchanged small talk about the rabbi and his family for a few minutes. Despite his roughed-up appearance, Cord was charming and affable. I wasn't so sure how I felt, but he'd clearly won Isaac's approval. "Come see me in Seattle," he said to Cord, handing him a business card. "Your aunt Miriam, she'd like some crystal goblets. I have a new shipment coming in soon. I can get her an inside price."

"It's a deal," said Cord. "As it turns out, I'll be up your way next week." He nudged me. "Kellie has invited me to go sailing with her."

I let his little white lie pass with a remarkably straight face. But I couldn't let Isaac's comment pass. "So you do plan to return to Seattle. On business?"

Isaac glanced at Pearl, then down at the table. An uncomfortable silence followed. "He wants to go home, we both want to," explained Pearl. "But we can't."

I never thought I'd ever hear Pearl Danielson say she couldn't do something. "Can't" wasn't in her vocabulary. She delighted in doing what others said couldn't be done. Gently I asked, "Why can't you come home, Pearl?"

"Because it would be like giving in. Admitting that our daughters were right. Adrienne and Rachel have never met, but they're made from the same bolt of cloth."

"How's that?"

"They both think they know what's best for their parents. Rachel was estranged from Isaac for many years, but they recently patched things up, and now she's trying to run his life. She wants him to retire, says it's time for him to relax and take it easy—especially since he's been so sick. But what she doesn't understand is that his business is his greatest joy in life." She patted Isaac's hand. "Retiring just isn't an option," she said.

"Feh! It would kill me."

Pearl continued. "And for a long time now, Adrienne has wanted me to move to Salem so I can be near her. She thinks I'm getting too old, too frail to be on my own."

The notion was so absurd that I laughed out loud. "Pearl, you're the strongest woman I know."

She sighed so deeply that her shoulders slumped. "There's some truth to what Adrienne says. I'm getting awfully forgetful these days. Sometimes I find myself doing the strangest things. One day I went into town with my slippers on."

I was about to tell her that that didn't sound so terrible, that it's normal to occasionally forget things. Then I remembered what I overheard Dennis Lancaster and Phillip Coughlin saying about her. Something to do with keeping her car keys in the sugar bowl. And there was the matter of the unpaid moorage fee in Olympia. Perhaps she'd simply forgotten to pay it. Maybe Pearl was slipping more than I realized.

"So that's what you meant when you said Adrienne and Rachel would try to break up your marriage?"

"Yes," she admitted. "We don't think they'll understand how we feel about each other." She sighed heavily again. "They'll come up with all kinds of reasons why we shouldn't be together—age, religion, health, take your pick."

"But it's *your* life," I said. "Surely they'll respect that."

In the telling silence that followed, it occurred to me that good intentions and disrespect are separated by just a single slender thread. The insight was jarring. Out of concern for Pearl's well-being, I'd entered her home and boat without permission, invaded her privacy by tracking her whereabouts, pestered her with questions, and pried into her relationship with the Reverend St. Paul. I'd already tugged at the slender thread. And here I was, about to cut it altogether. Did I really have the right to suggest that they come home despite their fears?

Before I could say anything, Isaac started coughing. Loud racking coughs. Coughs far too forceful for such a delicate frame. His breathing between coughs was labored, shallow, and scary.

Pearl quickly hooked her husband to the portable oxygen tank and said their goodbyes. Before leaving, she gave me a hug. "I'm sorry you came all this way for nothing, Kellie. I hope you understand."

# SEVENTEEN

AFTER THEY'D GONE, Cord said, "Nice couple." He checked the label on the bottle of wine. "Nice year, too," he said, pouring himself a glass. The effort caused him to wince. He rubbed his shoulder.

I eyed him suspiciously. "This little trouble you say you ran into. What'd you do? Take a photo of something or someone you shouldn't have?"

"Nothing so dramatic. Just an encounter with a wild Oregon driver. A white van ran me off the road. Luckily I had my seat belt on, or it could've been much worse."

My throat tightened. "Did you say a white van?"

He nodded. "Probably a drunk driver. He didn't stick around for a breathalyzer test. Took off like a shot when I rolled. There were all kinds of witnesses, but no one got a license number."

"Let me guess. The plates were too dirty."

"Hey," said Cord, setting his wineglass on the table, "how did you—"

"I think I know the van."

"How's that?"

I explained about the attempted carjacking.

He put his hand on mine. "Are you sure you're okay? You didn't get hurt?"

"Not to worry." His concern felt nice.

"Did you get a good look at the driver?" he asked.

"Oh, yeah. For about two seconds—but it was long enough. The guy was big, bad, and ugly. And probably insane."

Cord's bruised and battered face was pinched in thought. "No, he was very sane," he said, withdrawing his hand from mine.

"Look, I may not run across carjackers every day— in fact, this was the very first time, and hopefully the only time—but I saw his eyes. When I say he was crazy, he was crazy. Crazy dangerous."

"Dangerous I'll give you," said Cord. "But he was sane."

"How do you figure?"

"Think about it. What do you think the odds are that we both had a run-in with the same guy in the same vehicle on the same day?"

I had thought about it and didn't like the conclusion I'd come to. I shrugged it off. "Random acts of violence. It happens—even in the City of Roses."

"Granted. But these acts weren't random."

"Are you saying you think we were specifically targeted?"

He nodded grimly.

I'd had the same notion but favored denial. "Maybe you've made some enemies in Portland, but I just hit town. I haven't had time yet to piss anyone off."

"But you've had plenty of time to mess up someone's plans."

I waited, but he said nothing more. "Okay, I'll bite. Whose plans?"

"The good Reverend Paul St. Paul's."

Somehow I was expecting this answer. "And just what might those plans be?"

Cord's response was delayed while our waiter cleared the table. When I asked for the check, he informed us that our tab had already been taken care of by the Feldmans.

"In that case," said Cord, "what do you have for dessert?" He ordered some rich, artery-clogging chocolate specialty and tried to tempt me into doing the same.

I've never met a chocolate calorie I didn't like, but I opted for some tea. After the waiter left, I said, "We were talking about the reverend's plans."

"I don't know all the details yet, but I figure it has something to do with befriending Pearl and Isaac. Keeping them cut off from their families and friends for as long as possible."

"So he can dip his fingers into their lucrative bank accounts?"

"Exactly."

"But they claim that keeping their whereabouts a secret is their idea. They said St. Paul is simply doing what they asked of him." I related what they'd told me about how they'd met the reverend and his role in their marriage. "I admit that Pearl and Isaac seem fond of the man—his church is active in some of the same charities—but according to Pearl, that's all there is to their relationship."

Cord rolled his eyes. "Yeah, right."

Our waiter returned with his dessert and a second spoon and cup of tea for me. I ignored the spoon and sipped my tea while Cord satisfied his cholesterol cravings.

"So," I said, "you think the Reverend Paul St. Paul—the leader of the fastest-growing church in the area—is just a con man who preys (pun intended) on rich people. Gets them to buy into his 'follow your passion' philosophy and then separates them from their family, their friends, and eventually their money."

Cord nodded. "And when you came looking for Pearl Danielson, he panicked and got one of his minions to scare you off. Since I was tagging along with you, he must've figured I needed taking care of, too."

He paused to wipe a dab of chocolate from his chin. "He used Pearl and Isaac's interest in charity to get them hooked. It was his entrée. Remember how he grilled you on your passion? His eyes sure lit up when you said you owned a Hinckley."

"Yes, but—"

"That's how he does it. He finds out what drives you, what interests you the most. Then he uses the information to get at your purse strings. But don't get me wrong. I don't think everyone who winds up with Brother Dunk 'em Matthews in the baptismal font is rich. These programs are cleverly designed to appeal to the disenfranchised in our society, the loners, the kids or adults with problems. They make for devoted, if not fanatical, followers."

Rose had said essentially the same thing about her brother. Even Duncan Matthews had described himself as a kid with problems when he met the reverend. "Okay, maybe what you say about him is true. But that doesn't prove he had anything to do with the goon in the white van."

"Maybe not," Cord admitted, spooning the last dollop of ice cream from his dish. "But I have a damn good idea how we might find out."

What was this *we* business? "How?"

"Meet me at my office tomorrow morning, and I'll show you."

"Hmm. An invitation. Not quite as appealing as the sailing invite I supposedly gave you, but, hey, it's a start."

"I was wondering when you'd get around to that," he said, grinning through swollen, ice-cream-smeared lips. "Ever read *Moby Dick*?"

"About a million years ago. Why?"

"It doesn't matter. If you're a sailor, you know what Melville meant when he said, 'Whenever I find myself growing grim about the mouth; whenever it is a damp drizzly November in my soul—' "

" '. . . I account it high time to get to sea as soon as I can.' "

"Especially with a pretty woman," Cord added with a wink. "To sea or to . . ."

"Don't say it. Don't even think it."

"What?" he asked, feigning innocence.

BACK AT THE motel, I stripped off my clothes and climbed into bed—alone.

Grampy believed that there are two types of people in this world. And if both types were standing at the edge of a lake, ready to go for a swim, the first type would get a running start and dive right into the water. The second type would go to the edge and gingerly dip a toe in to test the water before slowly wading in. All things considered, I'd say I was the diving type, but when it came to men (read: sex), I was definitely a toe dipper.

Although Cord didn't take my refusal personally—considering the shape he was in, I think he was actually relieved—it bugged the heck out of me. I wanted to swim, even put on the swimsuit, but in the end I just couldn't take the plunge. *Face up to it, Kellie,* I thought. *You're a chicken. Squawk. Squawk. Squawk.*

I tried calling Cassie and got the answering machine again. I wasn't thirsty, but I grabbed a bottle of beer anyway and drank it while idly punching through the TV channels with the remote. The eleven o'clock news was on every channel. Same old cheery stuff—murder and mayhem made palatable for family viewing by picture-perfect talking heads. I clicked off the TV and turned on the air conditioner, which sputtered briefly and then died.

I was too keyed up to sleep, so I mulled over the day's events—the eleven o'clock news as anchored by Kellie Montgomery. Basically I'd accomplished all that I'd set out to do in Portland: I'd located Pearl Danielson and I'd met with Cassie's twin sister's adoptive mother. So beam me up, Scotty. I could hop in the Miata tomorrow morning with a clear conscience. Wrong. The job was only half done. Probably not even that if you added up all the loose ends dangling in front of my sleepless eyeballs.

I didn't think I could tie everything together with a neat little bow, but I was certain about one thing—I wasn't leaving Portland tomorrow until I'd made sure Pearl and Isaac were safe. Cord's comments and the reverend's not-so-veiled reference to the risks associated with following your passion didn't do much to reassure me that their plan to remain in Portland was a wise course of action.

The next morning I awoke to the sound of the phone ringing. I'd been dreaming about Cassie, and in my groggy state I thought she was calling. But when I got the receiver up to my ear, I realized it was a man's voice on the other end.

"Kellie? Did I wake you?"

I glanced at the clock radio. It was six A.M.. "Who is this?"

"Allen Kingston."

I sat up in bed. Fully awake. Heart pounding. "What's wrong? Has something happened to Cassie?"

"Relax, Red. Your daughter is just fine."

I didn't believe him. It was bad. Bad and breathing down my neck. "Then why are you calling?" I asked. "And how did you get this number?"

"Jeez, Montgomery, what's your problem?" He must've thought that came off a little sharp, because his next words were coated in sugar. "I got your number from Cassie and I called because I missed you."

I forced myself to take a deep breath. The effort didn't work. My blood pressure was shooting up the scale and into the red zone. "Excuse me? I didn't quite catch that one. You said you *missed* me?"

"Yeah, a lot. I've been meaning to call, but you know how it is with this job . . ."

It was too much. I thought about all the times I'd made excuses for him. And for why he didn't call: His job. His new boss. His new partner. His new *female* partner. "Oh, I know how it is, all right. I know perfectly well."

He was quiet a moment. I could picture him scratching his head, puzzled by my tone. "Uh, is something wrong? Did I call at a bad time?"

"As a matter of fact, I was just going to wash my hair."

"Hell, that sounds like something that can't wait."

"Kingston, what can't wait is me."

"Meaning?"

"Meaning this phone call is about two weeks too late."

He tried to apologize, but I cut him off, ending the call and our relationship in one fell swoop. Afterwards I sat on the edge of the bed and asked myself what the hell was the matter with me. It wasn't one of those mysteries-of-the-universe type questions. There was a fairly simple answer—I was stupid. A loser. I'd just blown it with one of the best men to come into my life since Wendell.

I felt a serious crying jag coming on. Determined not to give in to it, I got myself moving. I rolled off the bed and did ten pushups as fast as I could. Then I stood on my head until the air conditioner suddenly clicked on, and my naked, flabby butt shivered so uncontrollably that I was forced to hop into the shower and get on with my life.

As soon as I'd showered, dressed, and had a quick breakfast at Denny's, I headed downtown. Yesterday's travels had me fairly squared away with the lay of the land. Twelve bridges spanning the Willamette River connect east to west. Suburbs to downtown. Since my motel was closest to the Broadway Bridge, I chose it—along with a horde of early-morning commuters—as my route into the downtown core. I should have taken the bus.

Portland struck me as an artsy city. I passed brick-inlaid promenades, glass-canopied pavilions garlanded with floral displays, ornate statues, and fountains. Lots of fountains. Near the Pioneer Courthouse was a series of pools with small bronzed beavers, bears, ducks, and sea lions. On the south side of the square was a life-sized statue of a businessman with an umbrella—apropos of the Pacific Northwest's rainy reputation.

But no one needed an umbrella today. Although it was still early morning and dew-drop fresh, the sun perched in the sky like an eagle ready to pounce on its prey. I'd geared up for another scorcher by wearing shorts, a sleeveless blouse, and sandals.

Like Seattle, parking was at a premium. It took a couple of circuits around the Park Blocks—a series of small parks in the middle of a broad, elm-tree-lined avenue—before I found a vacant meter. Unlike Seattle, though, the downtown landscape was essentially flat. It was an easy hike to the 1300 block of SW Broadway, home to Cord Roberts' employer, *The Oregonian*.

As usual, I was winging it. But it seemed important to find out if there was a connection between our pal in the white van and the Reverend Paul St. Paul. Cord's invitation had me curious. At the very least I'd find out if it was based on anything other than some kind of sugar high.

Once inside the building, I pushed my way into an elevator filled with a bunch of bleary-eyed office workers carrying briefcases and dour expressions. As is the custom in office elevators all over America—no one talked or made eye contact under penalty of downsizing. I got off on the twenty-fourth floor feeling grateful that I had no marketable skills to offer the corporate world. Working at a marina definitely has its advantages.

I hadn't told him I was coming, but when I found Cord's office—a cubbyhole next to the photo lab—there was a little yellow Post-it note with my name on it stuck to the door. It said he was in the dungeon and that I should meet him there. The dungeon turned out to be the archives room, which was located in the bowels of the building. Also known as the basement.

The archives room was cold and dimly lit and, except for Cord, deserted. He sat at one of those microfiche readers that you see in the library. His crutches were propped next to the chair, but his head bandage was gone. I stood in back of him for a moment. He was too engrossed in what he was reading to notice. Finally I tapped him on the shoulder.

He jumped a mile high. "Jesus! Have mercy on a crippled man."

"Sorry," I said. "Find anything interesting?"

"You might say that." He twisted a dial on the machine and several pages of old newspapers rapidly scrolled across the screen. He stopped at a page with a small photograph at the bottom. "But I'd say it was proof."

# EIGHTEEN

"PULL UP A chair and take a look at this," said Cord, pointing to the photo. He scooted his chair aside to make room for me.

I plunked my shoulder bag on the floor, dragged a chair over to the reader, and sat down. The microfiche was blurry, the photo dark and the images hard to make out. I squinted at it for a moment, then gave up and—vanity be damned—fished my glasses out of my bag.

"What am I looking at?" I asked. The photo was taken from a distance. I could tell there were people in it, but that was about all.

"Recognize anyone?"

I bent over the glass so that my face was practically touching it. "Nope."

He nudged me aside and pointed to the first of three figures standing in front of a building. "That's the Reverend Paul St. Paul."

I examined the photo again. I couldn't see the resemblance. "He looks thinner."

"It's an old print—taken about five years ago by a freelancer working out of Houston—but it's our man."

"Are you sure?"

"Look at the caption beneath the picture."

Sure enough, the three figures were identified as the Reverend Paul St. Paul and two associates from the Church of the Passionate Life—Duncan Matthews and Tyrone Bonetti. "Okay," I said. "But what's so disturbing about the scene?"

"Look at what's in the background, behind the men." There was excitement in his voice, as if he were a kid pointing out what Santa had left under the tree.

The men stood in front of a church—not three houses joined together—but a real church with a steeple and everything.

"See it?" asked Cord impatiently.

"The church?"

"No!" he shouted. "Look again. You can't miss it."

"Maybe if I had a magnifying glass. Why don't you just tell me what it is?"

He pointed to the left of the men. "It's the van!" He was practically bouncing off his chair now. "The same van our pal was driving yesterday."

"What?" I pushed his finger out of the way. There was a van in the photo all right, but most of it had been cropped out of the picture. "I see some tires and a hood," I said, "but I'd be hard-pressed to say it's the same van."

Cord shrugged. "Suit yourself." He scrolled through several more pages of the newspaper. "Maybe this will convince you."

It was a lengthy article about the Church of the Passionate Life. The title read Church Pastor Faces Critics— As Membership Rolls Soar. I skimmed through the first few paragraphs rapidly. The author's tone was sympathetic. Essentially he asserted that the Reverend Paul St. Paul was the epitome of evangelical success despite the carping of critics. According to church leaders quoted in the piece, the reverend's unidentified critics had deliberately timed their accusations in order to cause dissension just as the church embarked on a major expansion of its ministry.

I stopped and said, "Cord, this is old news. I learned most of this stuff on the Internet. And I don't see how it relates to the van."

"Keep reading," he said.

I turned back to the article. The author asserted that the phenomenal growth rate of the church was due, in no small part, to the various outreach programs that the Reverend St. Paul had established. One convert was quoted as saying, "This bad-mouthing of the reverend that's going on, it's the work of Satan. The devil always tries to take down a soul-winning church." The article ended with a denial by the Reverend St. Paul that he'd ever encouraged members to break contact with their families and friends or turn over all their worldly goods to the church.

I took off my glasses and rubbed my eyes. "Cord, this article says absolutely nothing about a van."

"Check out the sidebar."

Sighing, I donned my glasses again. The sidebar was a short piece reporting the details of an ongoing police investigation into allegations that a high-ranking official of the Church of the Passionate Life was involved in extortion, bribery, and attempted murder. An arrest was purportedly imminent. The last line read "See photo on page 4."

Grinning, Cord asked, "Ready for page four?"

"Do I have a choice?"

Unlike the previous photo, this one was large and exceptionally clear. Two men in suits—their backs to the camera—stood alongside the rear doors of a white van. They appeared to be talking to a third man who was unloading a box from the vehicle. I leaned in for a closer look. The caption underneath the photo read "Two Houston police detectives question Tyrone Bonetti, associate in the Church of the Passionate Life, regarding an alleged plot involving extortion, bribery, and attempted murder.''

A chill passed through me like a knife. ''Oh, my God.''

''Convinced now? It's our van.''

''Maybe.'' I pointed to the man identified as Tyrone Bonetti. ''But I've definitely seen *him* before.''

''Right. The van's driver, your so-called carjacker.''

''No, no. He was much bigger. This guy,'' I said, pointing to Bonetti again—''this guy is T-Bone.''

''Huh?''

''He accosted me at my sister's condo.''

''Do these things happen to you often?''

''I'm a magnet for pond scum. Present company excluded, of course.''

We left the dungeon and took the elevator back up to the twenty-fourth floor. Cord said he wanted to introduce me to someone. ''He's an investigative reporter.''

Pond scum alert. ''Great,'' I said.

We found Billy Joe Peterson typing furiously on his keyboard. ''*The Oregonian*'s Woodward and Bernstein'' was how Cord described him. ''He won the Beaumont Prize last year.''

Cord made him sound like a big deal, but Billy Joe was just a kid. A scrawny preppy type in brand-new jeans, sneakers, and a button-down plaid shirt. He smelled of aftershave but I figured that was just wishful thinking.

He gave Cord a quick nod and said, ''You got those photos for me?'' He spoke with a slight drawl.

''Finished processing an hour ago.''

''Terrific.'' He continued his attack on the keyboard.

''I was hoping you'd have a moment to talk,'' said Cord.

''Can't. Tight deadline.''

''It's important.''

Silence punctuated by clicking keys.

Cord leaned against Billy's desk. "BJ, I want you to meet Kellie Montgomery," he said quietly. He got no response from the busy ace reporter.

I figured this for a no-go and turned to leave.

Cord stopped me with a shake of his head and a light hand on my arm. Then he said to Billy, "She's met T-Bone."

Billy Joe's flying fingers suddenly froze. He whirled around in his chair and looked at me for the first time. Picking up his coffee cup, he said, "I need a refill. Let's go to the break room."

It wasn't a break room. The term was in-house lingo for an interview area that had been set up in a little storage room. It might've contained supplies at one time, but all that the place held now were a small table and some chairs. No coffeepot in sight.

As soon as Cord shut the door, Billy whipped out a miniature tape recorder from his shirt pocket and placed it on the table in front of me. "Tell me about T-Bone," he said without preamble.

The tiny room had no windows, and the air was stale and hot. But it was the kid's intense stare that made me sweaty. He seemed the type who'd pull out my fingernails if I didn't start talking soon. "Can't we open the door?" I asked.

"Just a crack," he said to Cord. "And make sure no one disturbs us," he added in an authoritative voice. Cord opened the door slightly and then remained standing on guard duty.

The dramatics made me feel as if I'd been caught spying in enemy territory. I went on the offensive. "Why are you so interested in T-Bone?" I asked.

He looked at me as though I'd asked him his annual salary. After a moment's hesitation he said, "He's the central figure in a story I'm working on, but I've been unable to interview him."

"I'm not surprised." I laughed. "He didn't strike me as the chatty type."

Billy checked the tape recorder and then asked, "How *did* he strike you?"

"Listen," I said, "I'm willing to tell you all that I know about the guy—which isn't much, actually—but this has to be a two-way street."

"What do you mean?"

"I came to Portland to find a friend. Cord and I located her, but she seems to have gotten herself mixed up with the Reverend St. Paul. Cord thinks he may be after her money. We both had a nasty tête-à-tête with a thug in a white van yesterday. Although we don't have any proof that he was working for the reverend, we found some photos of the church leaders, in the archives, with a similar-looking van in the background. They were taken five years ago in Houston, so it could be just a coincidence or another van altogether. But the point is I recognized one of the church leaders in the photos— Tyrone Bonetti, a.k.a. T-Bone. I'm concerned that if he's still associated with the reverend, my friend could be in danger."

Billy Joe said, "You could be right."

"I'd like to know whatever you can tell me about this story you're working on that involves T-Bone." As soon as I'd said that, a lightbulb went on over my head. I looked over at Cord and gave him a mental kick in the shins. I now knew the real reason why he'd been on Pearl's boat, why he'd been so eager to help me locate her, why he'd been snapping so many photos, et cetera, et cetera, et cetera.

"You're working with him, aren't you?" I said to Cord. "He's doing some kind of exposé on the Reverend St. Paul and his church, and you're doing the dirty work. You knew all about Pearl's involvement with the reverend when I first met you in Olympia. You weren't on any boat-buying expedition that day. You were on

Pearl's boat, trying to track down her whereabouts, just like me. The photos you took of *Picture Perfect* were for Billy Joe. And you've been supplying him with photos ever since—and using me to get them.''

Billy Joe turned off the tape recorder and glared at Cord.

"Hey, I haven't told her anything," said Cord with his hands raised.

"That's true," I said, making my disgust clear.

The kid eyed me carefully, as if trying to come to some sort of decision. Uncertainty balanced on a razor's edge. Finally he said, "What I say can't leave this room." If he seemed intense before, he was dead serious now.

Billy Joe Peterson's story was this: He was originally from Houston and had been working for his college newspaper when he first encountered the reverend and the Church of the Passionate Life. There'd been all kinds of rumors floating around about the man and his ministry, but no one had been able to prove any wrongdoing. So Billy Joe decided to go undercover, become one of the "Passionates," and report his findings. His youthful appearance worked to his advantage, and he was eagerly accepted into the fold.

It was his inside information that eventually led to the arrest of Tyrone Bonetti on extortion charges. He was convicted of using his position in the church to force church members to sell their homes, cars, jewelry, or whatever other assets they might have and turn it over to the church. The bribery and attempted murder charges could never be substantiated. The rumors about the reverend having been convicted of murder were just that—rumors.

The arrest of T-Bone, however, was a major setback for the church in Houston, and so the reverend moved his ministry to Portland. By then Billy had graduated from college. He followed the reverend to Portland, secured a job at *The Oregonian*, and continued his investigation of the church.

"I believe T-Bone is working for the Reverend St. Paul again," said Billy. "He got his extortion conviction overturned on a technicality and never served any prison time. I haven't been able to link him to the church's activities in Portland, but I'm working on it." He clicked on the tape recorder. "Now it's your turn," he said. "What do you know about T-Bone?"

What I knew took all of two minutes to say, but Billy Joe peppered me with a million questions, dragging out the interview for another half-hour. When it finally became obvious that he'd completely purged my brain cells, he clicked off the tape recorder and slipped it back into his shirt pocket. "Gotta run," he said, standing.

To his credit, Cord tried to soften the kid's abrupt leave-taking. "Thanks for your help, Kellie," he said.

I jumped up and followed Billy to the door. "Wait a minute," I said, digging into my bag. I pulled out the photo of Rose's brother. "Have you ever seen this person at the church?"

Billy reluctantly examined the photo. "Brother James Randall," he said, his face splitting into a smile for the first time. "How do you know Jimmy?" he asked.

"He's the brother of a friend. She hasn't had any contact with him for a long time."

"That's church policy," said Billy. "She shouldn't take it personally."

"It's hard on his family. They miss him a lot."

Billy took that in and then said, "Look, I shouldn't say this, but tell your friend that Jimmy's okay. He's working with me."

I tried to get more out of him, but he clammed up. Something about protecting his sources. He did agree, though, to let Jimmy know that his sister had asked about him.

"And tell him she loves him," I said.

# NINETEEN

THE BROCHURE CORD handed me was a glossy three-page foldout. The front page featured an artist's rendering of *Stars & Stripes*, the Dennis Conner-skippered boat that had won the America's Cup.

"What's this?" I asked.

"A peace offering," he said, grinning. "You mentioned yesterday that you were thinking about starting a sailing club." He pointed to the brochure. "This tells all about the Wind Dancers, a club I belong to here in Portland. It's mostly for racers, but it might give you some ideas."

We were standing on the sidewalk in front of his office building. The noise was deafening. A slow-moving street sweeper and a stalled car in the intersection had tempers flaring and horns honking. A siren sounded two blocks away. I hadn't said more than a couple of words since we'd left the break room, and the street activity around us didn't make an extended conversation likely. Fine by me, I thought. I'd been used by Cord long enough.

It was my own fault. I'd suspected all along that the reason he gave me for being aboard Pearl's boat was hogwash. But I'd let myself fall for his loopy grin and big blue eyes. He might've been eager to find Pearl, but it certainly wasn't for any human-interest story. If he'd been up front with me in the beginning, maybe things would've turned out differently. Maybe I'd have realized right away that Pearl and Isaac's relationship with the Reverend St. Paul was potentially dangerous. Maybe I'd have been more insistent that Pearl and Isaac return to Seattle. Maybe I'd be helping them pack right now instead of standing in the middle of the sidewalk shaking with anger.

I stuffed the brochure in my shoulder bag without comment.

"I know you're pissed at me and I don't blame you," he said. "But for what it's worth, I do care about you. And I'm sorry if my actions have offended or hurt you. That wasn't my intention."

His apology stirred fresh anger. "I understand completely, Cord. You were just doing your job. Whatever it takes to get a good photo—crawling over walls, hiding in bushes, chasing after personalities with long-lens cameras, and, of course, lying."

He looked as if I'd punched him in the gut. When he spoke, his voice was tinged with sadness. "You've every right to your opinion, Kellie, but I consider myself a professional. Most people don't make the distinction between the paparazzi and legitimate photojournalists."

A better woman would've kept her mouth shut, but she wasn't there. "Really? There's a distinction? I must've missed it."

Cord sagged a little but kept on talking. "We all dream of capturing that heart-stopping, history-making photo that will propel us to fame and fortune. But legitimate photojournalists are honest, hard-working professionals who are offended by the photo-at-any-cost tactics of the paparazzi. They may get the big bucks chasing down movie stars and royalty, but the majority of us make only a modest living with our cameras and reporter's notebooks. You've seen my car. The dump I call home isn't much better."

"So why do you do it?"

A tow truck rumbled to a stop in front of the stalled car in the clogged intersection. Honks and cheers greeted the driver as he hoisted himself out of the cab. Cord watched the street scene unfold a moment. When his gaze returned to my face, he asked, "Why do you sail?"

"That's not easy to put into words."

Cord nodded in agreement. "Our friend the reverend may be a dangerous, thieving phony, but he's got one thing right: Pursuing your passion, your dream—that fire in the belly that just won't die—is what makes life bearable. Do anything less and you're just taking up space."

"Very eloquent, Cord. Do whatever you have to do to make life bearable for yourself. But as for me—"

"Cord!" The piercing yell startled us both. We whirled around to see Billy Joe Peterson barreling out the front door of *The Oregonian* building. He was lugging Cord's camera case in one hand and a small notebook in the other. He plunked the case onto the sidewalk and frantically waved his notebook at Cord. "Get over here. Quick!!"

Getting anywhere quickly on crutches is a trick, but Cord hobbled across the sidewalk at a surprisingly rapid clip. I was inclined to hit the road, but curiosity reared its old familiar head and I found myself following him.

"What's up, BJ?" he asked.

"Just got a call from Jimmy Randall. The reverend's dead."

Cord and I stared at him. After a beat, Cord said, "No shit! What happened?"

"Looks like murder, but we don't have time to stand around jawing about it. I'll tell you what I know on the way to the church. Let's go. My car's just down the street."

They took off, Billy Joe running and Cord crutch-footing it as fast as he could. I made it a threesome.

"Where are you going?" Cord asked me.

"With you."

"BJ's not going to like that."

"Tough. You both owe me one."

The ace reporter ran a couple of stoplights, but we made it to the church without an accident or a ticket. According to BJ, Jimmy Randall had found the reverend's body. It sounded like a scene from an Agatha Christie novel—the reverend St. Paul was sprawled out on the couch in the library. He'd suffered a terrific beating before he died.

"Jimmy says the reverend's head is split open like a watermelon," said BJ.

"Great photo op," joked Cord.

"Did Jimmy call the police?" I asked.

The reporter was incredulous. "Are you fuckin' crazy? I told Jimmy not to do a thing until we got there. Except to keep everyone out of the library, of course. We need time to work the room before all hell breaks loose."

"Smart move," said Cord. "Who else knows about this?"

"Just Jimmy and us—so far."

"And the killer," I muttered to myself. The men's comments were making me nervous, especially the part about working the room.

Once inside the church, we found Jimmy Randall blocking the entry to the library like a defensive lineman. He shared the same blond hair and fair complexion as his sister Rose, but while she was tall and lithesome, he was of medium height and build with a layer of baby fat rounding out his youthful face.

He opened the doors to the library and quickly ushered us inside. Although he hadn't asked, I responded to the nervous glance he gave me. "I'm with the photographer," I said. I don't know what he thought about all of us trooping into the room, but *I* definitely had trouble with it. Not enough to keep me out, though.

Billy Joe told Jimmy to go back outside and guard the door again. Judging from the look on his face, he was relieved to have the job. Like most people, Jimmy Randall probably hadn't had much experience with violent death. I've encountered my fair share—mostly during the two years I spent volunteering with a local paramedic unit—but on the blood and gore scale, this was one of the grisliest I'd ever seen. I ignored my queasy gut and forced myself to look around.

As near as I could tell, the Reverend St. Paul had been bludgeoned to death. The weapon of choice was anybody's guess, as it wasn't near the body or immediately obvious anywhere else in the room. Based on the carnage it left behind, though, it was one hell of a killing implement. Short of being taken out by an Uzi, the reverend couldn't have been more brutalized. Whatever the man might've done, no one deserved to die that way.

As Jimmy had reported, his head had suffered the most damage. The Reverend St. Paul lay facedown on the couch, his bruised and battered face turned slightly, exposing an eyeball that had been torn from its socket. It dangled like a gruesome Christmas ornament against his cheek. The top of his head, once as white as snow, was matted with blood and split nearly in half. His brain—at least I think it was his brain—resembled gray mush.

The couch and carpet were drenched in blood with bits of brain matter and bone fragments scattered about. None of the other furnishings in the room had been disturbed—except for the wall behind the couch. The killer had taken the time to scribble a message in the reverend's blood: *Isaiah 16:3.*

If the macabre sight bothered Cord or Billy Joe, it wasn't readily apparent. Neither made any comment as they proceeded to "work the room." Despite our unauthorized intrusion at the crime scene, both men diligently avoided disturbing crucial evidence. Cord took his photos from a discreet distance, being careful not to touch anything. Billy Joe, meanwhile, donned what evidently passes for investigative reporter's gear these days—surgical gloves—and rummaged through the reverend's desk. After removing an assortment of papers, an appointment calendar, and God only knows what else that happened to catch his fancy, he ran it all through the office copier. Once he was done, he pocketed the copies and replaced the originals where he'd found them.

Real considerate of him, but Allen Kingston would've had a hissy fit to end all hissy fits. I'd just made a comment to that effect, when BJ noticed the bloodied wall for the first time. "Shit on toast," he said. "Cord! Get a shot of that!"

Cord aimed his camera and fired away while Billy Joe studied the message.

"Isaiah, Isaiah," he muttered, scratching his head. After a moment, he turned from the wall and took in the rest of the room. "Where's a Bible?" he asked. "I need a Bible." His tone was frantic.

"Here's a radical thought," I said. "You might try the bookshelves."

He paused long enough to give me a sour look and then quickly scanned each shelf. "I can't believe it," he said. "A whole library full of books—in a church, no less—and not one goddamn Bible."

Jimmy poked his head in the door and whispered, "You guys about done in there? The reverend had a prayer session scheduled at eleven o'clock. It's gonna look odd if I won't let anyone in."

Cord said, "I've shot a full roll."

Billy Joe gave the room another quick once-over. "Okay," he said. "We're outta here." As we exited the room, he said to Jimmy, "We need to talk."

"Not here."

"You're right," agreed BJ. "We don't want to be anywhere near this place when the police arrive. Meet us at the burger joint down the street in ten minutes. And bring a goddamn Bible."

THE LAST THING I wanted to do was eat, but the murder scene had seemed to whet Cord's and Billy's appetites. While we waited for Jimmy, they stuffed themselves with burgers and fries oozing with grease. I sucked on a mint to settle my uneasy stomach and listened to them theorize about the reverend's demise.

"Who do you think did it?" Cord asked Billy Joe. "You know his followers better than anybody. It's gotta be one of those nuts, right?"

"Not necessarily. The reverend's no-family-contact policy didn't go over so well with a lot of parents. There's been more than one deprogramming attempt. Maybe Mom and Pop got fed up with being kept away from Johnny or Susie and took matters into their own hands."

"But I thought most of the Passionates were loners, already cut off from their families," I said.

"True," admitted Billy Joe, "but not every loner is poor. Some of the people he attracted to the fold brought big bucks with them. Maybe a family member didn't like being ripped off in the name of religion."

"Or one of the faithful had second thoughts about the reverend and his program," suggested Cord. "Look at Jimmy. He certainly has had a change of heart."

"That scriptural reference on the wall is what gets me," said Billy Joe, "I think it will tell us a lot." He pulled out the copies of the papers he'd confiscated from the reverend's desk. "Plus, some of this stuff is damn interesting."

"What is it?" I asked.

He gave me one of his intense stares. "I'm not so sure you should be involved in this."

I matched his stare. "I'm involved," I said. "Now, what did you find?"

He cleared away the debris from their fast-food feast and unfolded one of the papers on top of the table. "It's some sort of list—names, dates, and a brief notation beside each entry." He ran a finger down the page. "Recognize any of these names?" he asked.

Cord and I peered over his shoulder.

"You mean besides my own?" I asked. The entry was dated May 5, and after my name were the words "Sailing; owns Hinckley."

Cord said, "I told you the reverend pounced on that. He probably thought you're as rich as your friends, Pearl and Isaac."

"Their names are listed here, too," said BJ. "And a notation that says, 'Elderly newlyweds; HavenSafe.' " He looked at me and asked, "What's HavenSafe?"

"Pearl and Isaac's favorite charity."

"Their hot button, their passion," said Cord. "I wager that's what this entire list is all about—a menu of potential converts and/or donors to his personal treasury."

"With their probable conversion route duly noted," added Billy Joe.

"There's an asterisk next to some of the names," I said. "What do you think it means?"

Billy Joe said, "My guess is that it has something to do with the reverend's assessment of how likely they were to join the Passionates' fold or cough up some dough—possibly an indication of how wealthy they are. Hinckley or not, I notice there's no asterisk next to your name."

"I wear my poverty proudly. Like a badge," I said.

Cord laughed, but Billy's attention was drawn to the restaurant's front door. Jimmy Randall had arrived— with a Bible in each hand.

# TWENTY

"KING JAMES VERSION," said Jimmy, handing one of the Bibles to Billy Joe. "That's the version we use, but I thought you might want to do a cross-check with another version." He plunked the second Bible on the table. "So I brought the New American Standard just in case."

Billy Joe smiled and said, "See why I like this guy?"

He and Jimmy flipped open their Bibles and rapidly thumbed through the pages. As soon as he'd found the scripture, BJ read it aloud. "Isaiah, Chapter 16, Verse 3: *Take counsel, execute judgment; make thy shadow as the night in the midst of the noonday; hide the outcasts; betray not him that wandereth.*" He looked up at Jimmy. "What's your version say?"

"Same thing, different wording." He quoted from the Bible: '*Give us advice, make a decision; Cast your shadow like night at high noon; Hide the outcasts, do not betray the fugitive.*'"

Cord shrugged. "I don't get it."

"The verse is referring to the Moabites and Israelites," said Jimmy.

Something stirred in the dusty cobwebs of my brain.

"I'm not a biblical scholar," I said, "but I spent a lot of time in church when I was a kid. I think I remember something about this. Weren't Moab and Israel neighbors?"

"And long-time adversaries," said Jimmy.

"Yeah," I said, "that's it. The Moabites gave the Israelites a hard time during their forty-year trek through the desert—basically, they wouldn't give them refuge."

Jimmy nodded, "Correct. The Moabites wouldn't give the Israelites refuge, but now the Lord, in this Scripture, is asking the Israelites to forget all that and give them the help they need."

"Do unto others as they should've done unto you," said Billy Joe.

"So what does all that have to do with the killing of the Reverend St. Paul?" Cord asked.

No one said anything for a minute, each of us wrestling with the question in our own way: Billy Joe drank the last of his soda, Jimmy re-read the passage to himself, Cord fiddled with his straw as if it were a piccolo, and I sucked on another mint.

Finally I said, "I can think of several possibilities." I ticked them off on my fingers. "One, it's a warning of some sort. Two, it's an explanation. Or three, it's a diversionary tactic."

Cord snapped his fingers. "A warning! That's what I was thinking. The killer was saying, 'Betray me, and this will happen to you, too.' "

"You think the Reverend St. Paul betrayed someone?" I asked. "Who?"

"The verse talks about hiding the fugitive," said Cord. "The Church of the Passionate Life attracted all kinds of outcasts—maybe one of them felt that the reverend hadn't come through for him, hadn't made good on his promises."

"That makes sense," said Jimmy. "The reverend offered sanctuary to all kinds of people. If we had access to the membership rolls, I bet we'd find that quite a few of the Passionates have criminal records."

"Like Duncan Matthews," I said. "And T-Bone."

"Bonetti's not with us anymore," said Jimmy.

Cord cast a wary glance at me. "I wouldn't count on that," he said.

"Kellie, you mentioned something about the verse being an explanation," said Billy Joe. "What did you mean?"

"The killer is an arrogant SOB. He's using the Bible verse to tell us exactly why he killed the reverend. We know that the Moabites hated the Israelites and didn't give them the time of day when they needed help." I paused to collect my thoughts. "Perhaps the killer identified with the plight of the Israelites. Perhaps he wasn't an outcast or a fugitive, but he needed help and the Reverend refused to give it to him. Or her."

"And the diversionary tactic?" asked Cord.

"The killer used the verse to throw suspicion off himself and onto someone else—like whoever in the church fits the betrayed fugitive or aggrieved Israelite role."

Billy looked at Jimmy. "I've asked you this before, but it's really important now. Can you get me a copy of the membership rolls?"

"Brother Matthews is in charge of those records," said Jimmy, "and you know how secretive he is. He's got everything on his personal computer, safeguarded with an encryption system that he claims even the CIA can't break."

Jimmy paused and smiled broadly. "But nothing's impossible for an unrepentant computer hack." He pulled a folded computer printout from his pocket and handed it to BJ. "It's taken me a while, but I finally broke into his system."

Billy Joe laid a hand on Jimmy's shoulder. "Brother Randall, you're a high-tech saint."

After the meeting with Jimmy broke up, we drove by

the church to see what was happening. As Billy Joe had predicted, all hell had broken loose. Besides the police and emergency vehicles lining the street, the once peaceful neighborhood had been invaded by a throng of reporters and photographers from various news agencies, including a crew from a local TV station. The street in front of the church had been cordoned off, seriously reducing available viewing space. The media and the merely curious jockeyed for position behind the barricades like frantic shoppers at a going-out-of-business sale. Billy Joe said he had no desire to join the fray. "I've got my story angle," he said. "I just need to get it filed."

Cord figured that most of the photos he'd taken wouldn't pass muster with their editor—too gruesome for a family newspaper—but Billy Joe wanted them processed ASAP. "The Bible quote might make it," he said.

I left them at *The Oregonian* and hiked back to my car. Cord had promised to keep me informed of any developments in the case. I didn't know what to make of our relationship or the reverend's murder, but I figured it was high time to get myself out of Dodge—by way of the Dover Hotel.

ONCE THEY LEARNED of the Reverend St. Paul's murder, it wasn't difficult to convince Pearl and Isaac to come home. They'd both wanted to return to Seattle anyway, and his death seemed to be the jolt they needed to make it happen. But they were understandably upset, and I stuck around long enough to calm them down and help make the arrangements for their trip. They decided to travel by plane this time, and I reserved seats for them on the first flight out the next day. I also called the marina in Olympia and used Pearl's credit card to pay *Picture Perfect*'s moorage fee. I told the harbormaster that someone would sail the boat back to Seattle in a few days.

As I was leaving, Pearl asked, "Will you help us with one more thing, Kellie?"

"Of course. What is it?"

"Isaac and I have been thinking about something you said at dinner last night. We want and very much need to live our own lives. But we're still concerned about how our families will take the news of our marriage."

"So," said Isaac, "we want that you should be our emissary."

"Emissary?"

"You know, sort of a go-between," Pearl explained.

They wanted me to talk to their families. They would let their daughters know about their marriage, but they also wanted me to contact each of them and explain how they felt about each other, how they wanted to live their own lives without interference. I was a little uneasy about my role in this plan. I was willing to help, but it seemed a lot like poking my nose in their business again. This time around, though, they'd asked for my help, which I figured had to count for something. What I didn't figure on was how high a price we'd all have to pay for that help.

THERE ARE DAYS in Seattle that are so spectacular, so unbelievably glorious, that you feel like falling down on your knees and thanking whatever god you worship for the blessed privilege of living amidst such beauty. I came home on just such a day.

The marina was experiencing what we call the *carpe diem* syndrome—a burst of boating activity that inevitably occurs after a run of bad weather. The upside is that the marina's peripheral businesses—the sailing school, yacht brokerage, sports apparel shop—get a needed financial boost. The downside is that the parking

lot is always full. Since my usual spot was taken, I
wound up double-parking behind Bert's Jeep Cherokee
and hiking halfway across the marina to the sailing
school.

Cassie was on the phone when I came through the
front door. She treated me to one of her dimpled smiles
and then pointed to the phone and rolled her eyes. I got
the picture—she was stuck dealing with a long-winded
customer.

I helped myself to a soda from the machine in the
outer room and gulped it down as if quenching my thirst
was the primo thing on my mind. After a couple of
swigs, I gave up the charade and sat down in the office
area where I could eavesdrop, something I wanted to do
in the first place.

It sounded as if the caller was drilling Cassie on what
Sound Sailing had to offer. Considering that she's always claimed to have zilch interest in all things nautical,
she was doing a bang-up job describing our sailing program. She ran through the basics: curriculum, instructor
qualifications, boat types, class size, schedules, school
safety record, equipment needed, and post-course sailing
opportunities.

After she hung up, I gave her a big hug and asked,
"Are you sure you don't want a full-time job? You handled those questions like a pro."

"Ha! You left a pretty good cheat sheet to follow,"
she said. "I know you probably want a rundown on how
it went while you were gone, but I'm in sort of a bind."

"What's up?"

"Things are really hopping at the Topside, and my
boss called earlier to see if I could work a split shift.
I've got to leave in about five minutes."

"That's okay. I think I can handle things here on my
own," I said with a grin.

She eyed me expectantly. "Well? I can't stand the

suspense a minute longer. How'd it go with the Hamptons?''

I described my visit with some judicious editing. I was reluctant to tell Cassie that I'd met her twin. It seemed to me that if they ever did meet, she shouldn't be influenced by my own impressions of the girl. Instead, I told her about Deena's home, her mother, and the loss of her father.

"Did her mother think Deena would want to meet me?" asked Cassie eagerly.

"It's probably too early to say."

"Why?"

There was no easy way to break the news. "Cassie, your twin sister doesn't know that she was adopted. Her mother isn't sure yet whether she'll even tell her."

The look on Cassie's face told me that was the last thing she was expecting to hear. "But," she stammered, "how come she doesn't know? Why didn't her parents tell her?"

I gave her the explanation Flora gave me, but it didn't do much to satisfy her. She left for work confused and upset. And, I thought, a little resentful of my role in the affair. I wished I could've handled the situation better, but I was treading on unfamiliar ground myself. Fortunately the phone rang as soon as Cassie left, and I didn't have time to dwell on it. Another potential student was on the line. So it went the rest of the day. Thanks to the change in the weather, Sound Sailing was up and running again.

As soon as I had a spare moment, I called Kate. She wanted to hear all about my trip, but I just hit the highlights—that I'd found Pearl, and she was coming home. I avoided mentioning her marriage or I'd have been on the phone forever. Same with the Reverend St. Paul's murder, but she'd already heard about it on the TV news. "Isn't he that preacher you were going to talk to in Portland?"

"The very one."

"Oh, my God. What do you know about his murder?"

"It's very busy here, Kate."

"Okay, okay. I'll let you go. But promise me you'll come by my place as soon as you get off work. I have some news for you, too," she said.

# TWENTY-ONE

KATE WAS WAITING for me in the lobby when I arrived, looking healthy and upbeat for a change. When she told me that she had some news, I'd automatically assumed the worst. But I took her jaunty mood at face value—that she was feeling good and not putting on a false front for my benefit. She was dressed casually in pale green trouser-style walking shorts and matching short-sleeved linen shirt.

"I hope you haven't eaten yet," she said.

"Are you kidding? The phone's been ringing off the hook all day. I barely had time to feed Pan-Pan before heading over here. I'm starving."

"I feel like pizza and beer. Luigi's okay with you?"

"Perfect," I said, grinning. She knew Luigi's was one of my favorite spots—a small café near the marina that Wendell and I used to call "our place." The owners, Luigi and Lisa, were good friends.

"And," Kate said, "is it okay if Tony meets us there? It's sort of a celebration tonight."

Better than okay, I thought. Tony was just the man I wanted to see.

"So what's your good news?" I asked as we belted ourselves into her Mercedes.

She hesitated, but I could tell she was eager to spill the beans. A picture of Tony and Kate walking down the aisle suddenly flashed before my eyes. It was not a pretty sight. "You're not getting married again, are you?"

"Good God, no!"

"Well, what is it?"

Keeping one eye on the road, she turned slightly toward me and said, "My doctor called today with my test results. I didn't want to tell you this before, Kellie, because I knew you'd just worry, but they thought I had emphysema or possibly lung cancer."

"Oh, Kate."

"It's okay. I'm not dying or anything. My lungs probably look worse than any of those pictures they tried to scare us with in high school health class. But I knew I wasn't as bad off as the doctors seemed to think. And the tests proved it! I absolutely have to quit smoking, though. I have asthma."

Asthma's no picnic, I thought, but she seemed so happy that I congratulated her on the good news and added, "I know you can quit, Kate. Everything's going to be just fine."

Tony was at the café when we arrived. He greeted Kate with a "Hi ya, doll," and gave me a brief nod.

As soon as we'd ordered our pizza and a pitcher of beer (and Pepsi for Tony), I told them about my trip—meeting Cord, the Reverend St. Paul, and finally Pearl's new husband, Isaac Feldman. Kate was worse than BJ, pumping me for every little detail. I'd skipped over much of what I knew about the reverend's death—especially my visit to the murder scene, but I covered everything else. Except the biggie.

"So, Tony," I said eventually, "what can you tell me about your friend T-Bone?"

He shifted in his chair and shot a nervous glance at Kate. "He's not my friend," he said.

"Maybe that was a poor choice of words," I admitted. "But I am curious—why was he looking for you that day I ran into him at Kate's condo?"

Tony hemmed and hawed a bit, and then said, "I don't remember."

"What's this all about, Kellie?" asked my sister.

"When I was in Portland I was the victim of an attempted carjacking," I said. "Cord Roberts—the photographer I told you about—also had a run-in with the same van that my carjacker drove. When we were going over some old newspaper photos, trying to establish a link between the van and the Reverend St. Paul, I saw a photo of this T-Bone character. Only he was identified in the newspaper as Tyrone Bonetti, one of the leaders of the Church of the Passionate Life."

Tony shrugged and said, "So?"

"So T-Bone was booted out of the church after he was convicted of extortion. Now that the reverend's been murdered, I couldn't help wondering what T-Bone was doing in Seattle and if he still has ties to the Reverend St. Paul."

"I don't know a thing about this reverend guy."

Kate gave Tony a hard look. "Tell her about T-Bone, Tony."

"Hey, it's no big deal, okay? I had a little cash-flow problem and I took care of it."

Kate wasn't going to let him off the hook. "The gambling, Tony. Tell her about the gambling."

He looked like a little boy who'd been caught with his hand in the cookie jar. "Yeah, okay. I got in over my head, and T-Bone came to collect. But everything is just fine now."

"I bailed him out," explained Kate.

"Has he been back to see you recently?" I asked Tony.

"No way!" He raised a hand in the air as if swearing on a Bible. "I don't drink no more and I don't gamble no more."

"I'm glad to hear it, but is there anything else you can tell me about him? It may be important."

"Why? You an investigator or something?"

Kate had had enough. "Listen, Tony, when my sister says something is important, it's important. Now tell her everything."

"All I know is that he's a mean mother. He'd just as soon kill you as swat a fly. What I can't figure out is why he'd try to get me fired. I paid my debt."

"Fired! How?" asked Kate.

"I seen him with Dennis Lancaster in the lobby. Real friendly like. That dude don't chat with anyone unless she's wearing a tight skirt, if you know what I mean. So I figured T-Bone had gotten Lancaster's attention by feeding him an earful about my gambling."

"T-Bone was probably just looking for you," I said. "He cornered me in the lobby, too."

"Maybe, but why would he be coming around after I'd paid him off? It don't make sense."

THE NEXT DAY, Pearl and Isaac flew into Sea-Tac Airport and took a shuttle to Pearl's condo in Seattle. As planned, each of them contacted their daughters to let them know that they were back home, they were safe—and they were married.

My role as their "emissary" began almost immediately after their return. Before I had a chance to contact Isaac's daughter as he and Pearl had requested, Rachel Feldman called me. She asked if I could come see her at her office in Kirkland as soon as possible. Now that the weather was cooperating, Sound Sailing had a full slate of classes. My schedule was tight, but I managed to squeeze out a couple of hours between classes.

Rachel worked for SoftGen, a computer firm that, like Microsoft and a host of other high-tech companies, had established its corporate headquarters on the east side of Lake Washington. SoftGen had its own office park, a somber cluster of copycat gray-and-white-trimmed buildings platted within a woodsy thicket. Rachel's building was at the rear of the complex alongside a rock-strewn brook that looked cool and inviting. She was waiting for me when I arrived at the lobby of the two-story building.

"I'm Rachel Feldman," she said, extending a slender, ring-bedecked hand. She was about my height and age, but that was where the similarities between us began and ended. For Rachel Feldman was a strikingly beautiful woman with intelligent, obsidian eyes and a self-confident presence that spoke of private schools and old money.

"Let's go for a walk," she suggested. It was breezy outside, and her long black hair whipped about her face as she talked. "I usually eat my lunch here on days like this," she said as we passed a picnic table. We turned onto a shady path. "There are five miles of trails on the grounds."

"Do you jog?" I asked. She had an athletic build and was dressed in jeans, T-shirt, and running shoes—standard garb in the high-tech world.

"Sometimes, but not on a regular basis. I should do it more often—it'd help with the stress."

I didn't know whether she was referring to her job or personal life, but based on Wendell's experience at DataTech, I knew how stressful working in the computer field could be. I said, "Putting in some long hours?"

She nodded and kicked a rock out of our path. "It comes with the territory in this business, but damn hard when you have a kid," she said.

Isaac hadn't mentioned a grandchild. "How old?" I asked.

"Fifteen." She turned slightly as she walked and looked at me. "And, in case you're wondering," she said with some bitterness, "I'm not married."

I hadn't been wondering, but I let it go, and we walked on in silence for a few moments until we came to a wide spot in the path. She pointed to a wooden bench under a shady old oak. "We can sit here," she said, "and discuss the point of this visit. Father told me he'd gotten married, but he was rather short on details. Which is typical of him, by the way."

"I only just met your father a few days ago, so I don't know what's typical."

"Oh? I'd assumed that you were a business acquaintance of his. You're not in the import business?"

"No," I said, reaching into my handbag. I gave her one of my cards. "I teach sailing at Larstad's Marina."

"But—"

"Let me explain," I said.

When I was finished, she laughed out loud. "Father's married to a Gentile? This is unbelievable. Absolutely unbelievable!"

I wasn't sure how to take her reaction. "Your father was worried that you might object."

"Object? I'm delighted! In fact, I'm going to throw them a reception."

I warned her that Pearl's family might not share her enthusiasm for celebrating the nuptials, but she said she was going to have the party anyway. "Bring your significant other," she said. "It'll be fun."


WHEN I GOT back to the marina, I stopped by the repair dock to see if Tom Dolan had had a chance to look at *Sweet Reward*, one of several J22's in the school's fleet. The engine had been overheating, and I'd asked him to check out the cooling system for leaks or other problems. Tom was Sound Sailing School's lead and only mechanic, a job he took on soon after he retired from the Navy. At fifty-five, he was tall, wiry and quite athletic despite suffering from an arthritic hip. When it acted up, he could be as ornery as hell, but he never let it stop him.

"Hey, Kellie! Tom! Got a minute?" the Weasel called to us, trotting down the dock like a prissy poodle.

"Damn, he's back," muttered Tom.

Ever since Todd Wilmington had taken up with Danielle Korb, we hadn't seen much of him around the marina. No one believed that she'd keep him out of our lives permanently—the woman was bound to come to her senses and dump the guy—but the reprieve had been as good as an all-expense-paid vacation.

"You talk to him," Tom said. "I'm busy." He turned his attention to the strainer that keeps seaweed and other flotsam out of the cooling system and left me to deal with whatever Wilmington had on his mind. Tom's policy was to avoid the Weasel whenever he could. His belief was that if you gave the man a penny for his thoughts, you'd get change back.

"What can I do for you, Todd?" I said.

He waved a piece of paper in my face. "I understand from this that you haven't paid your moorage fee this month," he said.

"Wrong. The school's fleet is paid up in full." Even though the marina owned Sound Sailing, the slips for the boats were subject to various city and county taxes. I was responsible for paying the taxes from income generated by the school.

"I'm talking about the live-aboard surcharge," he said, "not the school's fees. You and Tom are both delinquent."

Tom dropped a tool and cursed.

The surcharge the Weasel referred to was a thirty-percent increase in moorage fees for live-aboards. Dennis Lancaster and his cronies had been trying to convince Old Man Larstad to approve the surcharge. Their argument was that the increase was needed to subsidize the costs associated with meeting environmental-impact requirements. If approved, Maritime Enviro Services stood to reap the benefits with an ongoing contract with the marina. But for many live-aboards, including Tom and myself, the increase would likely force us out of the marina.

"How can we be delinquent?" I asked. "The surcharge hasn't even been approved yet—if ever. Besides, what business is it of yours what we've paid and when? Last time I checked, Rose Randall was the marina's accountant, not you."

The Weasel puffed up his bony, pimple-sized chest. "You obviously haven't heard the news. I'm a leading finalist for the general manager position," he said proudly. "As such, it's imperative that I be kept abreast of all matters pertaining to the marina."

Tom popped his head up and spat a wad of chewing tobacco into an empty coffee can. "These matters you're keeping abreast of—" he said to Wilmington, "they include surveys?"

The Weasel eyed Tom suspiciously. "What surveys?"

"Guess you haven't heard the news, then."

I could tell Tom was gearing up for a drop kick, and the Weasel bent right over to receive it. "What news?" he asked.

Tom pulled a rag from his overalls and slowly wiped a grease smudge off his forehead. "Some bigwig on the selection committee decided that it would be a good idea if they found out what marina employees thought about the candidates—make us feel like we're part of the team, a way to let us have a say in who ought to be running the place. Surprised you haven't heard about it, being a GM finalist and all."

The Weasel looked as if he'd just been told he had a

week to live. "Of course," he stuttered, crumpling the paper he'd waved in my face. He wadded it into a tight ball and said, "Just forget the surcharge. It's not a done deal yet, and I'm not sure I approve of it anyway."

"Didn't think so," said Tom.

"Is there really a survey?" I asked after the Weasel had left.

"Damned if I know," said Tom, "but there oughta be."

# TWENTY-TWO

I'M THE ONLY full-time instructor at Sound Sailing.
But when the good weather hits, I sometimes have the
delicious problem of more customers than I can handle.
When that happens, I call on Jill Lessick. Jill is a twenty-
year-old prelaw student at the University of Washington
who got bitten by the sailing bug as a little kid in San
Diego. She first learned to sail in a little seven-foot din-
ghy called a Sabot and can now handle anything the
school has to offer. She's a great instructor, and I feel
fortunate to have her. Plus, she works cheap.

"Hey, Kellie," she called, waving when she saw me.
With her was a group of four students who were going
out on Elliott Bay for their first lesson.

"Have a good one!" I hollered.

My class—basic navigation—would be held inside
the school. Usually I schedule the classroom stuff in the
evenings so that the daylight hours can be spent out on
the water. But this was a small group of Boeing employees who worked a night shift and couldn't make an
evening class. The four-hour course covered navigational aids, charts, compasses, piloting techniques (such
as how to take a bearing and fix your position), and

using electronic devices. Celestial navigation—my favorite—was a separate class.

I usually start each class with some prefatory remarks about my sailing experience and then have the students introduce themselves and tell what they hope to get out of the course. Once that's finished, we move on to the meat of the program.

The students had just finished introducing themselves when I happened to look out the window. Dennis Lancaster was tearing across the parking lot and heading straight for the school. His tanned face was mostly scowl—a vile scar of unbridled rage.

*Oops*, I thought, the fit has hit the shan.

I quickly handed out some charts to my students, asking them to note all the different kinds of information displayed. Then I charged out the front door to deal with Lancaster.

A young kid pushing a dock cart momentarily blocked his path. Lancaster swore at the kid and elbowed him out of the way. He was breathing hard when he got to the school, but he had no difficulty shouting. "Just what the hell do you think you're up to?"

"About five feet four, but my mother always said I'd look at least an inch taller if I would just stand up straight."

"You can cut the funny stuff. I'm in no mood to deal with a lippy female."

"Fine by me. I need to get back to my students." I turned toward the door.

"Hold on! I want to ask you something. Why'd you butt into our family business when my brother and I specifically told you not to?"

"If I recall the conversation, I told you that Pearl was my friend and that I'd do anything for her."

"Oh, yeah?" he sputtered. "Maybe she won't be so friendly when she finds out you broke into her condo."

I wasn't going to go down that slippery slope. "My

students are waiting," I said. "Was there anything else?"

He tried to bully me some more, but I held my ground. "I'd be happy to talk to Adrienne or her husband if they're having difficulty dealing with Pearl's marriage. I promised Pearl I would do that for her. But I didn't promise her that I would take abuse from you."

I watched him stomp off and thought about how smoothly my meeting with Rachel had gone. If Lancaster's reaction was any indication of how Adrienne felt, I didn't think I'd have another walk in the park—literally or figuratively.

AS SOON AS class was over I checked for phone messages. Since I can't afford the luxury of a receptionist, I rely on voice mail to take care of business while I'm unavailable. I whine about this a lot. Making people wait until I can get back to them has cost me more than a few customers. The only saving grace is that my voice mail system doesn't have a long menu of options to wade through—no pressing buttons for fifty years only to wind up right back where you started, with no answers.

Callers to Sound Sailing are spared all that. They just get a short greeting, a beep, and the opportunity to unload whatever's on their mind for a full two minutes. There were five messages waiting. A banner day for Sound Sailing. Unfortunately, not a single call was business-related.

The first was from Danielle Korb. The love of the Weasel's life had called every day since I'd met her. The message was always the same: an urgent request for an interview, the subject of which was unspecified, but "of major import." Since I had no interest in the same old same old, I erased the message without bothering to listen.

The next was Andy of Andy's Auto Repair telling me that I could pick up the Miata anytime. I'd taken it into his shop as soon as I'd come back from Portland. "Bring cash," he said. As a mechanic, Andy is good and he's cheap—my personal requirements for just about everything—but he doesn't always play by the rules, especially those enforced by the IRS. If you're going to do business with the man, you can expect it to be conducted under the table.

The third message was from Rose. "Got something to tell you," she said excitedly. "Give me a jingle as soon as you can." I'd planned to call her anyway, to ask if she could give me a ride to Andy's.

The fourth message was a surprise. I sucked in some air and held it until the brief message ended. Allen Kingston's deep voice said simply, "Call me. We need to talk." I didn't know how I felt about that. Pleased? Curious? Scared? All of the above.

The last message was from Flora Hampton. She didn't say what she wanted. Just asked that I get back to her whenever I had the time.

I checked my watch. My class had run overtime, and I needed to pick up the Miata before Andy closed up shop for the day. I decided to call Rose and deal with Flora later. Kingston, I didn't want to think about just yet.

AS SOON AS I'd belted myself into Rose's Volvo, she handed me a postcard. On the front was a striking picture of a glistening, snowcapped Mount Hood, Oregon's highest peak.

"What's this?"

"It's from Jimmy! Read it."

I turned the card over. Jimmy's scribbled note to his sister was difficult to read—especially without my glasses—but as near as I could determine, he'd written:

*Dear Sis,*
*Tell everybody I'm okay. Sorry for all I've put you*
*guys thru—especially Mom. If everything works*
*out, I'll be seeing her soon. Love, J*

"This is great, Rose. I told you not to worry." I'd
reassured her at length that her brother seemed well
when I saw him in Portland. But the reverend's murder
had stirred fresh worry. So much so that I decided not
to mention her brother's connection to Billy Joe Peterson
or his role in the reporter's investigation.

"I'm so excited I can hardly keep my hands on the
steering wheel," Rose said. "This is the first word from
Jimmy we've had in nearly five years. We weren't even
sure he was still alive. Mom is going to be absolutely
thrilled."

She rambled on in much the same vein for a while
longer. At times, she was so emotional that tears
streamed down her face. "Hey, there," I said, handing
her a tissue. "Maybe I better do the driving."

"No, thank you," she said, smiling through her tears.
"I've seen you drive." She dabbed at her eyes with the
tissue and added, "Besides, we're almost there."

She turned onto First Street, and we passed the Pike
Place Market and a jumble of activity. Traffic slowed
and then came to a standstill in a frenzied blending of
cars, trucks, jaywalking tourists, and shoppers.

A traffic cop, standing in the middle of the intersection, waved us on. When we pulled into Andy's garage
and Rose turned off the engine, she gave me a hug.
"Thank you, Kellie. I owe you big time."

"Nonsense," I said. "All I did was pass your message to Jimmy."

She shook her head. "I know you haven't told me
everything. I think you took some risks in Portland—
that carjacking or whatever it was—for one thing." She

waved the postcard. "But without your courage, I wouldn't have this."

I thought she was overstating the case and told her so, but she continued to gush. Finally I gathered up my handbag, and when she paused to take a breath, I said, "Well, thanks for the ride, Rose. I'll see you later."

"Wait, Kellie," she said. "I need to tell you something else."

"That's okay, I get the picture. You think I'm a hero."

She laughed and said, "I guess I have laid it on pretty thick." Then she paused, her face growing serious. "But this is different, Kellie. It's about the marina."

No warm and fuzzy feelings now. "What about the marina?"

"Dennis Lancaster has forced the live-aboard issue to a head. It's become one of the deciding factors in who gets selected for the GM job."

I felt my spine tense, my body on high alert.

She continued, "And the selection committee is calling for a marina-wide meeting to be held Sunday evening. Each candidate has been asked to state his or her position on the issue—it's not a debate exactly, but questions will be taken from the audience. I've been told that old man Larstad's decision on the surcharge will be based on the outcome of the meeting."

I wanted her to reassure me that her position was clear—that as general manager, she would not favor the surcharge on live-aboards. That she felt we were an asset to the marina, not a liability. But she didn't do that. She eyed me carefully and said, "I'd advise you to be there, Kellie."

"Okay," I said, fumbling for the door handle.

"And one other thing before you go."

*Buck up*, I told myself. *It can't get any worse.*

"Have you read the *Times* lately?" she asked.

"No."

"You ought to take a look. They've been running a series of environmental articles by that reporter friend of Wilmington's. She's succeeded in stirring up a fair amount of controversy over how marinas affect the environment, especially those that allow live-aboards."

"That's ridiculous."

"Maybe so, but we've been told to gear up for a strong media presence at Sunday's meeting."

I mumbled my thanks for the warning and left.

I DROVE THE Miata back to the marina and then stopped by the Topside. When I arrived, I found an informal gathering of the clan in progress. Larstad Marina's live-aboard contingent numbers about twenty-five souls, a diverse group of men and women united by their love of the sea and the boats they call home. For the most part, though, we're an independent lot, preferring privacy above all else. Unlike the live-aboards at other marinas, the Larstad group has no newsletter, no regular meetings, and no social functions whatsoever.

It's not that we're unfriendly or don't socialize when we run into each other from time to time; it's just that we generally shun activities that require any sort of advance planning or organization. To find so many of my neighbors gathered together at the same time and place was not only unusual, it was unsettling—an indication of just how precarious our continued existence at the marina had become.

The group's mood was loud and boisterous. As soon as I walked in, John Holtzer stuck his hand in the air and waved me over to his table near the bar. There were already eight others at the big round oak plank, but John pulled up another chair and squeezed out a spot for me next to him. Holtzer was a gregarious chap in his midforties whose heart was almost as big as his beer belly.

He pointed to the half-full pitcher of beer in the mid-

dle of the table. "Push that thing on over here," he said
to one of our tablemates. "Kellie needs to get started if
she's gonna catch up with us."

"That'll take some doin'." The comment came from
John's wife, Helen. She was a plain, rail-thin woman
with gray hair and laughing blue eyes. "This bunch of
sea dogs has been lapping it up for the past two hours."

"Thanks," I said, "but I'll pass on the beer."

"I hear ya, Kellie," said Ray Rowan. Ray was a den-
tist who was going through a nasty divorce. "What we
need is something with a little more punch." He waved
the bartender over. "I'm going to have a Seattle mar-
tini."

"What's that?" asked Charlie Saunders. A big man,
Saunders was known around the marina as Charlie Tuna,
which was also the name of his sailboat.

"Three parts good gin, one part Kahlua, served with
a coffee bean," answered Rowan.

John shook his head. "You got the name wrong, man.
That's what they call a Magnolia mudslide: high-class
gin that goes downhill fast."

The table erupted in laughter, but last winter's mud-
slides weren't so funny. One of the couples at the table—Melissa and Don Fryer—had lost their home in
Magnolia when the hillside behind it collapsed in the
heavy rains. After the disaster, they moved onto their
boat, where they've been ever since. Nevertheless, Don
Fryer said, "We'll have one of those drinks, too. We
know it well."

Rowan motioned to the bartender. "Whatever it
takes," he said.

After we'd placed our drink orders, John asked me,
"Have you heard the news?"

I nodded. "I'm assuming you mean Sunday night's
meeting."

"Damnedest thing I ever heard tell of," said Charlie.

"They're trying to run us out of the marina, is what they're trying to do."

The ensuing talk around the table reflected Charlie's assessment.

"What I don't understand," said John, "is how they think we're a detriment to the marina. I can't even begin to count the number of times I've bailed someone out of trouble. Just last week, some nitwit left a towel saturated with fiberglass solvent in the sink of his aft cabin. Next day, the sun's rays caused the towel to start smokin'. It wasn't all that hot of a day, but it don't take much heat to start a fire. Anyways, if I hadn't been there to spot the smoke, we could've had a bad one on our hands."

Ray echoed John's comments. "During last winter's big storm, I was tying down my spring lines when I heard someone crying for help. A woman had slipped on some ice on the dock and landed in the drink. She couldn't swim and didn't have a life jacket on. No doubt about it, she would've drowned if I hadn't been there to pull her out."

The others related similar stories. "I think we can all agree that live-aboards are often the first to respond to an emergency at the marina," said Helen, "but it goes further than that. John and I live aboard our boat because we don't have the means to keep it otherwise. We consider ourselves upstanding and responsible citizens. We pay our fees on time, we conserve fresh water, and we do not pollute the waters of Puget Sound."

"Yeah," said Charlie. "What's with all this pollution stuff I've been reading about in the papers? This is a marina we live in, for God's sake. It's not like we're anchoring out in Elliott Bay, dumping our garbage and sewage overboard."

"It's a crock," said Rowan. "Live-aboards don't add to the pollution problem. If anything, we are the best enforcers of the rules. They ought to come down here on the weekend and take a look at how some of those fair-weather boaters treat the environment. That would be a real eye-opener.''

"What you've all been saying is true," I said, "but you're preaching to the choir here. Maybe we should focus on Sunday night's meeting and how we can effect a positive outcome. My grampy always said that we can either be creatures of circumstance or creators of circumstance. I'd like to think live-aboards are creators.''

Glasses raised and heads nodded. "Hear, hear!"

It was after midnight when we finally hammered out a strategy that we could all agree on. Someone tried to nominate me spokesperson for the group, but I declined. Adamantly. I'd had enough of the spokesperson role of late. I went straight home, climbed into my bunk, and crashed. Cassie came home soon after I did, but she tumbled into bed right away, too. The last thing I heard before I drifted off was Pan-Pan purring in my ear. She was curled up at my feet when the phone woke me the next morning.

"I'll get it!" hollered Cassie from the main cabin.

I pulled the pillow over my head. Ever since she'd come home from school, the phone rang constantly—always for her.

She rushed into my cabin carrying the portable. "It's for you," she said.

"Tell them to go away," I groaned. "I'm still asleep."

She cupped a hand over the receiver. "But I think it's Flora Hampton!" she whispered excitedly.

Shoot, I never got back to her yesterday. I pulled myself upright and took the phone from Cassie, who waited for confirmation by hovering at the edge of my bed, biting her lower lip. It was an old habit, recently resurfaced.

"Hello?"

"Hello, Kellie. This is Flora. Flora Hampton.''

I nodded to Cassie, and she sat down on the bed. "Flora, it's good to hear from you." I purposefully avoided mentioning her other call. I didn't think Cassie would understand why I hadn't said anything to her about it—or why I hadn't called Flora back right away.

"I called your business number yesterday," she said, "but I guess you didn't get the message."

"What can I do for you?"

"Nothing, really. I just wanted to let you know that I told Deena about the adoption."

I mouthed the words "she told her" to Cassie. She smiled and snuggled up next to me. "That's great," I said into the receiver. "How did Deena take the news?"

"Not so good, I'm afraid. She doesn't believe me."

I struggled to keep my voice and face neutral for Cassie's benefit. "Did you show her Cassie's picture?"

"Yes, I did. But she said that didn't prove anything. That Cassie looks nothing like her."

"But they're identical! How could she think . . ." I felt Cassie's body tense up.

"I know, I know," said Flora. "But Deena can be real stubborn. She said she doesn't want anything to do with your daughter." A short pause. "I'm sorry, real sorry."

I thanked her for calling, and we hung up.

Cassie looked at me. "It's bad news, isn't it? Tell me, Mom."

I put my arm around her shoulder and hugged her close. "Sometimes things don't always work out the way we'd hoped."

Cassie twisted out of my embrace. "Mom, just tell me what she said."

I told her.

"No! That's not possible. You said we were identical! And what about the picture you left with her mother? Didn't Deena look at it?"

"Flora said she did."

"Then how could she say something like that?"

"Cassie, I don't know. But think about what Deena must be going through. Not learning that you were adopted until you're twenty years old has to be quite a shock. It's possible that she'll eventually accept the idea. And you, too."

She started to cry. "I wanted to meet her, Mom."

"Oh, honey, I believe you will. Give Deena some time." I hugged her again. "Life is constantly changing, Cassie. It's like the wind. Just when we think we're headed in the right direction, something happens. The wind shifts, and we're—"

Cassie jerked out of my embrace again, tears streaming down her face. "Oh, stop it. Just stop it!" she screamed. "I don't want to hear about the stupid wind one more time. That's your answer for everything. But it's just a bunch of crap. Do you hear me? Crap!"

I reached out for her. "Cassie, please."

"NO! Just leave me alone."

She bolted from the cabin and didn't speak to me for the rest of the day. Thursday was a little better, and by Friday we'd declared an uneasy truce. By then I'd also reconciled with Allen Kingston. The mending of our relationship was sudden and unexpected—as was the case with just about everything that happened in the days that followed.

After Cassie's outburst that morning, I skipped breakfast and trudged off to the sailing school. I didn't have a class until midafternoon, but I wasn't up to dealing with my daughter one minute longer. The understanding mom I was not. Since everything I owned was in the dirty clothes basket, I grabbed whatever was at the top of the heap and slipped it on—an old, faded T-shirt and some ratty cutoff jeans. My hair was a tangled frizz ball, which seemed appropriate, given my attire and state of mind.

Kingston was standing in front of the school when I arrived. Perfect timing, I thought.

He took one look at me and broke into an amused grin. "Hey, there, Red. Glad to see you looking so well."

Ordinarily I would've made some sort of snappy comeback about the way he looked. But I just stared at him, completely at a loss for words. I'd only seen him from a distance the other day. He'd looked good then, but seeing him up close and personal like this took my breath away. When I finally got my mouth working, I said, "What are you doing here?"

"Same reason I called you on the phone—I've missed you," he said, his dark eyes locking onto mine.

He had me. He knew it, and I knew it. But, not wanting to make it too easy for him, I said, "Seems like we've covered this territory before."

"Not in person." He took both my hands in his and drew me to him, wrapping his big arms around me in a tender embrace.

Perhaps he'd simply caught me at a vulnerable moment, but as soon as I felt his touch, all the anger and hurt I'd held inside for so long melted away. I didn't care anymore what it was that had kept him from me. He was here now, and that was enough. I leaned my head against his chest and returned his embrace.

"I need you, Kellie," he whispered in my ear.

"I need you, too," I said.

The rest of our reconciliation process took place later that evening.

# TWENTY-THREE

THE RECEPTION FOR the newlyweds was held at Pearl's condo on the Saturday evening following their return to Seattle. Although she had only a couple of days to put the affair together, Rachel Feldman handled all the arrangements herself—from planning the menu and hiring a caterer to inviting the guests and decorating Pearl's home. "I want to make their homecoming special," she said. "This will be a celebration."

Besides family, the lengthy guest list included many long-time friends, business acquaintances, several prominent community leaders, and the entire board of directors for Pearl and Isaac's favorite charity, HavenSafe. Since there wasn't any time to send out invitations, Rachel had personally called everyone on the list.

She'd said formal attire was appropriate, so Allen Kingston and I went all out for the occasion. He rented a tuxedo, and I bought a slinky black silk dress. Cassie helped me with my hair and, when Kingston arrived, took our picture.

"I feel like a penguin in this thing," he groused.

"But you look like a prince," I said.

He gave my hand a squeeze and then kissed me. "I should. I'm with a princess."

His car, however, was definitely not a chariot.

"You're still driving this old rust-bucket," I teased. "Where's that Porsche I heard you'd bought?" *And saw you in*, I thought.

"Hey, there are some things too sacred to tamper with. Melody's the one who drives a Porsche, not me."

According to Kingston, all the changes he'd made recently had nothing to do with his new partner, Melody Connor—and everything to do with his job. His boss, Brian Saunders, had been riding him unmercifully for months. It was either shape up or ship out. "Believe me, I was tempted," he said. "But the thing is, I love my job. And despite his nit-picking, Saunders isn't all that bad. After all, I trained the guy."

I accepted his explanation at face value, but I still hadn't met Melody. And while my relationship with Kingston seemed to be back on track, I couldn't shake the feeling that his partner remained a threat.

We arrived at the Palisades West Condominiums early—just in time to see a familiar-looking black stretch limo pull away from the curb in front of the building.

"Kingston, I know that limo!"

"Aw, Red. Don't rub it in." He waved a hand at his car's torn and faded interior. "This is as good as it gets with me."

"No, no. I mean I know who owns it," I said. "Don't stop. Follow it!"

He pulled to the curb and parked. "What the hell are you into now, Montgomery?"

I watched T-Bone's limo turn a corner and disappear. "Nothing," I said.

Kingston gave me one of his famous stares. "This have something to do with that preacher's homicide in Portland?"

I'd told him very little about my trip. He knew that I went to Portland to locate Pearl and that I had a hand in convincing the newlyweds to come back home. But I hadn't said much about the Reverend St. Paul or his murder. I already felt guilty about my presence at the crime scene. It wasn't Kingston's jurisdiction or case, but if he knew what BJ and Cord had done, he'd have made it his business. So I'd kept my mouth shut, figuring there are some things that you just shouldn't share with a homicide detective.

"Forget it," I said. "Let's go party."

Rachel greeted us at the door, and I made the introductions. After we'd offered our congratulations to the newlyweds, we helped ourselves to some champagne and mingled with the other early arrivals. It wasn't long, though, before the entire room was filled with guests—a testament, I thought, to just how highly Pearl and Isaac were regarded.

A large buffet table had been set up in the formal dining room. It was heaped with food and lavishly decorated with a large floral arrangement in the center. In one corner of the great room, a teenage boy kept the few children who were present entranced with magic tricks. He also gave each child a balloon which he filled from a helium tank. Every once in a while we'd hear peals of laughter as he'd inhale a little of the helium and demonstrate his cartoon voice.

A pianist friend of Rachel's entertained the adults with a selection of Pearl and Isaac's favorite melodies. The atmosphere was lively and festive—until Dennis Lancaster and crew arrived.

I was beginning to think that they'd decided to boycott the shindig, when they suddenly strode through the front door—Lancaster leading the pack, his scowl as fierce as ever; Coughlin following close behind, his pitted face looking grim and determined; and finally, Adrienne bringing up the rear, a younger version of Pearl, but with rounded shoulders and dark circles under her eyes.

"Now there's a scary bunch," said Kingston.

"That's Pearl's family," I told him. I'd tried to contact Adrienne as Pearl had requested, but she'd refused to even talk to me on the phone, let alone meet with me. "I've never met Adrienne, but her husband and brother-in-law are real charmers. I hope they don't make any trouble tonight."

Kate, who was standing next to us, said, "Maybe we better head them off at the pass."

I agreed, and we split up. Kate cornered Lancaster, while Kingston and I joined Phillip and Adrienne Coughlin. I nodded to Phillip and extended a hand to Adrienne. "I'm Kellie Montgomery," I said, "a friend of Pearl's."

She gave me a tight, half smile. "I know who you are," she said. Her handshake was limp and her palm moist.

Phillip Coughlin looked at Kingston. "And who are you?" he asked bluntly.

"Allen Kingston," he said, offering his hand.

"*Detective* Allen Kingston," I said. "Homicide detective." It wasn't something I'd planned to say, but the way Coughlin ignored Kingston's outstretched hand ticked me off.

"You here on official business?" Coughlin asked.

It was an odd question, and Kingston ran with it. "Should I be?"

Coughlin seemed embarrassed. "No, no, of course not," he said.

Adrienne's gray eyes darted around the room until they settled on her mother and Isaac.

"They make a nice couple, don't you think?" I said.

She shrugged her shoulders. "What I think apparently doesn't matter."

"From what Pearl told me, she cares very much about what you think."

Adrienne made little quotation marks in the air with her fingers. "Just as long as I quote don't interfere with her life unquote."

"My mother-in-law has really done it this time," said Coughlin. "Getting married at her age." He shook his head. "My God!"

"Look at it this way," said Kingston with an amused grin. "At least it wasn't a shotgun wedding."

Adrienne drew back her rounded shoulders by half a mile. "I find that insulting," she said through pinched lips.

*Oh, lighten up.* "Don't take it personally," I said. "Allen insults everyone sooner or later."

Coughlin said, "My wife is the one who's going to bear the brunt of this fiasco."

"Oh?" I said with a tell-me-more look.

"Mother is not well," explained Adrienne, "and I can't be taking care of her long distance. She needs to move to Salem, where we live."

"Pearl isn't sick," I said. "Why do you believe you need to take care of her?"

Coughlin and Adrienne exchanged glances. "Not many people know this yet, but Mother has Alzheimer's," explained Adrienne. "The beginning stages."

I was momentarily stunned, but Kingston jumped in with a pertinent question. "Has her physician made this diagnosis?"

Coughlin's answer was a dodge. "We're familiar with the signs. My own mother went through the same thing."

Kingston said, "I see."

"I don't think you do, but it doesn't matter," said Adrienne. "I know my mother, and she needs us. Not some old geezer of a husband with health problems of his own."

I reined in my growing anger with difficulty. "What Pearl needs is your understanding, your love, and your good wishes."

Adrienne drew back her shoulders again. "I think we're in a better position to know what Mother needs. We're her family. We love her."

"And so does Isaac," I said.

"If you'll excuse us," said Coughlin. "I believe this conversation has run its course."

After they'd left us, Kingston said, "There go two good arguments for birth control."

We found Kate at the buffet table.

"I hope you had better luck running interference than we did," I said.

She dished some salmon paté onto a china plate. "Lancaster asked me out. The jerk."

A smile played at the corner of Kingston's mouth. "What'd you tell him?"

"That I'd rather date a serial killer."

"Don't hold back, girl," I said.

She gave me a sly grin. "That was the G-rated version. You don't want to hear what I really said." She popped an olive into her mouth as she heaped more food onto her plate. "I don't know why I'm even thinking of eating. Talking to that leering idiot has ruined my appetite."

We all moved aside so that an elderly lady using a walker could pass. When she reached the buffet table, she surveyed the various delicacies and sighed wearily.

"Do you need some help, ma'am?" asked Kingston.

She nodded gratefully as Kingston began filling a plate according to her directions.

I drew Kate aside and said, "I saw T-Bone's limo earlier."

"Oh?"

"Are you sure Tony's not gambling again?"

Kate sighed. "I don't think so, but who knows? He was supposed to be here tonight."

"Where is he?"

"Home, I guess. Said he didn't feel good." She took a bite of the paté. "Mmm. This is delicious. You should try some."

I helped myself to a plate and joined Kingston and the elderly lady. He'd finished his serving duties, and they'd settled themselves on a nearby couch to eat. She was a frail little thing, but next to Kingston's six-foot-four frame she looked positively Lilliputian.

"This man of yours—" she said after Kingston had introduced us, "you hold onto him. He's a mensch."

"That's a good thing, right?"

Yetta Bernstein proved to be a lively old gal—she'd turn ninety next month—who took great delight in gossiping about the other guests. "But this marriage of Isaac's," she said, waving her fork. "Who'd have thought such a thing? What *meshugenners*."

"You don't approve?" I asked.

"Oh, yes. I should be so lucky. I just thought it . . . What is the word I'm looking for?" She paused a moment. "Ironic. That's it."

"How so?" asked Kingston.

"Because Rachel did the same thing. Married a *goy*."

"A goy?"

"Non-Jew. It almost broke Isaac's heart."

"I didn't think she was married," I said.

"Not now. This was years ago. It didn't last. He was a no-goodnik, just like Isaac said. He begged Rachel not to marry him, but she did it anyway. Like her mother, she is. So headstrong." She shook her head sadly. "Rachel and Isaac didn't speak for years. Even after Joseph was born."

"Joseph?"

"Rachel's son," she said, gesturing toward the teenager manning the helium tank. "That's the boy over there."

"Looks like all is well between Rachel and Isaac now," I said.

"You think?"

I looked across the room to where Rachel was fussing with a flower arrangement that had been knocked over by one of the guests. "If this party is any indication, I'd say so."

"Ah, yes, the party." Mrs. Bernstein shrugged. "I'm just an old woman. What do I know?" Then she leaned in closer and motioned for us to do the same as she whispered, "But I wouldn't trust a thing that girl says or does."

We chatted for a few more minutes and then excused ourselves. I don't know what time the party broke up, but Kingston and I left at eleven o'clock.

"Did you have fun?" I asked on the way home.

"Yeah, I did," he said. "I thought I'd be uncomfortable. You know, all that money walking around in one room—but I held my own. I could get used to hobnobbing with the rich and famous."

"Where does that leave me? The poor and unknown."

"Well, now," he said, "I'm glad you asked that. Because I had something special in mind for you."

And he did.

THE CALL CAME early the next morning—as most calls do that bring bad news. It was Kate, breathless and stammering. I was certain that she'd suffered a relapse.

"What's wrong?" I asked. "Are you all right?"

"No. I mean, I'm okay. It's not me. Something's wrong with Pearl and Isaac. Medic One is here."

"What happened?"

"I don't know for sure, but the police just arrived. You better get over here."

I dressed in whatever I could grab in a hurry and stopped just long enough to tell Cassie what had happened before taking off. As Kate had indicated, Medic One and a patrol car were at the condo. I found Kate pacing a hole in the carpet outside Pearl's front door.

"Tell me what you know," I said, taking her arm. We found two chairs in the hallway and sat down.

"It's bad, Kellie. I heard one of the paramedics tell the police to call the medical examiner and advise him that there'd been a death."

"Was it Isaac?"

"I'm not sure."

"Is any of the family here?"

Kate nodded. "Just Rachel. She was the one who found them. I guess she came by the condo early this morning for some reason. Anyway, she called 9-1-1."

"What about Pearl's family? Have they been notified?"

"I don't know."

# TWENTY-FOUR

ISAAC FELDMAN WAS pronounced dead by the medical examiner at 8:03 Sunday morning. By then Pearl had been transported by Medic One to Virginia Mason Medical Center where her condition was listed as stable.

"Is she aware of her husband's passing?" I asked the nurse on duty.

"Yes, she's been told."

Kate and I were permitted to see Pearl only after she'd been moved from the emergency room to a private suite on the second floor. Adrienne and Phillip Coughlin were at her bedside when we walked in.

Phillip jumped up from his chair and met us at the door. "This isn't a good time."

"Mother needs to rest," said Adrienne.

I snatched a look at Pearl. She was lying flat on her back with her eyes closed. An IV tube was attached to her left hand. Her face was pale but otherwise unmarked.

Coughlin gestured toward the door. "She's not up to company right now."

"We're not company," I said. "We're friends."

Pearl stirred in the bed and opened her eyes. "Kellie? Is that you?"

"Yes, Pearl. And Kate."

Adrienne turned her head toward us and frowned. "Thanks a lot. Mother was sleeping."

"I wasn't asleep," said Pearl.

"Yes, you were."

Pearl raised her head from the pillow. "Where's that button?"

"What button?" asked Adrienne.

"The one that gets this bed tilted so I can sit up."

"Now, Mother, you don't want to do that. You need to go back to sleep."

Coughlin, who hadn't budged from his guardlike stance at the door said, "That's right. You shouldn't be greeting visitors right now."

Adrienne patted her mother's pillow. "So lie right back down here and—"

"Shut up!" shrieked Pearl.

The loud cry startled us all, but Adrienne recovered quickly. "Now, Mother, I know you're upset and—"

"Shut up, shut up, shut up!" As she yelled, Pearl balled her free hand into a fist and waved it at her daughter. "And get out! Right now!"

Adrienne reared back and shouted to her husband. "Find the nurse! Quick!!"

Coughlin pushed Kate and me toward the door. "Move it!"

Adrienne stood up but continued to hover near Pearl's bed.

Pearl stopped waving her fist and glared at Adrienne. "I told you to leave."

Adrienne turned toward us. "They're leaving, Mother. They're all leaving."

"Kellie stays," said Pearl.

"What?"

"You heard me. I want everybody out except Kellie."

"Don't be ridiculous."

I dodged Coughlin and walked over to the bed. "Adrienne,'' I said in a firm voice, "do what your mother says. Find a nurse. I'll stay with Pearl."

Adrienne looked at me and then at her mother. "I don't think—"

"Just do it, Adrienne," I said. "Do it now."

She turned abruptly and followed Kate and Coughlin out the door.

"Thank you," said Pearl softly.

I sat down in the chair that Adrienne had vacated.

"Can you get this bed up for me?"

I found the button and adjusted the bed to suit her.

"That's better," she said. "Adrienne just won't listen to me. Always telling me what she thinks I need. What I need is my husband back. But I've lost him, Kellie."

Her distress was hard to witness. She didn't cry, but the pain in her eyes and her voice was heart-wrenching.

"I know, Pearl. And I'm so very sorry. I liked Isaac a lot."

"He liked you, too. He said I'd always be able to count on you."

"That's true."

She glanced toward the door. "I'll have to make this quick—Adrienne and Phil are going to be dragging some poor nurse in here any minute. What I'd like you to do is find out who killed Isaac."

I looked at her carefully. She seemed rational, but her words made no sense. "I was told that his death was due to oxygen deprivation—from the emphysema."

"I know what the doctor said. But Isaac was feeling just fine. He didn't have to use his oxygen tank at all yesterday. In fact, he hasn't had any problems since we returned from Portland."

I couldn't imagine how she figured that made a case for foul play, but I wasn't about to argue with her. "Why do you think someone would want to kill Isaac?"

"Not just Isaac. Me, too. Someone wants us both dead."

I didn't know how to respond, so I just nodded for her to go on.

"The doctor thinks I passed out because I was upset over Isaac, but I'd felt woozy much earlier—when I got up to go to the bathroom. Isaac was in the small bedroom on the main floor, but he snores so badly that I slept upstairs. Anyway, when I got up I was groggy, like I'd been drugged. I don't know what happened last night, but somebody tried to kill both of us. I'm sure of it. And I want you to find out who. Don't worry about money or my privacy or anything else. Just do whatever you think is necessary."

Our talk came to an abrupt halt when Pearl's nurse—followed closely by Adrienne and her husband—trooped into the room.

Pearl gripped my hand with a strength that surprised me. "You'll look into it, then?"

My brain was screaming *No, absolutely not! This is the request of a grieving, delusional woman*. But I heard my mouth saying, "Of course, Pearl. I'll do what I can."

I FOUND KATE with Rachel Feldman in a small waiting room near the nurses' station. Despite having just lost her father, Rachel looked quite lovely in a brown floor-length peasant skirt and a billowy white blouse. Her long dark hair was tied with a white ribbon and worn in a loose ponytail at the nape of her neck. From all outward appearances, the morning's events hadn't seemed to upset her unduly. When she'd told us earlier that her father had died, she'd simply said, "In itself, death is not a tragedy—no matter how great the loss or sorrow. Father had a long and full life." I didn't think anything of her demeanor at the time, for I believe that we all grieve in our own way. But with Pearl's words still ringing in my ears, I couldn't help wondering if Rachel Feldman's calm exterior had another, more ominous significance.

Both women stood as I approached.

"How is she?" asked Kate.

"Hard to say."

"Did she talk about the arrangements?" asked Rachel.

"Arrangements?"

"She had Father's body taken to the morgue instead of the funeral home. Perhaps she doesn't realize it, but Father must be buried right away—in keeping with our faith."

"Rachel," I said, "we need to talk about that." I motioned toward the chairs, and after we all sat down, I said, "Based on what Pearl told me about your father's death, I can only surmise that she has requested an autopsy."

"An autopsy!" Rachel's calm exterior suddenly disappeared. "That's totally unacceptable," she said angrily. "Autopsy is prohibited by several centuries of rabbinic rulings."

"I don't know much about the Jewish faith, but it's my understanding that exceptions are allowed. Especially if required by civil law."

"That's true, but it's required by law only when and if foul play is suspected. The police have made no such determination in Father's case. He was eighty-one and suffered from emphysema for years. Everyone knows that. His death was due to natural causes—with absolutely no need for an autopsy."

"Pearl thinks otherwise," I said.

"What are you saying?"

"That Pearl has some serious concerns regarding the nature of your father's death."

Rachel stood suddenly and placed her hands on her hips. "I'm not even going to ask what kind of concerns. The woman is obviously nuts. I suppose the next thing you'll tell me is that she wants him cremated, too."

"No, she didn't say anything about that."

"Good," she said, flinging her bag over her shoulder. "Because you can tell Pearl for me that the Torah is quite emphatic on that point."

After she'd huffed out of the room, Kate said, "What the heck is going on?"

"Pearl thinks someone murdered Isaac, and whoever it is wants her dead, too."

"You've got to be kidding."

"No, I'm not. And it gets worse. Pearl asked me to find out who the culprit is."

"What did you tell her?"

"That I'd look into it."

"But why would anyone want to kill Pearl and Isaac?"

"I can't imagine, and Pearl never said."

"So what are you going to do?"

"I guess I'll start by going back to the condo to take a look at the scene of the death. And I'd sure like to get a copy of her will."

"I can help with the will," said Kate. "I helped her hide it."

"She hid her will? Whatever for?"

"She was afraid her daughter and son-in-law would try to get their hands on it."

TONY LET US into Pearl's condo with his passkey. "It's a damn shame about Mr. Feldman," he said as he disarmed the alarm system. "How's Pearl doing?"

"As well as can be expected under the circumstances," said Kate.

Tony closed the panel door to the alarm's keypad. "Well, ladies, I gotta get back downstairs. Anything else you need?"

"Before you go," I said, "I have a couple of questions."

He looked at me warily. "What kind of questions?"

I motioned to the alarm system. "First of all, how come the alarm was on? Pearl couldn't have set it before she left for the hospital. They wheeled her out of here on a stretcher."

He scratched his head. "I guess Mr. Feldman's daughter must've set it. She was the last person to leave."

"How did she know the code?" asked Kate.

"I told her," said Tony.

"Why on earth would you give out that information?" I asked.

He shrugged. "She asked—and she is a relative now. I just assumed it was okay."

"Jeez, Tony," said Kate.

"What? Did I do something wrong?"

"Where were you last night, Tony? How come you didn't come to the party?"

He glanced at Kate. "I . . . uh, I was sick."

"Feeling all better now?" I asked.

"He wasn't sick," said Kate.

"Kate, don't," Tony protested.

"Tony, she saw T-Bone's limo."

"Okay, okay. I had business with T-Bone last night," he said. He wiped a bead of sweat from his brow. "But I'll tell you this: I wasn't the only reason he came calling."

"What do you mean?"

"I said I'd seen T-Bone talking to Lancaster before. Well, last night I seen the two of them together again. And they was arguing something fierce."

"What do you make of that?" I asked.

"At first I thought T-Bone was trying to get me fired, but . . ."

"But what?" asked Kate.

"But now I'm thinking that I'm not the only one around here with a gambling problem." He looked at Kate. "Can I go now?"

The doorbell rang before she could answer.

"I'll get it," offered Tony. He opened the front door and laughed. A clown with frizzy orange hair and a big red rubber nose stood in the doorway. "Party's over, bud," Tony said.

"Exactly," said the clown. "And I need to pick up the tank."

Tony waved him inside. "Oh, man, you're gonna have to talk to the ladies about that. I'm outta here."

"What did you say you wanted?" asked Kate.

"The helium tank. It should've been picked up last night. I got a kid's birthday bash on tap for today."

I gestured to the corner where Rachel's son was filling the balloons last night. "It should be right over there," I said. "Help yourself."

His giant-size clown shoes flip-flopped across the room. "It's not here," he said.

Or anywhere else that we could determine. We stood in Isaac's bedroom with an unhappy clown. "This is the last room," Kate said, "but I can't imagine why the tank would be in here."

The clown's mood—which wasn't all that great to begin with—had steadily deteriorated as we'd searched the house. "Damn, my boss is gonna shit bricks over this," he said. He kicked at a large gray blanket on the floor and then grabbed his foot. "Oh, man. Oh, man. That fuckin' hurts."

"But the good news is you found your missing tank," I said.

After treating us to a few choice words about his boss, clowns, birthday parties, and bratty little kids, he bent over to pick up the tank. "Hey," he said. "The tank's empty. There should've been enough helium in here for five fuckin' birthdays." He examined the tank. "Well, no wonder. Some nitwit left the valve open."

"Maybe your boss should've sent you last night," said Kate.

"He tried, but the lady doing all the arrangements said her kid could handle it." He lifted the tank onto his shoulder. "Damn. Where am I gonna get helium on a Sunday?"

We escorted him to the door. "Better tell that kid to be careful next time," he said. "Leaving a valve open like that could be dangerous—especially in a small, closed-up bedroom. He could've gotten hisself killed."

# TWENTY-FIVE

PEARL DANIELSON'S LAST Will and Testament was located exactly where Kate had helped her hide it—inside the toilet tank in the guest bathroom. They had rolled the will into a large, plastic waterproof tube and weighted the whole thing down with a rock.

"Whose idea was this?" I asked.

"Mine. I hide all my rings this way." Kate pulled the tube out of the water and dried it off with a towel.

"Did Pearl hide any other paperwork in the toilet?"

"I don't know. Why?"

"Because there's another tube in here." I extracted the second tube and handed it to her.

"What do you think it is?" asked Kate.

"Only one way to find out."

The first tube contained Pearl's will, dated a couple of days before she left on her trip to Portland. Isaac Feldman's will, dated a year ago, was enclosed in the second tube.

"He must have thought our hiding place was a good idea," said Kate, smiling. "Martha Stewart, take note."

We carried both documents into the dining room and unfolded them on the table. As we carefully smoothed out the papers, I began to have second thoughts about what we were doing. Although Pearl had given me carte blanche as far as her privacy was concerned, I couldn't shake the feeling that I was trespassing in the worst possible way. It made me feel sneaky and guilty.

Kate had no such qualms. "Let's read Pearl's first," she said eagerly.

Basically Pearl had left the bulk of her estate to her favorite charity, HavenSafe, with additional donations to a variety of other worthy causes.

"Look at this," said Kate. "She's even left money to Sound Sailing."

That surprised—and embarrassed—me. While I appreciated her largesse, it was humiliating to learn that Pearl thought of my struggling little business as needy. I quickly scanned the rest of the document. Besides the charities, Pearl had a lengthy list of individuals she'd remembered with varying amounts of money. "I don't recognize any of these people," I said.

"I guess you didn't see his name."

"Whose name?"

"Antonio R. Carmine. Pearl's earmarked over one hundred thousand dollars for him—provided he joins Gambler's Anonymous."

"That's interesting. But what about family members?" I asked. "Do you see where she's left anything to them?"

"It looks like she'd planned to leave the rest of her estate to her daughter and son-in-law. But that was all changed when this was drawn up." She handed me a separate document that had been attached to the back of the will with a paper clip.

"What is it?" I asked.

"A codicil to her will, dated a week ago," said Kate.

I read through the document. The codicil revoked the provisions for her family and directed that their portion of her estate be given instead to the Church of the Passionate Life. Cord Roberts was right, I thought. The Reverend St. Paul had succeeded in getting access to her fortune after all.

"How much do you think she's worth?" asked Kate.

"Millions."

"Many millions, I'd say. She's not famous, but she's right up there with Oprah when it comes to wealth."

I was more concerned with whether Isaac's will had a codicil, too. I flipped through several pages and found it. As I suspected, he'd revoked all provisions he'd previously made for Rachel and her son, Joseph. While I didn't expect that Isaac would donate his estate to the reverend's church, he had essentially accomplished the same thing by designating Pearl as his sole beneficiary. The Reverend St. Paul was one shrewd cookie.

"What do you make of all this?" asked Kate.

"The answer to that depends on just who, besides Pearl and Isaac, knew what was in these documents."

"Well," said Kate, tapping the plastic tube, "if the family knew about the codicils, that lets them off the hook as far as murder goes," said Kate.

"How do you figure?"

"They didn't stand to inherit anything. Murdering Isaac and Pearl wouldn't do them a bit of good—financially speaking."

"No," I agreed, "but they still might have wanted them dead for another reason."

"What's that?"

I told her about the scriptural reference scribbled on the reverend's wall. "It was all about betrayal. Someone killed the Reverend St. Paul because he or she felt betrayed somehow. Being cheated out of your inheritance might make someone feel betrayed, don't you think?"

"Are you suggesting that Adrienne or Rachel had something to do with the preacher's murder?"

"No. They didn't even know that their parents were

in Portland, so how could they know about the reverend?"

"But," said Kate, "it's possible that they learned about the codicils when Pearl and Isaac returned from Portland. If so, they could've had something to do with Isaac's death."

"If he was murdered. We still don't know that for sure."

"What about the helium tank? That valve being left open is rather compelling evidence."

"That could've been just a simple mistake," I said. "Joseph is only fifteen."

"But what if it wasn't a mistake? What if someone had deliberately left it open and placed it in Isaac's room? Who do you think might have done that?"

I hadn't seen anything to indicate that the condo had been forcibly entered. "It would've had to be someone who knew how to disarm the alarm system."

Kate grabbed a paper and pencil from the telephone stand. "Let's make a list," she said. "After what Tony said, I'm thinking everyone in town had access to this place."

"Speaking of Tony . . ."

"Right. His name goes at the top."

After we'd finished, our list contained five names: Tony Carmine, Rachel Feldman, Dennis Lancaster, Phillip Coughlin, and Adrienne Coughlin. We put an asterisk next to Adrienne's name because we could only assume she knew the code. A fairly safe bet, though, since her husband knew it.

"Okay," said Kate, "where does this leave us?"

"Exposed," I said, pointing to the front door.

Dennis Lancaster stood in the entryway glaring at us. "What the hell are you two doing here?"

"Quick," I whispered to Kate. "You distract him while I get rid of this stuff."

She stood up from the table and moved (as only Kate

can) toward Lancaster. "Denny," she purred, "just the person I wanted to see."

WHEN I JOINED them in the great room, Kate was snuggled up to Lancaster on the couch. He shot me a dirty look and whispered something in her ear.

Kate giggled like a silly schoolgirl. "Oh, Denny, you're so funny."

"Sis," I said, "we need to get going." I held up a small suitcase. "I packed the clothes Pearl wanted."

Kate extricated herself from Lancaster's embrace. "Sorry, punkin, but Kellie's right. Pearl's expecting us at the hospital."

"Wait a minute," Lancaster said, grabbing her hand but addressing me. "How do I know there are just clothes in that suitcase?"

"You think I'm robbing the place, Dennis?"

"I think you're a nosy little broad who should mind her own business or—"

"Or what? You'll sic T-Bone on me?"

He let go of Kate's hand and stood up. "You know T-Bone?"

"Only by reputation," I said. "Which makes me wonder why a nice guy like you would have anything to do with him."

"What makes you think I do?"

"Because," I said, "you were seen arguing with him last night. Not a cool move, Dennis."

"I'll tell you what's not a cool move," he said, taking a step forward. "Fuckin' with me."

Kate latched onto his arm. "Denny, there's no need to get into a pissing contest with my sister." She gave his arm a squeeze. "We have to go now, but I'd really like to see you later, okay?"

* * *

"WHAT A PERFORMANCE," I said to Kate. "Considering how you rebuffed him last night, I'm surprised Lancaster fell for it."

"He's stupid, that's why." She sniffed at her hand. "Jeez, I can smell him on me. I need a shower."

"Want to stop off at your place?"

"No, let's get the hell out of here. I don't want to run into him again."

We drove to the marina and stashed Pearl's suitcase aboard *Second Wind*. Kate was ready for lunch, but I needed to check my phone messages first. Kate couldn't get to the head fast enough. "I still stink," she said. "I hope you have lye soap in there."

While she was busy washing, I listened to the solitary message on my machine: "Hey, Kellie. This is Cord Roberts. Need to talk to you right away. You can reach me at work." I'd been hoping he'd call and give me an update on the reverend's murder investigation. I dialed the number he left, but he wasn't in, so I left a message on his voice mail. Kate walked out of the head just as I hung up.

"Feel better now?" I asked.

"The idiot must bathe in aftershave. It even rubbed off on my clothes." She looked around. "You don't have something here I could wear, do you?"

All I had was an old sweatshirt that Kate declared stank worse than Lancaster's aftershave. "Come on," I said. "We can eat our lunch outside. There's a good breeze blowing. That should freshen you up."

The Topside's decor is marginal, but it does have a great deck overlooking the marina. We found a table underneath a green-and-white-striped umbrella and ordered lunch. I looked for Cassie, but she didn't appear to be working.

After we'd finished eating, Kate asked, "So what's our next move, Sherlock?"

"I'd sure like to talk to Rachel and her son, but I have a class this afternoon."

"I can do it for you," she said eagerly. "What would you like me to ask them?"

I thought it over for a moment. Pearl had said to use any means necessary. And Kate was pretty good at getting what she wanted—at least with men. Maybe she'd have luck with Rachel, also. "Okay, Kate. Here's what I'd like to know."

She listened for a minute, and then I lost her when she waved at someone behind me. "Hey, look who's here."

When I turned around, Allen Kingston and the blonde I'd seen him with a couple of days before were walking toward our table.

"Oh-my-god, Kellie, who's that with him? She's gorgeous."

"Undoubtedly the one and only Melody Connor, his new partner."

After introductions were made, Kate insisted that they join us. They accepted readily, apparently missing the pained look on my face. All I wanted to do at that moment was to crawl under my chair. Even on my best days, I don't exactly set the fashion world on fire. But in this morning's rush to Pearl's, I'd wound up wearing a faded pair of blue jeans and a Sound Sailing T-shirt that was big enough for Kingston. I might as well have wrapped myself in a bedsheet.

Melody Connor, on the other hand, was perfect. She was dressed in an outfit similar to what she'd worn the other day—a conservative, dark-blue power suit that showed off her long legs and trim figure.

"So what have you two been up to this fine day?" asked Kingston.

"We're investigating a murder," blurted Kate.

I gave her foot a swift kick under the table. "Not exactly."

Kingston's dark eyes narrowed. "Montgomery, what's going on?"

My helpful sister jumped in before I could answer. "Haven't you heard? Isaac Feldman died last night."

Kingston frowned. "He looked just fine when we left the party."

"Died in his sleep," I said. I shot Kate a meaningful glance. "Peacefully."

"So, where does the murder come in?" asked Melody.

"Pearl thinks he was killed and that someone is out to get her, too. She's asked Kellie to investigate."

Now I really did want to crawl under my chair. And keep on crawling until I was no longer on the deck.

Kingston and Melody exchanged looks. It was just a quick glance, but what passed between them was pretty clear: *What we have here, folks, is amateur hour at its finest.* But that didn't bother me half as much as what the exchange told me about Kingston and Melody's relationship. In their short time together as partners, they'd developed a closeness that often takes years to achieve— a knowledge of one another so intimate that it allowed them to pick up on what the other was thinking. I'd been able to do the same thing with my husband, but the realization that Kingston and Melody operated that way was hard to take.

Kingston looked amused. "What kind of evidence do you have that points to murder?"

"None," I said quickly. "Pearl is understandably overwrought right now. I told her I'd look into the matter because I thought it would ease her mind."

"But, Kellie," said Kate, "tell them about the helium."

There are times when I could commit murder myself.

"What about the helium?" asked Melody.

"It's nothing. Probably just an honest mistake. The helium tank that was used to blow up balloons at the party last night was left in Isaac's bedroom. When the worker came to pick it up, he discovered that the valve had been left open."

"So Isaac Feldman could've died from lack of oxygen," said Melody.

"Feldman suffered from emphysema," said Kingston. "Most likely that's what took him out."

"That's what the doctors think," I said.

Kingston dismissed the subject with a shrug. "Well, there you go," he said.

But Melody's interest was piqued. "Is there any money involved?" she asked. "Anyone stand to gain by his death?"

"That was Kellie's first question," said Kate. "We read their wills and—"

Kingston cocked an eyebrow. "You did what?"

I felt my face flush. "It's not as bad as it sounds," I said. "Pearl asked me to do whatever I thought necessary."

To Kingston's obvious amusement, Melody egged me on. "Tell me about the wills," she said.

I felt myself becoming defensive, as if I needed to legitimize my actions somehow. "Well," I said, "they were interesting."

"I'll bet," snorted Kingston.

I ignored him and directed my comments to Melody. "Pearl and Isaac are both very wealthy—we're talking megabucks here. Anyway, the answer to your earlier question is yes. Quite a number of people stood to benefit from Pearl's and Isaac's deaths—handsomely."

"Go on," said Melody.

"But the kicker is this: The people who would benefit the most—the close family members—have been virtually eliminated as beneficiaries."

"How so?"

I told her about the codicils. "So, either way, Pearl and Isaac's families are suspects. Depending upon what they knew about the wills, they could've killed because they thought they would inherit a fortune or because they felt that they'd been unfairly cut off from their inheritance.''

"And," said Kate, "they were all at the party last night. All of them had access to that helium tank.''

"What about the others mentioned in the will?" asked Melody. "Were any of them at the party?''

"Lots of people were there," I said, looking at Kingston. "*We* were there."

"Yeah, but we're certainly not the beneficiaries of any fortune," he said.

"Kellie is," said Kate.

*Thank you, Mary Kathleen.*

Kingston's jaw dropped about ten feet. Melody shifted forward in her chair and said, "Oh?''

"Sound Sailing benefits," I said quickly, "not me.''

Kate, now realizing the implication of what she'd just said, tried to make amends. "That's not important. What's important is the list we made.''

"Oh, jeez," said Kingston. "I've heard enough." He gathered up his sunglasses.

"Wait," said Melody. "I want to hear this. Go on, Kellie.''

"It's just a list of names—the names of five people who knew how to disarm Pearl's alarm system.''

"And you feel this is important because . . .''

"Because," I said, "they could've let themselves into the condo after the party and fiddled with the tank. There was no evidence that the condo was broken into.''

"Let me get this straight," Melody said. "You have a list of five names. Five people who thought they would either benefit from Pearl's and Isaac's wills or had somehow discovered that they'd been cheated out of their inheritance. Five people who also knew how to disarm the alarm system.''

"Correct," I said, suddenly feeling uneasy.

Melody eyed me closely and asked, "Was your name on that list?"

"My name?"

"You said your sailing school was mentioned in the will and that you were at the party. But you haven't said whether you know how to disarm the system." She smiled and leaned across the table. "So, tell us. Do you?"

# TWENTY-SIX

MY FIRST IMPULSE was to slug her. She'd set me up big time, and I'd been too stupid to see it coming. The worst part was, Kingston had done nothing to stop her. I left her question dangling in the air and stared at her. After a moment it occurred to me that Melody and I were like two sailboats competing in a race. She was the upwind boat that—by drilling me with questions—had rushed ahead to take the wind out of my sails. As the downwind boat, I had the right of way. I could've turned and forced her to change direction. Instead, I decided to come about and take a different tack. "You'll have to excuse me," I said. "I have a class to teach."

My class consisted of just two students—a married couple who owned their own sailboat. Although they were fairly experienced sailors, Dan and Sue Costers had signed up for lessons—as they put it—"to save our marriage." Like many couples, Dan had taken on the role of captain while Sue served as crew. Dividing up responsibilities is based on a sound premise—the boat will be better organized, and there will be less confusion if the authority to make decisions and give directions rests with just one individual. But the role of captain has nothing to do with testosterone levels. A good sailor is one who is able to perform all functions on the boat.

In the case of Dan and Sue Costers, their one-sided division of labor had cheated them out of enjoying sailing to its fullest. In addition, Dan had succumbed to an interesting psychological phenomenon that sometimes occurs when an otherwise normal person gets behind the wheel or the tiller: He'd turned into a power-hungry maniac, screaming orders at his wife, and treating her, and anyone else who was unfortunate enough to be onboard, like waterborne vermin. On the highway it's called road rage. On the water it's called the Captain Bligh complex. My job was to help the couple learn how to work with, rather than against, each other. "Today," I said, "we'll switch roles. Sue will be captain, and Dan and I will crew."

Sue, a petite brunette in her early thirties, looked startled. She cast her big brown eyes at her husband as if to seek his approval. Dan was about his wife's age, but at six-feet-two he towered over her—and not just physically. He stroked his scruffy, lumberjack beard thoughtfully. I thought for sure he was going to object, but he said, "That's why we're here, Sue."

I began by talking about the role of captain, or skipper. "The most important thing to keep in mind is that you are in command. Your crew will respond to your directions ably and willingly—*if* they're given properly. This means that you must treat your crew as you would want to be treated."

Sue's head bobbed vigorously.

" 'Tacking!' and 'jibing!' are important commands," I said, "but the 'Ready to tack/jibe' command is equally important. Your crew needs some time (thirty seconds or so) to get in position before you start the turn."

"And no yelling," said Sue, giving her husband a pointed look.

"But if it's windy, you have to yell to be heard," protested Dan.

"True," I said. "There's a big difference, though, between a firm, in-control command and an angry shout." I gestured toward the school's burgee flapping wildly in the breeze. "Today will be a good test of how to give commands properly."

Sue assumed her position at the helm, and we cast off, departing the marina for the open waters of Elliott Bay. After some initial trepidation, she settled into her new role with confidence. It was only when we were sailing close-hauled that she began to experience some difficulty.

Sailing close-hauled is perhaps the most difficult point of sail for a helmsman, because it is the least forgiving. If the helmsman steers too close to the direction of the wind or too far from it, or if the crew pulls the sails in too tight or not tight enough, the boat will not perform efficiently. The happy medium of best angle to the wind is often referred to as the "groove."

For crew members, close-hauled is a relatively easy point of sail. Once the sails have been sheeted in, the crew's main duty is to watch for other boats. Sue's job as helmsman, on the other hand, required her to continually steer the boat, making small course adjustments for the inevitable wind shifts. Her main problem was that she was oversteering.

I prefer to let students experiment and get the feel of what they're doing before stepping in with advice. When I noticed Sue becoming frustrated, I said, "As a rule, the closer you sail to the wind, the slower the boat will go. For upwind sailing with the sails trimmed, you should head up, easing the tiller to leeward and turning the boat until the sail just begins to luff. When the sails luff, bear away slightly until the sails stop luffing."

She did as I directed.

"Great job, Sue. Now you've found the upwind

groove.'' For his part, Dan had found his groove, too. Namely, he kept his mouth shut and followed his wife's commands. And, as the lesson progressed, they began to find their groove as a couple. Watching them work together as a real team for the first time was gratifying, but I found my mind wandering back to the exchange I'd had with Melody and Kingston. Despite (or maybe because of) the way Melody had so cleverly played me for the fool, I was determined to figure out whether or not Isaac really was a murder victim. And if so, who killed him.

KATE WAS WAITING in my office when I came back from the Costers' lesson. I tossed my sailing gear on the floor and said, ''How'd it go with Rachel?''

''She wasn't home, but I had a nice little chat with her son. Joseph is a talkative kid. Handsome, too. We hit it off *real* well.''

*Jeez, sis, not a teenager.* ''Kate, he's only fifteen!''

She gave me an indignant look and flounced into a chair. ''Give me a break. I didn't seduce the kid. I didn't have to, anyway. He answered every single question I asked.''

''Okay,'' I said, sitting down at my desk. ''What did he say about the tank valve?''

''He swears on everything holy that he closed the valve. He knew it could be dangerous, so he made sure it was secured tightly before he left for the night. I believe him, Kellie. He struck me as an honest kid. Besides, what reason would he have to lie?''

''To cover for his mother.''

''It sounds like you're suggesting Rachel had something to do with her father's death. I thought you weren't convinced it was murder.''

''I'm still not, but I'm reconsidering it. Especially after our little conversation with Melody and Kingston.''

Kate shifted in her chair. "Look, Kellie, I'm sorry for my part in that fiasco. I shouldn't have opened my big mouth."

"Don't worry about it. But the episode did cause me to do some thinking while I was out sailing."

"And?"

"And I have a lot of questions about Rachel—beginning with her reaction to her father's marriage. Isaac was concerned she would be upset. So much so that he and Pearl were reluctant to come back home. They were afraid that Rachel would try to break up their marriage. From what I heard at the party, Isaac had tried to do something similar when she married outside their faith. I'd have thought Rachel might be a little resentful, at the least. Yet she didn't say a word about that—only how happy she was for him."

"So she forgave him. Maybe she only did what she wished her father had done for her. Joseph claims that his mother was pleased his grandfather had finally found someone he cared about after all these years. That's why she threw the party."

"Maybe. But she'd told me that she was really busy at work, with lots of overtime and pressure on her to perform. Yet she dropped everything and organized one of the best parties I've been to in years—all within two days of their homecoming. Why the rush?"

Kate shrugged. "I don't know, but Joseph said she'd planned on working today in order to make up for the time she'd taken off. That's why she stopped by the condo. She'd left her purse there with her ID badge in it."

"Did you ask him about the alarm system?"

"Yep. According to Joseph, his mother had to have access to the condo for the party. She was in and out a lot."

"Then why ask Tony for the code? Why not just have Pearl give it to her?"

"Joseph didn't know."

"Whose idea was it to put the tank in the bedroom?"

"Joseph's. He said he started to put the tank in a closet, but the bedroom was closer, so he just stashed it there."

"Interesting."

"What are you thinking?"

"Just that whoever planned this thing was either very lucky or incredibly smart. There is no way to know for sure who did what or when. The clown not only hauled off the tank, but also all of the evidence."

"Right," said Kate. "And even if an autopsy was able to show helium in Isaac's system, what would that prove? There is nothing to indicate that his death was anything other than an unfortunate accident."

The sun was low in the sky, casting reflections on the windowpane. It would've been a pretty moment except for the fact that the sunlight also reflected how badly the windows needed washing.

"What about the other people on our list?" asked Kate. "Do you have questions about them, too?"

"Lots. As I see it, every one of them had a reason or reasons to kill Isaac and Pearl. Let's start with Tony. His inheritance would get T-Bone off his back."

"I can't see Tony as a killer. He really likes Pearl, and besides, how would he know what was in her will?"

"He had access to her condo, didn't he? Maybe he found it."

Kate slapped her forehead. "He's the one who gave me the idea!"

"What idea?"

"How to hide valuables. I'd been thinking about getting a safe for my jewelry, but Tony told me not to bother. Then he showed me how to rig a safe in the toilet."

"Motive and opportunity," I said. "Next, we have Adrienne and Phillip Coughlin. They certainly weren't happy about Pearl's marriage to Isaac. Was that because they thought the marriage would affect their inheritance or, as they claim, put another burden on Adrienne?''

"Burden?''

"Adrienne and Phillip think Pearl is suffering from the first stages of Alzheimer's.''

"That's ridiculous,'' said Kate.

"Maybe so, but Pearl has admitted that she's been getting forgetful and doing some strange things—like going to town in her slippers.''

"So if Adrienne and Phillip killed her, they'd have all the money to themselves and be free of any responsibility for her care.''

"Exactly. Then there's your favorite person—Dennis Lancaster.''

She made a gagging gesture with her finger. "He's too stupid to commit murder.''

"Don't sell the man short. He's wheedled himself a spot on the GM selection committee and he's one step away from convincing old man Larstad to agree to a plan that would effectively oust most of the live-aboards at the marina.''

"But how would he benefit from Pearl and Isaac's death? He wasn't even mentioned in their will.''

"Are you forgetting that he owns Maritime Enviro Services with his brother, Phillip? A business that is rumored to be in financial difficulties. He's trying desperately to secure a contract with Larstad Marina. If that fails, they're going to need money from another source. I don't know how much they need, but Adrienne's inheritance would certainly be a big help.''

"Do you think he knows about her will?''

"I think that's what he and Phillip were looking for the day I ran into them at Pearl's condo. I can't prove it, but I believe the brothers also searched Pearl's boat when it was moored in Olympia. For that matter, why do you think Lancaster showed up there today?''

"He came back to look for the will again?"

"I can't imagine any other reason why he'd be there. Can you?"

She shook her head.

"This is the way I look at it: We have five viable suspects—and absolutely no way to prove there was a murder, let alone which of the five committed it."

"So what are you going to do?"

"I don't have the faintest idea. As Melody Connor so aptly implied, detective work isn't for amateurs."

The phone rang.

"I gotta run," said Kate. "Let me know if I can be of any further help."

I waved goodbye and picked up the receiver. "Sound Sailing."

"Kellie, is that you?"

"Hi, Cord."

"Sorry I wasn't here when you called back. Things have been real crazy today." He paused a moment. "You'll probably hear this on the news tonight, but I wanted to give you a heads-up. Duncan Matthews is missing—absconded with all of the church's funds."

"Hmm. That's interesting."

"But not surprising—he was about to be arrested for the murder of the Reverend St. Paul."

"How do you know that?"

"Police informant—BJ has sources everywhere."

"Why do they suspect Matthews?"

"Remember those computer files he was so secretive about? Turns out the files contained more than just membership rolls. When Jimmy finally got everything decoded, he discovered that Matthews had been swindling the church for years—very profitably, I might add."

"Sounds like he took up where Tyrone Bonetti left off."

"You got it. And when old Paul St. Paul found out that Matthews had been stealing from him, he was one pissed preacher. The police believe he threatened to turn Matthews in if he didn't stop. But Matthews went ballistic and killed him.''

"So I was right. The killer left that message on the wall to tell everyone why he'd killed the reverend.''

"We think there's more to it than that—and that's the most important reason why I called." He hesitated. "I guess there's no easy way to break this. Matthews found out about BJ's undercover role and how Jimmy was helping him decode the files. BJ is dead.''

My heart beat wildly. "And Jimmy? Is he okay?''

"He's in the hospital.''

"Oh, my God.''

"He's all right. Matthews gave him a nasty beating, but he's going to make it.''

"You should've told me this up front, Cord. I need to let his sister know right away.''

"Kellie, be careful. Your life could be at risk.''

"My life? I don't understand.''

"BJ had suspected T-Bone was involved with the church again. And Duncan Matthews' records prove it. But it was Matthews that T-Bone had teamed with—not the reverend.''

"How does that put me in danger?''

"The police think T-Bone had originally come to Portland on another matter. He and Matthews formed their little partnership afterwards.''

"I repeat, how does that put me in danger?''

"Because the matter that brought T-Bone to Portland was an MFH. It got sidetracked when you came looking for Pearl Danielson.''

"What's an MFH?''

"Murder for hire. Someone in Seattle hired T-Bone to kill Pearl.''

"Who?''

"That's what I hoped you'd be able to tell me.''

# TWENTY-SEVEN

ACCORDING TO CORD, Pearl Danielson was safe—the Portland police had already notified the Seattle P.D. about the murder-for-hire plot. But I called Kingston anyway. I wanted to make absolutely sure that Pearl was under police protection at the hospital. Melody Connor answered Kingston's phone and interrupted me midway through my first sentence.

"Everything's under control," she said brusquely. "A guard has been posted outside Pearl Danielson's hospital door."

"Thank God."

"It isn't really necessary, but Kingston insisted."

Her cavalier manner shocked me. "Are you crazy? Of course, it's necessary. T-Bone was hired to *kill* Pearl."

"I suppose you're referring to Tyrone Bonetti?"

"Yes, yes!" I felt as though I were drowning, struggling to breathe and talk at the same time. "He also goes by the name T-Bone."

"Calm down, Kellie. As I said, everything is under control."

"But—"

"Listen, I'm in a hurry. I shouldn't be telling you this,

but Tyrone Bonetti is not going to hurt anybody. He's just been found shot to death. Kingston's at the scene right now, and I'm on my way to meet him.''

"Oh." After a beat I said, "Well, could you let Kingston know I called?''

"Kellie," she said with an exasperated sigh, "you've got to understand something here. Allen Kingston and I have work to do. It's best if you leave these things to the professionals.''

Her "butt-out" attitude did nothing for my own attitude. *Understand this, Ms. Professional: Eat my dirt.* She was spared this uplifting sentiment when someone in the background called her name.

"Be right there," she said.

"Wait, don't hang up!" I shouted. But I was talking to a dial tone.

I put a lid on my anger and quickly dialed Rose's number to break the news about Jimmy. Afterwards, I called Cassie. When she didn't pick up the phone at home, I called the Topside to see if she was at work. "She was supposed to be here for the afternoon shift," said her boss, "but she didn't show. Is something wrong?''

I ran all the way down the dock to *Second Wind*.

"Cassie!" I shouted as I clambered aboard. "Cassie, are you here?''

Pan-Pan was in the cockpit, meowing loudly. She nudged my legs. "Not now, Pan-Pan," I said, roughly brushing her aside. The hatchway to the cabin was open. I grabbed hold of the rails and hurtled down the ladder.

"Cassie!''

The silence was deafening. I stood in the galley and tried to calm myself. It didn't work. I couldn't think of any reasonable explanation for Cassie's absence. *She's so conscientious*, I thought. *If she'd had a sudden change in plans, she'd have called her boss. At the very least, she'd have left me a note.* I checked all the usual spots in the galley and then searched the entire cabin. No note.

And no suitcase.

But the stink from Dennis Lancaster's aftershave was everywhere.

I didn't know what to do. Cord's phone call had upset me, but the realization that Lancaster had been inside *Second Wind* had me panic-stricken. My mind raced with terrifying possibilities. Had Cassie been here when Lancaster showed up? Had she tried to stop him from taking the suitcase? Did he harm her? So what if T-Bone was dead? Whoever killed him could be out to get me—and Cassie, too. Was that Lancaster or someone else?

My only thought was that I had to get hold of Kingston somehow. I reached for the phone, but the red light on the answering machine was blinking. When I pressed the play button, Kate's voice filled the cabin. She sounded frightened.

"Tony's in big trouble. Call me!"

I hesitated for half a second, then dialed her number. "What's going on, Kate?"

"Oh, Kellie, I'm so glad to hear from you. Some goon just took Tony!"

"What do you mean, 'took' him?"

"Came here to the condo and forced Tony to leave with him." Her voice faltered as she added, "Kellie, the guy had a gun. I'm so scared for Tony. He's really messed up this time."

"Have you called the police?"

"Yes, but they haven't shown up yet."

Cassie's disappearance was still uppermost in my mind, but I had a very bad feeling about Tony's abduction. Could the two events be connected somehow? "Tell me everything," I said. "What did the guy look like? Did you see his car?"

"That's the weird part. He wasn't one of the creeps who usually come around looking for Tony. Nothing like that T-Bone character. He was young and good-looking. Tall with close-cropped blond hair and a cute smile. A real charmer. I thought he was harmless—until he pulled the gun. God, it scared me to death!''

''And his car? What was he driving?''

''It wasn't a car. He shoved Tony into a van.''

My heart beat wildly as I asked, ''A white van?''

''Yes! How did you know?''

''Listen, Kate. When the police get there, tell them everything you've told me. And tell them that the guy's name is probably Duncan Matthews.''

''Who's that?''

''I can't go into it right now. Just give them that name. Duncan Matthews. You got that?''

''Yes, yes. Duncan Matthews.''

After I hung up, I was trembling. I filled a glass with water and sat down at the table. As I drank, I tried to compose myself and make some sense out of what had occurred. Melody was right. I wasn't a professional, but I felt if I could just calm down I'd figure out the puzzle.

I didn't know what had happened to Cassie (if anything), but I was certain that Matthews had abducted Tony. The question was: Why? Did Tony know something about the Reverend St. Paul's murder? The biblical verse that Matthews had scribbled on the library wall kept running through my mind. So far, everything he'd done—from killing the reverend and Billy Joe to nearly killing Jimmy—had been tied to that verse and his concept of betrayal. Did Tony's abduction mean that he'd betrayed Matthews, too?

Oh, hell, I thought. It's impossible. I couldn't figure anything out. Nothing made sense. Pan-Pan came into the cabin and wound herself around my feet. ''Where's Cassie, Pan-Pan?'' I asked. ''Did you see what happened?'' Good Lord, what was I doing? Anything—running down the dock, screaming for my daughter—would have to be more effective than talking to a cat. I stood up and then sat back down again. No, I had to figure this out.

I gulped some more water and thought about T-Bone's murder. If Matthews killed him, was it because of something that had happened in Portland? Or did T-Bone's death have something to do with the murder-for-hire plot? Tony Carmine and Dennis Lancaster both knew T-Bone. Did one of them hire him to kill Pearl? But why would Tony or Lancaster murder T-Bone? Because he'd failed to kill Pearl? Or for some other reason?

Then it hit me.

I reached for the telephone and dialed Allen Kingston's pager, punching in my phone number.

A minute later, the phone rang.

"Kingston, I know who killed T-Bone!"

"Mom? What are you talking about?"


OUR CONVERSATION WAS brief but reassuring. Cassie didn't go into much detail about where she was except to say that she had a big surprise for me. And that she was sorry for causing me worry. The relief I felt was overwhelming. Now that I knew Cassie was safe, my anger kicked in. I was still pissed at Melody for putting me down, but most of all, I was furious with Dennis Lancaster. He must have figured that the story I gave him about Pearl's suitcase was a ruse when he couldn't locate the wills at her condo. So he broke into *Second Wind* and stole the suitcase. And Cassie had made it easy for him. According to her, she'd left the boat in such a hurry that she'd forgotten to shut the hatchway.

It was bad enough that he'd brazenly boarded *Second Wind*, but I also believed that he was the one who hired T-Bone to kill Pearl. Although I still couldn't figure out what Tony's relationship to Duncan Matthews was, I was certain that Lancaster had more to gain from Pearl's death than Tony did. If Maritime Enviro Services went belly-up, my guess was that Lancaster, unlike his brother, Phillip, wouldn't have the smarts to survive. He desperately needed Adrienne's inheritance to save himself from financial ruin. But when Lancaster stole Pearl's suitcase and found out about the codicils, he realized he'd been double-crossed. If he'd made the connection between T-Bone and the Church of the Passionate Life, he would've had a nice little motive for murder.

Unfortunately I couldn't prove anything. That was made quite clear to me when the call I'd placed to Kingston's pager was returned by Melody Connor.

"Kingston asked me to answer your page. But I really shouldn't be talking to you, either. In case you've forgotten, Kellie, we're investigating a murder."

I swallowed my pride and tried to explain. "That's why I called. I've figured out who killed Tyrone Bonetti." I went on to give her my reasoning.

She cut me off before I was finished. "What kind of proof or evidence do you have that Dennis Lancaster is involved?"

"I know he took Pearl's suitcase from my boat."

"How do you know that?"

"His aftershave is quite distinctive."

She laughed. "And that makes him a murderer?"

"No, but I feel—"

"Let me be blunt, Kellie. Gut feelings do not carry any weight in a court of law. We need proof. So do us all a favor and let Kingston and me handle this investigation."

"Okay, okay," I said. "Handle it. But could you do me a favor, too?"

She sighed wearily. "What?"

"Tell Kingston that there's a meeting at the Topside tonight at seven o'clock. I'd like him to come. Dennis Lancaster will be there, too." Maybe I could convince Kingston that my reasoning was based on something other than gut feelings.

"Sure, sure," she said.

"Please, Melody. It's important."

AS ROSE HAD predicted, the media was well represented at the meeting. And the Weasel's reporter friend, Danielle Korb, was leading the pack. Besides reporters, the huge crowd that had gathered in the Topside's only meeting room was a mixture of marina personnel, boat owners, some folks who lived near the marina, and a couple of city council members.

The live-aboard contingent was well represented, but definitely outgunned by a strident group of environmental activists from the Blue Water Warriors. Although he'd been carted off to jail for the antics he'd pulled in my office, I half-expected to see Noah sitting with the Warriors. I didn't spot him in the crowd, but I couldn't help wondering if any of his fellow activists were suffering from the same delusions. If so, it could prove to be an interesting meeting.

As head of the general manager selection committee, Dennis Lancaster had organized the meeting. Since one of the stated purposes of the gathering was to give the GM finalists an opportunity to answer questions from the group, he'd arranged for them to sit on the dais with him at the front of the room. I had to give the guy credit. If he was a murderer, he was one cool customer. He looked totally in control—a smiling, savvy politician, glad-handing the assembled crowd and chatting up the reporters.

He made me sick to my stomach. But I was determined to help my live-aboard friends with the plan we'd concocted for tonight's meeting. The Weasel had already taken a seat on Lancaster's left side when Bert Foster and I walked into the room at five minutes to seven. I followed Bert onto the dais and sat down on Dennis Lancaster's right side.

Lancaster cupped his hand over the microphone and gave me a hard look. "Wait a minute," he said, clearly surprised by my presence. "You're not supposed to be up here. Where's Rose Randall?"

"Family emergency," I said. "She asked me to fill in for her."

"I can't allow that."

The Weasel leaned forward in his chair and craned his neck at me. "He's right. You're not qualified to take Rose's place."

Once a suck-up, always a suck-up.

I smiled sweetly and said, "Look at it this way, Wilmington. I can only make you look good."

Lancaster raised an eyebrow at Bert Foster.

Bert shrugged and said, "I have no objections."

The pre-meeting buzz had died down, and the audience had settled into their chairs, waiting for things to start.

Lancaster managed a tight smile as he whispered to me, "I don't know what you're trying to pull, but any funny stuff and I'll have you ejected."

I eyed him carefully. "Don't worry about me, Dennis. There's nothing funny about murder."

His smile disappeared, but he managed to keep a cool exterior as he clicked off the microphone. "What the hell are you talking about?" he asked through clenched teeth.

I pointed to the jagged, ugly red scratch on his hand. "How'd you get that? Wrestling Pearl's suitcase away from my cat or killing T-Bone?"

"You little bitch," he spat. "Get the hell out of here."

"Not on your life."

"You're in way over your head."

"We'll see about that." I caught Tom Dolan's eye and nodded.

"Hey!" Dolan shouted. "You gonna get this dog-

and-pony show on the road or what?'' The rest of the live-aboards joined in with similar comments.

Lancaster cleared his throat. "Uh, ladies and gentlemen, I want to thank you for coming tonight."

So began the meeting.

After Lancaster had rambled on for several minutes without saying anything worth repeating, he introduced the GM finalists. The plan was to have the candidates read a brief statement about their qualifications for the job and then state their position on various marina issues, the proposed live-aboard surcharge being item number one. Questions would be taken from the audience after each of the candidates had had a chance to speak.

Wilmington went first. As expected, he played up his relationship to old man Larstad and his long-time affiliation with the marina. Basically he compensated for his lack of qualifications for the job with good-old-boy schmooze. As far as his position on marina issues went, he waffled on everything except the live-aboard surcharge which he supported.

Lancaster introduced Bert Foster next. Bert's not a public speaker, but he did a decent job outlining his experience as harbormaster and his position on the issues. He did not support a surcharge, which got a loud round of cheers from the live-aboard crowd.

When it came time to introduce me, Lancaster couldn't keep the disdain out of his voice. "Our next speaker is definitely not a candidate for the GM position. Kellie Montgomery is just a sailing instructor."

My sailor- and live-aboard friends yelled, "Way to go, Kellie!"

Lancaster hurriedly quieted the group. "All right, all right," he said with upraised hands. "Kellie is substituting tonight for Rose Randall, the marina's accountant."

I read Rose's prepared statement. Understandably her

position on the issues reflected her business background. She did not favor the live-aboard surcharge, stating that it simply wasn't necessary. To prove it, she had prepared a spreadsheet that showed the marina's income and outgo. If it were shown to be necessary (and she did not believe that was the case), the marina was financially able to contract with an environmental clean-up service without raising mooring fees—at least for the next two years.

After I'd finished reading Rose's position, Lancaster opened the meeting to questions and comments from the audience. Things got out of hand quickly; the comments became accusations, the questions, challenges. Although I felt obligated to represent Rose, I couldn't keep my mind focused on the so-called discussion raging around.

My mind was on Lancaster. I knew in my heart that he was a killer. And I desperately wanted to prove it. Mostly because of Pearl and Isaac, but also to make Melody Connor eat her words. Unfortunately I still had absolutely no idea how I was going to prove anything. I'd only mentioned the scratch on Lancaster's hand to try to get him rattled. But he'd recovered well enough. So far, he'd controlled the meeting with a cocky, take-charge attitude that brooked little dissent from those who disagreed with his position.

The guy had to be nervous, though. His whole future depended upon the outcome of tonight's meeting. He now knew that Maritime Enviro Services would not be receiving a bail-out from Adrienne's inheritance. If he thought that his contract with Larstad's Marina was in jeopardy or a dead issue, I might be able to force his hand. My only hope of accomplishing this depended upon my fellow live-aboards. As we'd planned the other night, they each took the floor and spoke from their hearts.

Lancaster effectively shut them up by giving dispro-portionate mike time to representatives from the Blue

Water Warriors. The party line they pushed was that marinas were not good for the environment, particularly those that allowed live-aboards. As proof, they produced two vials of water—one that was supposedly drawn from Larstad's Marina and one that was drawn from another marina—an unnamed marina that did not allow live-aboards.

They passed around copies of a chemist's analysis of the two samples. Not surprisingly, the water from Larstad's was so thoroughly polluted that it was a wonder it supported any marine life at all. They also circulated graphic photographs depicting what water pollution can do to marine animals. The mood of the audience was shocked outrage.

Lancaster immediately followed up their presentation by delivering a blatant, self-serving commercial for Maritime Enviro Services. He had the audience in the palm of his hand—until Don Fryer rose to speak.

Fryer was a nerdy sort with short-cropped hair and glasses held together with the proverbial adhesive tape. But when he spoke, he spoke with authority. A live-aboard ever since his home took a muddy nosedive off Magnolia Bluff into Elliott Bay, Fryer was also a chemist. He'd been chosen by the live-aboards to represent us at the meeting.

Fryer waved the copy of the report that the Blue Water Warriors had circulated. "I have some questions about this analysis," he began.

Lancaster cut him off. "We've already discussed that issue. On behalf of the selection committee, we thank you all for coming tonight. This meeting is adjourned."

I grabbed the microphone. "Let him speak. What he has to say is important."

Lancaster shook his head. "I repeat, this meeting is adjourned."

A booming voice came from the back of the room. "Just a cotton-picking minute."

Every head in the room whipped around. Old man Larstad stood by the door. At sixty-five, Lawrence Larstad was as bald as a grapefruit, paunchy, and stoop-shouldered. Although he'd given up day-to-day management of the marina in favor of the golf course, he was far from a doddering old man. His voice was clear and firm. "I want to hear what Fryer has to say."

Lancaster stammered, "But we've already—"

"*Now.*"

Someone handed Fryer the microphone. He was an impressive speaker who listed his extensive experience as a chemist before launching his attack on the flaws in the Warriors' presentation. He specifically questioned the chemical analysis of their water samples, debunking it as essentially meaningless.

To prove his claims, he produced two other water vials. "The chemical analysis of the water in these vials shows that the water at Larstad's Marina is not only *not* polluted, but is of the highest quality in the area."

Lancaster started to protest, but old man Larstad cut him off. "I've heard enough," he said. "There'll be no live-aboard surcharge." A huge cheer drowned out the last of his statement: "And there'll be no clean-up contract."

Lancaster most certainly heard Larstad, but it didn't matter.

Duncan Matthews had just walked into the room.

# TWENTY-EIGHT

IT'S SO NICE when a plan comes together.

Although Duncan Matthews' sudden appearance at the Topside had nothing to do with the live-aboards' plan—or my desire to prove Dennis Lancaster guilty of murder—it was the catalyst that would ultimately change everything. I'd tried to get Lancaster rattled and had failed miserably. All Matthews had to do, though, was walk into the room, and the man began to unravel.

Of course, the fact that the guy was brandishing a gun in one hand and dragging a bruised and battered Tony Carmine with the other might have accounted for some of Lancaster's nervousness.

There were over fifty people in the room, but everyone, including the reporters, sat in stunned silence while the gun-toting Matthews took over the meeting. I don't know if they thought he was a robber or a drug-crazed wacko, but no one did or said anything that would draw his attention. Especially when he waved his gun at the crowd and shouted, "Don't any of you pissants move a muscle!"

I, on the other hand, had a pretty good idea why he was here. If I was right, things were going to get nasty.

Matthews eyeballed the room's occupants for a brief moment. Then, jerking Tony by the arm, he asked, "Where's Lancaster?"

I cast a sideways glance at the object of Matthews' quest. Gone was the cool exterior, the unflappable politician. He'd blanched a pasty white and was even trembling.

Tony winced as he struggled to respond. He appeared barely able to function, and if Matthews hadn't been holding onto him, I'm sure he would have collapsed. My guess was that Matthews had snatched Tony because he couldn't find Dennis Lancaster. Just why he was looking for him didn't immediately leap out at me, but I figured it had to be tied to T-Bone's murder somehow.

"Come on, come on," Matthews said to Tony. "I want my money back and I don't have a lot of time to fool around."

"Hallelujah, Brother!" shouted a man near the front of the room. I hadn't recognized him in his spiffy new suit and tie and neatly combed hair, but there was no mistaking his voice. That the courts had seen fit to put Noah out on the street again didn't surprise me. Seattle has a history of shortsighted dealings with mental health cases.

Matthews looked at Noah. "Shut the fuck up!"

If Noah heard him, it wasn't readily apparent. He climbed onto his chair and began swaying back and forth with his hands raised in the air. "Thus saith the Lord: To every thing there is a season, and a time to every purpose under the heaven. A time to be born and a time—"

"To die, sucker!" shouted Matthews.

He let go of Tony and pushed him out of his way. Then, with the gun leveled at Noah, he moved toward the front of the room. He was so focused on getting a clear shot that he failed to notice Tom Dolan sitting near the aisle.

Dolan stuck out his foot as Matthews passed. He went down with a thud, and his gun skittered across the floor. Several men immediately pounced on him, and a terrific struggle ensued.

The room erupted in screams and shouts. Some people scrambled for the door, but most stayed to watch the unfolding action as if it were a TV thriller. The melee on the floor came to an abrupt end when Charlie Tuna plopped his considerable bulk on top of Matthews. He was a good anchor. And just to make sure, someone retrieved the gun Matthews had dropped and pointed it at his head.

Several people yelled, "Call 9-1-1! Call the police!"

Tony Carmine's knees had buckled after Matthews pushed him, and he'd collapsed onto the floor. A couple of folks had come to his aid. "He needs a doctor!" they shouted. "Call an ambulance!"

To add to the noise and confusion, Noah was still standing on his chair shouting, ". . . a time to kill and a time to heal; a time to break down and a time to build up . . ." His sermon ended only when one of his fellow Blue Water Warriors coaxed him down from his makeshift pulpit.

Next to me, Lancaster exhaled deeply. Some of his color had returned, and he wasn't shaking anymore. But his sense of well-being was premature. Danielle Korb and the other reporters swarmed around the dais. Their little environmental story had suddenly taken a bizarre twist, and they were on a feeding frenzy. While a photographer snapped pictures, the reporters peppered Lancaster with questions. "Who was the guy with the gun? Why was he looking for you?"

"I have absolutely no idea," said Lancaster. He pointed at Noah being led from the room. "He's obviously a nutcase, just like that fellow."

"His name is Duncan Matthews," I said.

Danielle Korb turned to me. "You know him, Kellie?"

I nodded. "We've met."

"What was he doing here?" she asked.

I locked eyes with Lancaster. "Why don't you tell them, Dennis? Something about money, isn't it? Or perhaps T-Bone's murder?"

That got the reporters going. "Murder? Who's T-Bone?"

"Tyrone Bonetti." The answer came from Melody Connor. She'd walked into the room with her handcuffs in one hand and her pistol in the other. At first I thought she was after Matthews. But she threw her handcuffs to Charlie Tuna and made her way toward the dais.

"Dennis Lancaster," she said, "you're under arrest for the murder of Tyrone Bonetti."

That she'd finally acted on my hunch was gratifying, but I had no time to relish the feeling. Lancaster suddenly grabbed hold of my arm and jerked me to my feet, using my body as his shield.

"Stand back, bitch!" he yelled at Melody. I felt him pull a gun from his jacket and jam it into the small of my back. "Stand back, or she dies."

Once again, everyone froze in stunned silence and then scrambled for cover as Melody raised her weapon to assume a shooting stance.

"Let her go, Lancaster!" she yelled.

I was the one who was trembling now. I knew he wouldn't listen to her. He blamed me for everything. I'd interfered with all his plans and now I'd have to pay. He'd use me as a hostage to make his getaway and then kill me.

Melody repeated her demand. "Let her go. Kellie has nothing to do with you."

"That's where you're wrong, sister," he said. "The little bitch has everything to do with me." He turned me slightly with his free hand and aimed his pistol at Melody.

"You're only making things worse for yourself. Let her go and drop your—"

He fired.

When Melody fell, the room erupted. The Weasel ran off the dais and into the arms of Danielle Korb. Bert and several others tried to rush Lancaster, but he brandished the pistol at them and they retreated.

Tightening his hold on me, he backed us off the dais and toward the rear door. "Move it!" he shouted.

I obeyed, stumbling over my feet as he dragged me outside and onto a narrow walkway leading to the deck. I fully expected Kingston to be there, to rescue me and take Lancaster down. But we were alone.

My mind raced. Had Melody come by herself? Without backup? Could she be *that* arrogant? The possibility was terrifying. But there was no time to second-guess her motives. I'd have to save myself—and fast. Hostage time was over.

As we backed onto the deck, I slammed my foot down on Lancaster's instep as hard as I could. The sudden pain startled him, and he released his grip slightly. It was enough.

I twisted around to face him, and with one quick move shoved both my fists under his chin. The *coup de grâce* was a knee slam into his crotch.

The dual-action punch propelled him backward onto the deck's low railing. He teetered a moment and then fell off. It was a short distance to the bottom, but he landed hard on the concrete walkway below. The gun clattered out of his hand.

Lancaster moved slightly, but Allen Kingston was on him like dirt. He pinned him to the ground belly-side down with his foot. Once he had Lancaster's hands behind his back and handcuffed, Kingston looked up at me and grinned.

"Nice move, Montgomery."

• • •

A WEEK LATER, he was grinning at me again. We were aboard *Second Wind* and had just rounded Bainbridge Island on a starboard tack. But the stiff breeze we'd enjoyed earlier in the day had slacked off to a gentle whisper, and we now sliced through the water at a boring two knots.

Kingston was at the helm. "Hey, this is fun," he said. "I can take a nap and not miss a thing."

"You win some and you lose some," I said. "But the wind always determines when."

"Slow suits me just fine," said Tony as he exited the cabin and joined us in the cockpit. He was moving slowly himself these days. His injuries—several cracked ribs, a broken arm, and numerous cuts and abrasions to the face and torso—were still causing him discomfort. Although Kate was not a boater, the day sail was her idea. She thought it would do Tony good to get out of the house. More to the point, she was tired of playing nursemaid.

Although we'd diligently tried to avoid it, our conversation turned to the events of the past week.

"You always claimed that Dennis Lancaster was too dumb to commit murder," I said to Kate, "but you were only partly right. He was too dumb to get away with murder."

Kate looked at Kingston. "I know Kellie pegged him as T-Bone's killer," she said. "But what convinced you?"

Kingston laughed. "The idiot had neglected to remove the incriminating evidence—the numerical code to Pearl's alarm system. His handwritten note on Maritime Enviro Services stationery was still in T-Bone's wallet."

"Phillip Coughlin owns that business, too. What

made you think it was Lancaster and not Phillip who'd written the note?''

"Because," said Kingston, shaking his head, "Lancaster had signed his own name."

"No way," said Kate. "No one could be *that* dumb."

"Strange as it seems, it happens all the time. These psychopaths never think they're going to get caught. That they're somehow smarter than everyone else. It probably never even occurred to Lancaster that we'd find the note."

"He didn't leave the money behind, though," said Tony.

"Yeah," said Kingston, "and that was the beginning of his undoing. The Portland P.D. thought Matthews had absconded with all of the church funds, but T-Bone had beat him to it."

"Is that why Lancaster was arguing with T-Bone the night of the party?" Katie asked.

"No," answered Kingston. "Lancaster didn't know anything about the money T-Bone had stolen at that point. He was just pissed because Pearl was still alive. He was afraid that her marriage to Isaac would ruin any chance he had of getting at her money. Lancaster wanted both of the old folks killed, but T-Bone had only contracted for one hit. He demanded more dough—that's why they were arguing."

"So Lancaster coughed up the extra cash T-Bone wanted and gave him the alarm code," I said.

Kingston nodded. "That's right. When T-Bone came back to the condo after the party, he spotted the helium tank and decided to make their deaths look like an accident. In his haste, though, he either didn't notice or didn't care that Pearl wasn't in the bedroom."

"And when Lancaster killed T-Bone for double-crossing him, he took the church money," added Tony.

Kate looked confused. "But how did Matthews know that Lancaster had taken it?''

"He didn't, but he knew Lancaster had hired T-Bone to kill Pearl," said Tony. "When he found T-Bone dead, Matthews concluded that Lancaster had done him in and taken off with the money."

"Which was exactly what happened," Kingston said.

"And Phillip Coughlin? Did he know what his brother was up to?" asked Kate.

"Not a clue," said Kingston.

"But I saw them together in Pearl's condo," I said. "They were searching for something—I assumed it was her will. I think they also tracked her to Olympia and searched her boat for the document as well."

"Yeah," said Kate. "They were both sniffing at Pearl's bank account."

"Right," agreed Kingston. "But Coughlin had hoped the will would somehow prove Pearl's incompetence, while Lancaster was trying to find evidence of her largesse. When he couldn't get his hands on her money, he took the funds T-Bone had stolen from Matthews. We found Pearl's suitcase stuffed with cash at his condo."

Tony said, "Speaking of being stuffed . . ."

Kate gave him a gentle nudge. "Hungry again, are you?"

"Hey, I have to build up my strength."

"There's plenty of food in the galley," I said. "Feel free to help yourselves."

Tony turned to Kate with a hangdog expression.

"Hey, do I look like a cook?" she asked.

"No. You look like a pretty cook," said Tony.

*Oh, brother*, I thought, *that's weak*.

But Kate smiled broadly. "Okay, okay. Let's go below and see what we can find."

Ever since that night at the Topside, Kingston and I had skirted the subject of what had happened to Melody Connor. Her wounds had not been life-threatening, but she was still on medical leave. I took a deep breath and asked the one question that had been on my mind ever since the shooting. "How come Melody arrived at the marina before you did?"

Kingston eyed me a moment. "Well, Red, I was wondering when you'd get around to asking about that. The truth is, Melody never gave me your phone message. I had no idea that Dennis Lancaster was at the marina. It was just pure luck that I wound up there when I did."

"Why didn't she tell you? Aren't you partners?"

"Good question. The captain asked the same thing."

"And what was the answer?"

"That she messed up, Montgomery. She messed up big time."

"Are you still partners?"

"That's not clear at the moment. A review board is investigating." He turned the wheel slightly to port. "Think that'll make a difference?" he asked.

"The review board or your port turn?"

He laughed, and we let the answer ride.

Kingston pulled his baseball cap over his eyes. "Wake me if I need to do anything," he said.

I kept my eyes open, but my thoughts wandered. Although Melody was still recuperating, Jimmy Randall and Pearl Danielson had both been released from the hospital. Jimmy was staying with Rose, the marina's new general manager. His future plans were uncertain, but he was thinking about accepting a job offer from Microsoft.

Pearl was staying with her daughter and son-in-law in Salem—temporarily. Just until they'd worked out an arrangement for Pearl's medical care. The concern that Adrienne and Phillip had expressed about her health was not without merit. She didn't have Alzheimer's, but her doctor advised that it would be best if she didn't live by herself anymore.

Although I'd been suspicious of Rachel Feldman's swift and warmhearted acceptance of her father's marriage, she proved to be entirely without ulterior motive. She and her son, Joseph, moved into Isaac's home on Mercer Island. And when Pearl generously signed a new will, reinstating their inheritance from Isaac, Rachel suggested that Pearl move in with them. That didn't make Adrienne and Phillip happy, but Pearl said she was still capable of making her own decision about where she'd live.

Cassie poked her head out of the hatchway. "Hey, you two. What do you want on your sandwiches?"

"We're at your service," chimed in Deena.

"Whatever you're having is fine," I said.

Kate and Tony elected to eat below, but Cassie and Deena joined us in the cockpit. Deena set a plate stacked with sandwiches in front of Kingston.

He popped one eye open. "Don't tell me it's peanut butter and cucumbers again."

The girls laughed. "Don't you approve? It's our favorite."

I looked at the two girls and marveled at how well they were getting along—and that they were together. Deena's phone call had come out of the blue. "I hadn't planned on calling," she told us later, "but I just couldn't get Cassie's photo out of my mind. We looked so much alike that it was hard to deny that we weren't related somehow."

Finally curiosity won out. She borrowed her mother's car and drove to Seattle. Cassie had been so excited to get her sister's call that she raced off to meet her without even thinking about her job or anything else, including a note to me.

Since their impromptu reunion, the girls had discovered that a love of peanut butter and cucumber sandwiches wasn't the only thing they had in common. Though raised apart, they were more alike than different. They shared many of the same mannerisms, food preferences, interests, and talents. Even their choice of future careers was similar. Cassie was an architecture student, and Deena was hoping to become a fashion designer. After some initial wariness, the two girls were giggling and acting as if they'd always been together.

But today Deena seemed sad. She sat in the cockpit looking out at the water without eating.

Cassie picked up on her mood. "What's wrong, Deena?"

"I was just thinking how different everything is now," she said.

"What do you mean?"

"I thought I knew who I was, but I'm just a fake," she said. "My parents should've told me I was adopted. If they lied about something that important, I have to wonder what else they haven't told me."

Cassie put her arm around her twin. I could tell from her expression that she was struggling to think of something comforting to say. My heart went out to the two sisters as they sat together in awkward silence.

Cassie's eyes caught mine, and I knew she wanted me to fix things somehow. But I was struggling to think of something to say, too.

After a moment, Cassie said, "I can't begin to understand how you must feel, Deena." She glanced at me. "But there's something my mom taught me that might help you."

"What's that?"

"It's going to sound kind of corny, but hear me out. Okay?"

Deena nodded.

Cassie looked up at our sails, barely fluttering in the delicate breeze. "Mom says that there're two kinds of wind." She paused. "True wind—I think that's what it's called—is the wind we feel when the boat is at anchor or in its berth."

I smiled, suddenly realizing where she was going with this analogy.

"And then there's the other wind. It's apt wind." She shook her head. "No, that's not right." She thought a moment. "Apparent wind. That's it. Apparent wind is a combination of true wind and the wind that the boat creates as it moves through the sea. Mom says that the able sailor will sail the apparent wind."

"What are you trying to tell me?" asked Deena.

"Just this: You're not a fake, Deena. Your adoptive father's love for you was very real. Flora's love is real, too. Knowing that you're adopted won't ever change that. The main thing is that you're loved."

My heart swelled with pride as Cassie continued.

"You can carry on about what might've been, what should've been, forever and ever, but it won't get you anywhere. That's true wind. But here's the kicker: To really live, you've got to let go of the past and move on. When you understand that, you'll not only surge through the sea, you'll soar."

As if on cue, a sudden burst of wind billowed out our sails. Kingston turned the wheel over to Cassie and sat down next to me. He put his arm around me and squeezed.

"Like mother, like daughter," he said.

# ABOUT THE AUTHOR

VALERIE WILCOX WAS born and raised in the Pacific Northwest. She currently lives in the Seattle area. A graduate of the University of Oregon, Wilcox was a teacher and management training consultant for over twenty-five years.

Much like her Montgomery protagonist, Wilcox is a lifelong boating enthusiast. She and her husband David were living aboard their sailboat when she began the sailing mystery series.

As the mother of three adopted daughters, Wilcox drew upon personal experience to help her character, Kellie, deal with her adopted daughter's search for her birth mother. During the course of writing her first novel, *Sins of Silence*, Wilcox teamed with her own daughters to locate their birth mothers.

*Sins of Betrayal* is her second novel.

Valerie Wilcox welcomes reader feedback and may be contacted via e-mail (vjwilcox@nwlink.com) or in care of Berkley Prime Crime. Readers are also encouraged to visit her web site (www.nwlink.com/~vjwilcox).

EDGAR AWARD-WINNING AUTHOR

# DANA
# STABENOW

# HUNTER'S
# MOON

A KATE SHUGAK MYSTERY

PUTNAM

# DANA STABENOW
### EDGAR AWARD–WINNING AUTHOR

___BREAKUP___                  0-425-16261-3/$5.99

April in Alaska is the period of spring thaw, what the locals call *breakup*. First, the snow uncovers a dead body near Kate's home. Then a woman is killed in a suspicious bear attack. Kate is drawn further into the destruction of breakup—and into the path of a murderer...

___BLOOD WILL TELL___          0-425-15798-9/$5.99

When a member of the Native Association dies mysteriously, Kate is thrown into the thick of tribal politics. The more she learns, the more she discovers how deeply she is tied to the land—and to what lengths she will go to protect it.

___PLAY WITH FIRE___            0-425-15254-5/$5.99

Kate must break the silence of a close-knit community to find out who would want one of its members dead.

___A COLD DAY FOR MURDER___     0-425-13301-X/$5.99

Kate returns to her roots to find out if a national park ranger lost to the harsh Alaskan snowscape was killed by more than the cold.

___A FATAL THAW___               0-425-13577-2/$5.99

Nine bodies lay dead in the snow. Eight are victims of a crazed killer. But it's the ninth, a woman with a tarnished past, that's troubling Kate Shugak.

___DEAD IN THE WATER___         0-425-13749-X/$5.99

Kate goes to work on a crab fishing boat to try to find out why part of its crew disappeared on the Bering Sea.

___A COLD-BLOODED BUSINESS___    0-425-15849-7/$5.99

Kate goes undercover to investigate drug trading on the TransAlaska Pipeline that's causing overdoses and deadly on-the-job errors.

# EARLENE FOWLER

introduces Benni Harper, curator of San Celina's folk
art museum and amateur sleuth

## __FOOL'S PUZZLE       0-425-14545-X/$6.50

Ex-cowgirl Benni Harper moved to San Celina, California, to begin
a new career as curator of the town's folk art museum. But when one
of the museum's first quilt exhibit artists is found dead, Benni must
piece together a pattern of family secrets and small-town lies to catch
the killer.

## __IRISH CHAIN       0-425-15137-9/$6.50

When Brady O'Hara and his former girlfriend are murdered at the San
Celina Senior Citizen's Prom, Benni believes it's more than mere
jealousy. She risks everything–her exhibit, her romance with police
chief Gabriel Ortiz, and her life–to unveil the conspiracy O'Hara had
been hiding for fifty years.

## __KANSAS TROUBLES    0-425-15696-6/$5.99

After their wedding, Benni and Gabe visit his hometown near Wichita.
There Benni meets Tyler Brown: aspiring country singer, gifted quilter,
and former Amish wife. But when Tyler is murdered and the case comes
between Gabe and her, Benni learns that her marriage is much like the
Kansas weather: unexpected and bound to be stormy.